BROTHER TO DRAGONS

CHARLES SHEFFIELD

BAEN BOOKS

BROTHER TO DRAGONS

A Baen Books Original

Baen Publishing Enterprises
P.O. Box 1403
Riverdale, NY 10471

ISBN: 0-671-72141-0

Cover art by Stephen Hickman

First Printing, November 1992

Printed in the United States of America

Distributed by Simon & Schuster
1230 Avenue of the Americas
New York, NY 10020

To Eleanor Wood,
who only pesters me
for my own good

• Chapter One

Let the day perish wherein I was born,
and the night in which it was said,
there is a man-child conceived.

— The Book of Job, Chapter 3, Verse 3

Bed Nine. Infant pulse rate 139 and falling.

The charity delivery ward was on the lowest floor, a level where no modernization program would ever reach. Sweating walls and low ceiling softened and yellowed the reflection of overhead fluorescents. Light gleamed off racks of steel-cased equipment cabinets, battered by use, repair, and endless reuse.

Bed Nine. Infant blood pressure 48 over 20 and falling.

Eleven P.M. on December 31st, and the final minutes of the old year were fluttering away.

In the hour before midnight, the birthing urge moved towards its maximum. Down the middle of the long room, on a bank of screened table-beds, a dozen women lay in every stage of parturition. The loudest sounds were the hum of lights and the women's groans of pain and effort.

Bed Nine. Infant pulse rate arrhythmic, 112 and falling.

The soft mechanical voice of the in situ uterine sensors contained no suggestion of alarm, but it was insistent. As it spoke in her ear, one of the nurses moved to the head of the ninth bed. She glanced at the monitors, rolled her eyes above the white protective mask, and swore into her throat mike.

"Damnation! Doctor Brisbane! We're close to losing one."

"Coming." The throat mikes permitted the doctors and technicians to exchange information, no matter how ominous or final, without any patient hearing it. The physician moved to the bed and began to probe with delicate fingers between the supine woman's legs.

"Need to get the head showing, need to take a look at the cord. Not breech, position feels normal." He spoke as though to himself, but every word in the throat mikes formed part of the continuous medical record of the ward. "I don't think the umbilical is around the neck. Nurse Calder, tell her she has to do more work. She must push harder."

"Huh? Sure, I'll *tell* her to push. But how do I get her to *listen*?" An audible snort came from the other end of the table-bed. "Look at her. Think this one's been doing her Lamaze regularly?"

The doctor did not answer. He had seen enough as soon as he came to the bedside. Thin white quivering arms and legs, asymmetrically swollen belly, flushed face, far-off dreamy eyes, and a half-smile showing brown-stained teeth. The brief admitting report served only to confirm his immediate diagnosis: seventh month, alcoholic, malnourished, heavy smoker, crack addict.

One thing the admissions report did not say: the woman was high *now*. She must have jammed cocaine in the waiting room while she was being admitted, to mask the pain of contractions.

Bed Nine. Infant blood pressure 40 over 14 and falling.

"You're right." He made brief eye contact with the nurse at the other end of the bed. "We're going to lose this one unless we do something quick. Come give me a hand."

The long, curved forceps were a device from a medieval torture chamber. The nurse held them as the doctor adjusted their position within the expanded vaginal canal.

"Gently." He nodded. "Almost got it."

The woman on the bed gave a gasp.

Bed Nine. No pulse. Blood pressure indeterminate.

"Holy Mother of God. No time. That's as good as we'll get — give 'em to me."

He swept the uterine sensor out of the way, allowing it to fall to the floor. His right hand was probing, touching the malleable plates of the head and avoiding the soft fontanelle, while his left hand tightened the forceps and steadily applied tension.

"Hold her!"

A force stronger than drugs was at work in the woman's body. She grunted as shuddering contractions rippled bands of muscle across her belly.

"Come on, come on . . . " Brisbane's whisper sounded like a curse. "Come on — all right, here we go . . . right *now*."

Gripped at the sides of the soft-skulled head by the forceps, a tiny purple-red body was slithering free. It came fast, emerging completely in just a few seconds. The nurse grabbed and lifted it, assessing weight and condition.

"Stillborn male," she said into the mike. "Estimated body weight, three pounds. Anoxic. Nasty forceps marks, jaw appears abnormal. No other visible deformities."

Even as she spoke she was turning the shrunken body upside down, attaching sensor electrodes, slapping the fibrillator into position and massaging the little chest. Fluid began to drip from the open mouth, on past the eyes to the bulging and naked skull, and down to the floor.

"Don't waste your time. He's gone, we have to look to her." Doctor Brisbane bent over the mother. He grunted in surprise. She was asleep, sprawling splay-legged and slack-mouthed on the table-bed. After a quick inspection he turned back to the baby and the furiously active nurse. "Nothing to do here. Poor little bugger, he never had a chance with a mother like this. Lung damage for a certainty, probably liver, too, undersized even for seven and a half months. No wonder he didn't make it. If she'd bothered to look after herself one little bit, or if she'd just held him to full term, maybe we could have — well, I'll be damned."

His angry words had been interrupted by a weak, wavering cry.

Nurse Calder grinned behind her mask, and her eyes showed fierce triumph as she glared up at the doctor. *Don't ever give up too soon.* The long room had gone totally silent. It broke out now in excited chatter. Every woman had caught that faintest mewl of new birth.

"Got a pulse." The nurse had her finger at the baby's groin. "Faint, fast, maybe 150 — little irregular."

"Need an incubator, ASAP." Brisbane took the baby and spoke rapidly into his throat mike. "First order service: high oxygen, liver stimulants, blood transfusion. Additional monitors. Bed Nine mother to recovery room. We're on the way up."

He severed and tied the umbilical as he spoke and handed the baby again to the nurse. She wiped slimy mucus from eyes and mouth, cleared the little blocked nostrils, and checked ears, caul, limbs, anus, and genitals. She gently wrapped the newborn in a swaddling cloth and held him out tentatively toward his mother.

"Don't bother. She's off and floating — still high." The doctor walked along the whole length of the row of beds, checking each monitor. The in situ uterine sensors were all silent. "That looks like our last one for tonight — thank God. Next delivery will probably be Bed Two, but that looks like an hour or two to go. Next shift's problem. Come on." He gathered up the patient records for the five deliveries they had made in the past ten hours, handed them to Nurse Calder in exchange for the baby, and headed for the exit.

The incubators were three floors up from the charity ward. By the time the baby had been installed there and the battery of monitors and telemetry units were hooked up, midnight was approaching. When the transparent plastic film was at last in position over the incubator unit Doctor Brisbane sighed, rubbed at his eyes, and removed his mask.

"Thanks, Nurse. You deserve all the credit for this one. That does me for the day. Just let me send word downstairs that the mother can visit as soon as she feels up to it, and we'll be off."

"Don't hold your breath." Nurse Calder removed her mask and was revealed as a plump-faced woman of fifty. Her expression had become angry, with no sign of earlier euphoria. "Did you read these?" She held out the patient records.

"What about them?" He was removing his gown and surgical gloves, and he made no move to take the papers.

"The mother. Her name is Nina Salk. This is her *fifth time* in the charity ward. She's eighteen years old, unmarried, and the father of the child is unknown."

"So?" Brisbane had done enough *pro bono* work in the charity ward to recognize the pattern.

"So the last *four times* she was here for a delivery, she walked right out of the hospital as soon as she could stand. And she never came back. One child stillborn, one died at four days, two placed with foster parents. But I'll bet she doesn't know any of that. Damn her, she never even went to look at them, never came back to see if they were alive or dead."

"She's an *addict*, Eileen." With masks and gowns off, the formal relationship was replaced by familiarity. "A bad one, too — I'll be surprised if she sees twenty."

"I don't care what she is, or how long she lasts. She owes something to her kids — she didn't even stay long enough to give them *names*. I bet this one won't have a name."

"Then it's our job to name him if she won't do it. I'll name provisionally, just in case you're wrong and she does come here." He unclipped the ID card from the side of the incubator and took a pen from his shirt pocket. "Any ideas? John Salk? Not bad, and it's safe, but it sounds a bit too anonymous."

She was not listening. She had moved back to the incubator and was staring down into it. The monitors were doing their job, the status reports already appearing on the display screens.

"Little boy," she said softly. "You're so tiny, and so frail."

"That's not the worst." Brisbane waved his pen at the display. "See, that's what I was afraid of."

Weight at the fifth percentile for full-term delivery. The computer was integrating the reports made by the doctor with prior information on the mother and its own telemetry data of the child's condition. *Length at the tenth percentile. X-rays reveal ribcage defects, malformation of jaw and dental structures, incomplete development of lungs. Liver, heart, and kidney abnormalities. Diminished retinal sensitivity. Prenatal cocaine addiction symptoms. Immediate postnatal survival probability, nine percent. Long-term survival probability, two percent. Maximal life expectancy, thirty-one years plus or minus three years.*

"He's a total mess." The excitement of life snatched from death had died away. She was exhausted, reaction was setting in, and she was close to tears. A thousand healthy births could not take away the pain of a single sick baby. "You say you give me credit for this one — credit for what? He's ailing and weak, and doomed at birth. If everything went *perfectly*, he'd not live much past thirty."

"Christ was dead at thirty-three. So was Alexander the Great. How much more do you want him to do in the world?"

Still she was not listening. "Why do we do it? — drag the poor babies into the world, fight to save them, breathe life in them, operate on them — when even before we start we know they can't live a normal life, maybe can't live for an hour. Why do we *bother*?"

"You're tired out, Eileen." He took her gently by the arm. "We're not gods. Just medics. It's our job to save lives. That's all we can do, all we ought to do."

"We didn't save *anyone*. Look at him, and those displays. He's dying while we watch." But as she spoke, one miniature brown hand was raised in the air. The little head squirmed round on its negligible neck and the diminutive toothless mouth opened to deliver a cry of protest. One brown eye opened a slit.

"Oh, look at him." Eileen Calder gasped and leaned over the incubator crib. "See him, Doctor? He's looking at us." She smiled down and waved her fingers. "I'm sorry, baby. You heard me, didn't you? I shouldn't have said what I did — we wrote you off once tonight already, and we were wrong."

She turned to Brisbane. "He's a tough little thing, and he's a fighter, or he wouldn't be here now. I hope he makes it. But what sort of a life will he have? Poor little sweetheart, a few minutes old and already he's in trouble. He was born to trouble."

"Then we ought to call him Job, rather than John. 'Yet man is born unto trouble,' that's what the Book of Job says. If he's off to a bad start, he needs a better-than-average name, one with some weight to it. *Job Salk*." Doctor Brisbane was still holding the ID card, and now he wrote on it, his eyes blurring with fatigue. "Job Salk. No, that's not bad but it's not grand enough. Job *Napoleon* Salk. How about that? He was a little guy, too, and it didn't hold him back. Yes, I like it." He wrote again, and clipped the card back onto the incubator. "Come on, Eileen, let's go home. We've done all we can. I'm ready to drop."

The nurse took one last look at the squirming baby. "You keep right on fighting, babe, you hear me?" She

blew a kiss through the scratched plastic cover of the
incubator. "Good night, Job Napoleon Salk. I'll see you
tomorrow."

She turned to the attendant who watched over the
babies needing incubator care. "You look after this one
really well. He's had a tough time."

Eileen Calder blew another kiss at the incubator and
hurried out after the doctor, into the corridor and onto
the elevator that would take them up past Administra-
tion to the hospital roof and the helicopter pad.

In the twelve hours since Brisbane and Calder had
arrived for duty a weather front had been and gone,
pushing high winds through the area. A balmy noon
and low cloud had given way to cold, starlight, and
crystal-clear air. When the two emerged onto the roof
they found that the midday smog had vanished and the
whole city lay spread out before them. The shuttle
helicopter was already in take-off position. As they hurried to it they glanced to each side, out and down over
the edge of the flat roof.

The area beyond the hospital's solid and windowless
walls was poorly lit and gloomy. Most street lights had
long since been smashed and never replaced. One mile
to the southwest, in vivid contrast to the dark streets,
the floodlights, landing pads, and flashing control
beacons of the Mall Compound formed a bizarre blaze
of red, white, yellow, and blue illumination. Brisbane
and Calder were a little too far away to make out the
barricades, wire, and watchtowers, but they could see
the roaming beams of searchlights, sitting on their long
poles and systematically scanning everything on the
Compound's boundaries. While the doctor and nurse
were climbing into the waiting helicopter, a sudden
scream and a clatter of sirens, bells, and horns rang out
below. It came from the Mall Compound and from all
the darkened streets.

BROTHER TO DRAGONS

"What the hell. What sort of trouble is *that*?" Brisbane jerked to a halt and froze with one foot on the helicopter's bottom step.

Behind him, Eileen Calder laughed and waved her arm to take in the whole city. She poked him in the back. "You've seen too many emergencies, Doctor. It's midnight. Remember? Happy New Year!"

More sirens and Klaxons were sounding. From all sides, church bells rang out through the chilly night. Brisbane stepped down from the helicopter, turned, and kissed Eileen Calder smack on the lips. "Happy New Year, Eileen."

He walked to the edge of the roof, leaned over, and shouted into the noise-filled night. "Happy New Year, everyone. Happy New Century!"

His cry vanished unanswered into the darkness. But in homes and bars and hotels and restaurants, in freezing log cabins and tall tents and stifling squat mud huts, in churches and chapels and synagogues, in hospitals and prisons and asylums and refuge shelters, on and under land and sea, in the air and out in the vacuum of space, with raised glasses and held hands and songs and cheers and prayers and tears, Brisbane's unheard words were echoed and reechoed. It was a night for jubilation, for reflection, for assessment, for rededication; a night for old memories and new commitments.

As midnight rolled on around the world, the people of Earth were celebrating the arrival of the Third Millennium.

● Chapter Two

Cloak House Child

Lights-out in Cloak House was eight P.M., enforced to the minute. But in the long evenings of summer it was too light and too hot to sleep, and that's when the big kids told the little ones what they knew about Mister Bones, which was a lot, and about the Tandyman, which was very little but all horror.

Job knew about Mister Bones before he could speak, but it was a long time before he was singled out by that figure of ultimate authority at Cloak House, the pencil-thin man who prowled the dining hall, led the morning prayers and hymns in a deep, cracking bass, and once a week examined everyone's hair, ears, and teeth.

The big meeting with Mister Bones took place on Job's fourth birthday.

He did not know that it was his birthday. All he knew was that in the late afternoon he was thoroughly washed by the dormitory attendant, dressed in a clean shirt and pants, and taken downstairs to a part of Cloak House that he had never seen before.

"You sit right here, Fish-face." With thirty-nine other kids to attend to, the fourteen-year-old attendant could not hang around. "Stay where you are, and wait. Someone will come and get you in a few minutes."

The big door slammed behind her. Job ran over and tried to open it. The handle was at the limit of his reach, and it would not move. He went back and sat, knees tightly together, on the old black chair. He stared at the

heavy dark wood of the other door to the room and
wondered what might come through.

Someone will come and get you, that's what Cobby had
said. But what did she *mean*?

Spick 'n' span, Tandyman,
Blin' your eyes an' burn your wan',
Night-time watch say one-two-three,
Tandyman, you won't catch me.

The big kids all agreed that what they chanted was
true, that the Tandyman with his white-hot hands
came only when it was dark, at three o'clock in the late
night-time. Now it was still light, and Job had not even
had dinner. But still he trembled. Sometimes, he knew,
even the big kids were wrong.

As he sat silent he began to hear a voice from the
other side of the wooden door. He stopped shivering.
That voice he knew, and it was not the Tandyman. It
was the woman who came to see him and sometimes
brought him presents; not food — Mister Bones would
take away any food that was not served in the big hall —
but toys; little figures of carved wood, a metal chain and
cross to wear around his neck, and once a box that you
could shake, look into, and see something like spar-
kling lights. He did not know the woman's name, but
she would not let anything bad happen to him.

"I don't know how you do it, Father Bonifant."
When Job leaned back to the wall, he could hear the
reassuring voice more clearly. "You are paid no more
money than any of the other Houses. This building is
older than most, and I haven't see a dime spent on it by
the government in the years I've been coming here.
But — "

The next sentence was drowned for Job as the
wooden door creaked open. He jerked forward off the
chair.

"And yet Cloak House is clean, and the children are
healthy," went on the woman's voice, much louder

now. "Or as healthy as some of the poor bairns will ever be. How do you manage to feed and clothe and clean, on so little?" She had moved through the door and was smiling down at Job. "Hi. Remember me?"

She reached for him. But he had not seen her for a long time (almost three months) and, suddenly shy, he ran and hid his face against the other door.

"Job Salk! Come back here at once. You are four years old now — not a baby." The other voice was Mister Bones's rough, crackly bass. It reassured Job, even as it scared him. Everyone in Cloak House did what Father Bonifant told them to do. *Fast.* He returned, to stand by the black chair.

"You ask how we manage it," went on Mister Bones, as though Job did not exist. "Nurse Calder, I do not know if you expected an answer to that question, but I will give one. We have two great forces working for us in Cloak House. They are called *prayer* and *discipline*. Together they can produce miracles."

He bent down towards Job. "And you, Job Napoleon Salk, you are a very fortunate boy. Today is your birthday, and you have a visitor. Not many children at Cloak House are so lucky. Can you say hello to Nurse Calder?"

Job nodded dumbly. All he wanted was to go back upstairs and join the other children. He was hungry, and soon they would be eating dinner. But the nurse had grasped his arm and was leaning over to inspect him, just as Mister Bones inspected all of them, every week. She took his jaw in her right hand, turning it slowly from side to side. She opened his mouth wide, peered inside, and looked up at the man standing in front of her. Her eyebrows arched in question.

"I know, I know, I *know*." Father Bonifant sounded angry. Job prayed that it was not with him. "Better than you imagine, Nurse Calder, I know. I am not blind."

"Then you know that these at least are solvable

problems? It is too soon for reconstructive surgery, the bones are still growing fast, but standard dental work would help that awful overbite." She saw Bonifant's face. "I'm sorry, of course you know. But is there no grant that he could get, or some free treatment?" She pulled Job onto her knee, and he did not resist. "Job, can you eat all right, with your teeth and jaw?"

He nodded eagerly, misunderstanding the question. But she made no move to offer him food.

Mister Bones was leaning over them. His dark eyes went right through Job, who leaned back against Eileen Calder's comforting chest.

"Are you still at the same hospital, nurse?" said Father Bonifant. And, at her nod, "Then you tell me: are *your* facilities improving, or are they getting worse? Do *you* have grant money, or extra free services available? Are there *less* destitute charity cases, begging for your time and your resources? Are there *less* penniless and pathetic pregnancies? Do not bother to answer. The golden eighties ended a long time ago, for all the poor. What do you do with *your* most hopeless cases?"

I bury them, thought Eileen Calder. But she would not say it, not with Job snuggling up against her as living proof that such an answer was sometimes wrong.

"Father Bonifant, I know the problems. But it would be wrong if I did not at least *ask*." She stroked the boy's black hair. "Father, can I take Job for an hour?"

"Outside Cloak House? No. He is too young, and the AQI today is dreadful. We have been pumping in from the highest level."

"I know the ground air is bad — I walked here through it. I didn't mean outside. I mean up, to the roof. Last time I was here Job said that he had never been, and there will be lots of Mall activity tonight for him to look at." She turned Job's head, so that he was looking up at her. "Would you like that, Job? To go up on the roof with me?"

Job said nothing. His eyes flickered from her to Mister Bones.

"Answer Nurse Calder. Be honest. Tell her what you would really like."

"I would really like dinner."

Father Bonifant smiled, for the first time since Job had entered the room. "Of course you would. You can see the roof after dinner. Nurse, I should have had more sense. He has had nothing since lunch, and everyone else is upstairs, eating. I should have recognized a child's priorities. Come on."

"Here. I brought this." Eileen Calder reached forward into her purse and produced a big transparent sack of hard candy.

Bonifant reached out a long, skeletal hand. "That is very kind of you. I accept it, gladly. But you know that the rules of Cloak House require that this be shared equally among all the children."

He led the way up two flights of uncarpeted stairs. The beige paint on the walls had peeled away in places, the light fixtures were cracked and patched with plastic, and the stair treads were worn; but everything was neat, scrubbed clean, and dust-free.

They entered the dining room. Food had already been served on the long formica-topped tables, and two hundred seated children of all ages from two to sixteen were busy eating. The conversations died as Father Bonifant's arrival was noted.

"Continue!" He waved his arm, as Job ran to take a place beside a little girl of Oriental appearance who was sitting alone. A filled plate was set in front of him. Eileen Calder walked to stand behind him and heard the girl chattering to Job in an unfamiliar tongue. He replied with his mouth full.

Nurse Calder turned to Bonifant, who had moved to her side. "What language is that?"

"I wish I could tell you. She was deposited at the

front door of Cloak House two months ago, frightened, badly beaten, and undernourished. The only word she could say that made sense to us was *Laga*, which is now her name."

"But she's talking a blue streak to Job, and he's jabbering back like nobody's business!"

"I know. She is learning English — slowly — but for the time being Job is her interpreter. He is the only one here, child or adult, who understands her."

"But how?"

"By God's good grace — that is my only explanation." Father Bonifant's cadaverous face wore an expression of real pleasure. "Nurse Calder, when Job Salk came here from the hospital, you told me your fears: that his mother's addictions during pregnancy would add mental retardation to his physical problems.

"I told you that it was useless to worry, and that the Lord tempers the wind to a shorn lamb. I said that we would pray for him. We did, everyone here at Cloak House. Maybe you thought that it accomplished nothing. When you looked at Job, you still saw that deformed jaw. But look inside his head, and you will find no defect, but a great God-sent gift. He picked up the street argot — which the children here are officially forbidden to speak — through his pores, before he was two years old. No one knows how he came by it. He has had no tutoring, but he speaks Spanish as well as he speaks English."

The plates of food had been rapidly emptied as Bonifant was speaking, and were disappearing back into the kitchen hand-to-hand, like a well-run assembly line. Within two minutes the food was gone and cups of milk had taken its place.

"Everyone helps," said Father Bonifant, at Eileen Calder's nod of approval. "It is one of my rules. By two years old, a child can understand enough to contribute."

"Understanding is one thing, but children are children. How do you make them obey you?"

"You will be horrified to hear my answer. I told you that Cloak House works through prayer and discipline. Both are needed, if we are to survive. I can scour the city for cheap meat and three-day-old bread and give-away furniture and condemned cleaning materials, but even so Cloak House sits at the very edge of survival. I cannot afford to waste anything, or see anything wantonly destroyed. If a child who is more than two years old wilfully breaks something, or dirties something and does not clean it, or wastes food or drink, he or she joins me in prayer. And he forfeits the next meal. I make no exceptions."

Eileen Calder said nothing, but her lips tightened with shock.

Father Bonifant could see her grim-faced disapproval, and then her skepticism. She did not really believe him. He had expected nothing less. As the cups of milk were emptied and vanished back to be washed, he walked forward to collect Job.

What he had told Eileen Calder was exactly true. He did not see the need to mention that whenever any child missed a meal, so too did he.

"Come on, Job. There's nothing to be afraid of, it's quite safe up here."

Eileen Calder could not understand why Job was so reluctant to take the last few steps. He had walked up the stairs willingly enough, although he had been forced to stop frequently for breath — those lungs, flawed at birth, would never have normal efficiency. But Job seemed excited at the idea of visiting the very top of Cloak House. He had wanted to look out of each window as they moved higher and higher, and he had paused and gaped with pleasure and amazement at the great, noisy air handlers, drawing their intake at the top floor of the building, above the smog layers, and pumping air down to provide tolerable breathing for all the lower levels. The handlers were not so necessary now, at night, but in the afternoon Eileen Calder had been forced to wear a filter mask when she walked over to Cloak House.

They had finally arrived at the door that led out into the night and onto the flat roof. And now Job was hanging back. Was he afraid of the night itself?

She had an inspiration. It was not just the roof. Job had been brought to Cloak House when he was six weeks old; Father Bonifant had made it clear that he still considered Job too young to go out into the streets. So this must be a completely new experience for the boy — he had lived all his life *inside*, in this building, without ever seeing open sky or breathing fresh air!

"Job, it's all right. Look." She let go of his hand and took the last few steps herself, to stand on the rooftop in the warm night air. "See, up there — stars."

They were not much to see. The muggy damp of air, even ten stories up, was still thick with smoke and dust. But Job came hesitantly forward and stared up and around in wonder.

"That's the city, Job. *Our* city." Taking his hand again she led him around the perimeter of the roof, with its five-foot guard rail and thick wire mesh.

"Over there." She pointed northwest. "That's the hospital where you were born, and where I work. And way over there — you can't see it, because it's too far away — is the suburb where I used to live."

She felt a stab of nostalgia for her house and flowers, followed by a stronger rush of anger. When the charity work at the hospital was done, most of the medical staff flew out on the shuttle helicopter to cleaner air and safer streets. She had done exactly that herself until last year, when compassion for the children she was leaving behind every night became stronger than fear or comfort. If she chose, she could still return to her old life. But Job and the other children of Cloak House had no place to run to if the area became too tough or the air too dirty. They were stuck with this, like it or not.

She moved on quickly, past the dark secrets of the northern and eastern ghettoes. If Job had asked her what was in those unlit urban canyons, she could have offered no more than the unpleasant rumors passed on to her by welfare patients at the hospital. And she would not have told those to Job. Maybe they exaggerated, and only a fifth of what they said was true; but that fifth was too much.

They arrived at the western edge of the roof. Eileen Calder had deliberately kept it for last.

As usual, the Mall Compound was brilliantly lit. Tonight there was an added attraction. Helicopters by the dozen were landing, loading, and taking off for the airport that lay across the river, its runway lights visible far to the southwest of the Compound's mile-long rectangle.

Job had never seen anything like it. He gazed enthralled at the swarm of choppers, lifting, hovering, and darting away like gigantic dragonflies.

"What are they? What are they doing?"

"It's the final day of Congress — the people who run this country have been living there, and now they're going home. They'll be back again in a few months."

She felt again the stab of anger. Sure, *they* could leave here, exchanging the barricaded security (and rumored luxuries) of the Mall Compound for forests and deserts and mountains, and the great river valleys. But how long since a congressman or congresswoman had been to visit her hospital? How long ago, if ever, had one been to Cloak House?

She could tell that Job didn't understand what she was saying, that he was obviously too young and the words "Congress" and "country" and even "month" still meant nothing to him. No matter. His bright eyes were fixed on the dazzling lights of the Compound, and on the swarm of cars and trucks around its floodlit helicopter pads.

"I like that. I want to go there." He spoke so quietly that she could hardly hear him. "I'll take Laga with me, too."

"You will, Job. One day you will go there."

He wouldn't, of course. Not with his background and his appearance and his physical problems. For him the doors to the country's treasure chamber were already locked, the glittering prizes of life already denied. But you could not tell that to a small child.

And you should not even think it *yourself*.

I'm getting old, thought Eileen Calder. Old and worn out and cynical. And being cynical is a lot worse than being old or worn out.

She took the little boy with his receding chin and marred jaw-line and weak lungs, and lifted him in her arms.

"You will, Job Salk." She hugged him to her. "You'll go there when you grow up, you and Laga. And then the brightest lights in the world will be switched on, just for you."

• Chapter Three

> And behold, there came a great wind
> from the wilderness, and smote the
> four corners of the house, and it fell
> upon the young men, and they are dead;
> and I only am escaped alone to tell thee.

— *The Book of Job, Chapter 1, Verse 19*

When Job was nearly ten years old, four bad things happened within a few months. They were all consequences of a single badness, but it was years before he realized that.

The first came one misty September day, when Nurse Calder arrived at Cloak House for a final and tearful meeting. "They've closed the hospital, Job." She hugged him to her. "No more funding, not for babies, not for emergencies, not for anything. I've got to find another position. I know I can't do it in the city. I have to leave. Goodbye, little love. Look after yourself."

Job knew that she was very sad, but she only came to see him every few months, anyway, and at the time he did not understand the finality of this visit.

Much worse than Nurse Calder's leaving, and a shock that overturned his whole universe, was the second bad thing: the loss of Mister Bones.

Father Bonifant populated Job's earliest memories; he was the bedrock on which the boy's whole life rested, the one constant element of a changing world. He had sat with Job at one year old, when wheezing attacks turned breathing into agony; six months later he had

prayed and bathed the little body with cold water
through one endless night when fever had thrown Job's
frail limbs into muscle-tearing convulsions.

When Job was six, Father Bonifant had given him
the assignment that transformed the boy's life. The
high point of Job's week became Saturday morning,
when he accompanied Mister Bones on shopping
expeditions, wandering from the richer western sub-
urbs to the worst parts of the eastern ghettoes,
searching for anything that was being given away,
thrown out, or available for tiny amounts of ready cash.
Job soon realized why he had been singled out from
two hundred children for this privilege. Father
Bonifant had struggled for years with *chachara-calle*, the
gabble of the street people, and never mastered it. Job,
don't ask him how, had found that it came to him as
easily as breathing — more easily, what with the bad air
and his weak lungs. He became the interpreter, learning in the process how to find his way around the city,
how to negotiate, and how to crack the jokes against
himself and Mister Bones that made him acceptable to
the ghetto-dwellers. And when he returned to Cloak
House, he relived each of those exciting Saturday
mornings for Laga. She was now English-speaking,
but still shy and much smaller than she should have
been. Job had appointed himself her special friend and
protector.

It was during those street expeditions that Job first
heard the phrase, *Quiebra Grande*. The street language
had no words to describe the concept of global
economic decline and depression, and so the "Great
Crash" suggested to Job not a financial failure, but the
collapse of some real but far-off structure of
unimaginable size. It seemed totally unrelated to anything that might happen to Job or to anyone he knew.

Those Saturday rambles of the city also revealed
another side of Father Bonifant, a seldom-seen man

who hid behind the stern disciplinarian and guardian of Cloak House morality.

"You might say we have something in common, you and I." It was a sweltering summer morning, and Mister Bones was sweating a metal-wheeled hand-cart through a narrow alley, while Job sat on it and enjoyed — or endured — a bumpy free ride. "I'm referring to our *boniness*."

And then, when Job showed no sign of understanding what he meant, "You were named for a great general, Napoleon Bonaparte. Old Boney, his enemies used to call him. And I, of course, am known as Mister Bones."

Job was shocked to silence. No one at Cloak House would dream of saying "Mister Bones" anywhere within a mile of Father Bonifant — yet he knew the nickname. And he was making a *joke* about it!

"But do not let Napoleon Bonaparte become your hero, even though you are his namesake." If Father Bonifant had seen Job's reaction, he did not let it show. "Napoleon was a great general, one of the most famous in history. But a general becomes famous by killing. Remember this, Job Salk: your friend, Nurse Calder, is more of a hero and a greater person than Napoleon."

"How do I tell who is a great person?"

"That is a very difficult question. A complete answer now would confuse you. Remember, an easy question can have an easy answer. But a *hard* question must have a hard answer. And for the hardest questions of all, there may be no answer — except faith. I tell you this: one day you will know how to tell who is a great person."

Job had puzzled over that statement for the rest of the day, as he haggled for a great heap of old furniture and persuaded himself that none of it was stolen. (The latter at Father Bonifant's insistence; Job had sadly turned away over the months a score of wonderful deals for hot property.) This time he finally came to an agreement and they loaded the cart. Back at Cloak

House the goods would be carefully sorted, the seats of ancient armchairs examined (a sure source of lost coins), and the springs and iron frames removed for sale as scrap metal.

The load when it was in position was too much for Father Bonifant. Job had to go off and find a couple of *basura*, the "street garbage" homeless who lived in one of the alleys, and persuade them to help to push.

"What did you offer them?" asked Father Bonifant, as Job rode in grandeur on the topmost armchair. "Not food, I hope. This is a very bad month."

"Nothing. I just asked them if they were bored stiff and wanted something to do. They called me *chico feo* — little ugly — but they said they were."

All that had happened only one month before Nurse Calder came to see Job for the last time, and just two months before the dreadful, world-shattering day when Father Bonifant called a meeting in the big assembly room, to tell them that he was leaving.

"Tomorrow will be my last day at Cloak House," he began. As the babble started, he glared around him. He was still Mister Bones, and the incipient hubbub died to an awful silence. "I have been here for seventeen years, seventeen happy and fulfilling years. It is only fair to tell you that I will leave unwillingly. I love Cloak House, and I love all of you. Although I do not expect most of you to understand what I am about to say, I hope that you will remember it and reflect on it when you are older.

"For some years I have found it necessary to speak out against the actions of our own government. Within the Mall Compound there has been an increasing callousness towards the less fortunate of our country by the most fortunate. I have seen a widening gulf between rich and poor, between have and have-not, between our Congress and the people whom they are supposed to serve. I saw that gulf clearly. I denounced it.

"In the past few months, sure that no one was

listening, I became more outspoken and specific. I named individuals in the Congress who are the worst offenders. Now I find that I was mistaken. My words *were* being followed, more closely than I dreamed. They were far from acceptable.

"Yesterday I was summoned to appear before the trustees of Cloak House, which operates under congressional control. I was told that the stewardship of this institute must be nonpolitical, and that in view of my 'intemperate, not to say treasonous' words I would be relieved of my position, and reassigned.

"Word of my reassignment came this morning. It will be far from here. I will serve as a spiritual guide to those who dwell within the Nebraska Tandy."

Tandy. A ripple of horror ran around the room at that dread word. Father Bonifant ignored it.

"The Nebraska Tandy was the first disposal site in this country, and has become one of the biggest. My guess is that more than a hundred thousand people now live within the restricted area. Thus assignment to the Nebraska Tandy carries a great responsibility, and I choose to regard it as an equally great honor. But it is unlikely that I will return here, or that we will ever meet again."

He took a long, stern look around him at the wide-eyed faces.

"That is all I have to say, except to tell you again that I love you all very much. Now let us pray together; for each other, for our great country, and for its wonderful people."

Mister Bones vanished from Cloak House that night. He never returned.

For Job, that was the second bad thing. The third bad thing was the arrival of Colonel della Porta, the new Chief Steward of Cloak House.

At first the children thought he was a very good

thing. He was a fat, comfortable-looking man, triple-chinned and always smiling, and he did not have Mister Bones's addiction to discipline. Lights-out became a random event, and people stayed up as long as they liked. Colonel della Porta also abandoned the weekly inspections of hair and teeth, which had been seen by the kids as nothing but a nuisance. Best of all, with his advent the food at Cloak House, always scarce under Mister Bones, became more plentiful. It sometimes tasted funny, and the colonel ate his own meals in his private suite of rooms rather than with the children, but who cared, if there was plenty for everyone?

Only Laga was wary. "He smiles, even when there's nothing to smile at," she said to Job. "And he looks funny at some of the big girls."

Job dismissed her comments. His own view of the dark side of the colonel did not come until the new chief had been running Cloak House for three weeks. One afternoon Job was called downstairs for a meeting. There had been no foraging expeditions since Father Bonifant left, so Job assumed that was the reason for the call.

He was summoned at once into the big room, where Colonel della Porta and a visitor were sitting in new and plushy armchairs. After a nod to show that he had registered Job's arrival, the colonel went on with his business. Job was left standing for the next hour and a half, marvelling at the plates of fruit, cakes, and savories that covered the long sideboard.

The long wait was designed to make Job uncomfortable, and it would have succeeded if the conversation between the two men had been in English, Spanish, Japanese, Mandarin, or *chachara-calle*. But della Porta and his visitor spoke a tongue new to Job, a smooth, liquid voice that often suggested Spanish but differed from it in both sounds and words. Job listened hard. By the time the visitor was given his marching orders and made ready to leave, Job was identifying cognates, picking up cadences and speech rhythms, and making guesses at some phrases. The two had been talking about food and cooking — no, food and food *supplies*, because they mentioned trucks and deliveries. Job wanted to hear more and learn more. He was disappointed more than worried when the man left, and he was at last alone with della Porta.

"You know who I am?" The fat man eased himself up from the armchair and came to tower over Job.

"Yes, sir."

"You will call my assistants *sir*. I am to be addressed always as 'Colonel,' or as 'Colonel della Porta.' "

"Yes, Colonel."

"And you are Job Napoleon Salk, whom the others call Fish-face." The colonel walked slowly around the standing boy. "With good reason. What happened to your jaw, to make it recede like that?"

"Nothing, sir — Colonel. I was born this way."

"And you are the boy who has been described to me as Father Bonifant's favorite. Well, certainly not for the reason that I suspected. Tell me, Salk, is it true that you accompanied Bonifant when he went and bought food?"

"Yes, Colonel. Food, and other things, too."

"Indeed." Della Porta wandered over to the sideboard and helped himself to a handful of chocolates. "Describe those trips to me."

"Yes, Colonel." Job's mouth was watering, but he did his best to tell everything, about buying, bargaining, scrounging, wandering through the whole city (except the proscribed zone of the Mall Compound), sometimes to return with a laden cart, sometimes — though rarely — empty-handed. When he explained his own role in obtaining the junky furniture and old food that were their usual prizes, he saw della Porta's expression change.

"You are telling me," said the colonel when Job was done, "that you — an uneducated and ugly runt of a nine-year-old — were permitted to serve as Father Bonifant's chief *negotiator*?"

"Yes, sir . . . Colonel."

"Then Bonifant was an even bigger fool — or you are a bigger liar — than I thought. Anyway, that nonsense is finished. You will receive other assignments. Do you admire Father Bonifant, and what he did?"

"Yes, Colonel." Job sensed a trap, but what could he say?

"Then since you are so great an admirer of my predecessor, I will allow your work to be judged and rewarded as I understand that he rewarded it."

Job didn't know what that meant. But he was dismissed and sent back upstairs. The next day he learned that he had a special assignment at Cloak House. He was to work in Colonel della Porta's own suite of rooms, cleaning and dusting.

"Light duties, compared with other work," said della Porta's assistant. But he was grinning to himself.

At first it seemed easy to Job, too. When the colonel had a meeting, Job was not allowed to do any work. He made himself inconspicuous, said nothing, and listened hard. The language that Colonel della Porta spoke for most of his meetings, Job learned, was called Italian. In less than a month he could follow the conversations, and he mouthed phrases and then whole sentences to himself as he worked.

By the end of that month he knew two other things. First, he understood the source of Cloak House's food supplies. A visitor had spoken of a shipment that was ready for delivery. That night, long after official lights-out, Job stood at a second floor window and watched as a truck backed up to Cloak House's rear entrance. A dozen of the older boys unloaded bale after bale and box after unmarked box.

Second, Job learned that his assignment to Colonel della Porta's quarters was no favor. When the colonel was in meetings, Job was not allowed to do any cleaning. And no matter how well Job cleaned and dusted and polished in the limited time that was left, the colonel would find fault.

Job learned of that at dinnertime, when he and he alone was denied a meal. Every other night he went to bed famished. Within the month he realized that the colonel was starving him deliberately. Della Porta made a point of eating the delicacies on his sideboard and offering them to visitors while Job was watching.

"No, he gets more than enough food already," the colonel said, when one man commented on Job's longing look. He laughed. "He's a greedy little devil, you know, he'd eat all day if I let him."

It could not go on. Job was losing weight. He found it hard to think of anything but food. But it was forced starvation that saved him, when the fourth bad thing happened.

The bread at Cloak House under Father Bonifant's rule was always two or more days old, and often so stale that it had to be toasted to make it edible. Mister Bones had done an economic analysis, and found that even if he bought flour in bulk, fresh bread was more expensive than old bread, and more than Cloak House could afford. Under Colonel della Porta, all that had changed. Great sacks of flour were delivered to Cloak House late at night, and bread was fresh-baked for the day's needs in the kitchens. It was made by the older children. Since the colonel's arrival they were no longer taught "useless and seditious" mathematics and science, so there was plenty of time for the government-approved "domestic sciences" of cooking and cleaning. After a few failed experiments, which the colonel seemed to consider amusing rather than annoying (though the children went without bread for a day or two when it happened), the level of competence rapidly increased. New bread, once an unknown luxury, soon began to be taken for granted.

One Friday afternoon, Colonel della Porta found or imagined a smear on a sideboard that Job had polished. He declared that Job's attention needed to be sharpened, and ordered that his evening meal be withheld.

Baking had just finished. The aroma of piping-hot loaves was percolating through every room of Cloak House. Job, ravenous and salivating, fled for escape to the roof. It was unnaturally warm for the end of November. He stayed on the rooftop for a long time, gazing out at the sprawl of the city, and only ventured down long after dinner was over.

Cloak House was oddly quiet on the upper floors. All the usual sounds of active children with minimal discipline were absent. Laga was not in her dormitory with smuggled scraps of food for him, nor was anyone else to be found there. He kept going, and on the fifth floor found half a dozen children lying on the floor, or leaning against the cement walls. They did not reply when he spoke to them. He heard the sound of retching from the toilets, and looked inside. Every stall was occupied, and other kids were throwing up in the sinks and on the tiled floor. Five children lay in their own spew, facedown and unmoving.

Job ran to the next floor. He found Laga there alone on the landing, feebly crawling towards the stairs.

"Laga!" At his call she turned her head. She lifted herself to her knees, but as he moved to her side she fell forward again and started to vomit, near-dry heaves that dribbled something like a handful of dark coffee-grounds from her mouth. He lifted her so that she was facedown on his knees. As he did so her stomach muscles knotted with a great convulsion. She whimpered in agony.

Stay with Laga, or try to get help? He was useless here. He laid her gently on the floor.

"I'll be back, Laga, as soon as I can."

She gave no sign of hearing. Job ran on down the stairs. Where were Colonel della Porta's assistants, the ones who were supposed to oversee Cloak House? And where was the colonel himself? Surely he must have heard the sounds from the floors above.

Job came to the colonel's quarters and ran in without knocking, something he would not have dreamed of doing normally. The colonel was standing by the long sideboard, and he was shiny-faced and sweating. Job could smell him from twenty feet away.

"Colonel, something awful's happening upstairs. Kids are real sick — some look dead."

Della Porta took no notice. Job realized that the colonel was clutching the telephone in one hand, and with the other was cramming handfuls of bonbons into his mouth and convulsively swallowing them.

"Don't tell me that!" The colonel's mouth was so full of sweetmeats that his hysterical Italian roar into the telephone was hard for Job to follow. "I paid for *stolen* food. You bastards sent me *condemned* food!" He added a string of oaths, too fast and too unfamiliar for Job to catch. "Condemned and *contaminated*! A dozen dead, maybe scores more to come. How am I supposed to explain that?"

He fell silent, listening hard.

"Cheap!" His voice rose to a higher scream. "What the hell has that to do with it, when you sell me poison? I could have been killed *myself*. What do I care what it was contaminated with?"

The individual at the other end of the telephone made another long speech, loud and excited enough for Job to know that it was a man, and to catch the tone, if not the words. Colonel della Porta quieted considerably, and his face paled.

"All right, all right," he said at last. "Sure, so I pass it on. That's easy for you to say. Who the hell do I pass it on *to*? Some of the kids — some of the ones who've died, maybe?"

He took notice of Job for the first time, and switched to English. "What are you doing in here? Get the hell out, and back upstairs!" And then in Italian into the telephone, "No, no, it's just one of the dumb kids. He don't understand squat. Look, if I'm to do it your way I'll need a lot of help, here and over on the Hill. And if I don't get that, you better remember you're in as deep as I am."

Another torrent of words burst out of the telephone, but Job could wait no longer. He ran back upstairs at top speed. By the time he came to the fourth floor he was wheezing and his lungs were aflame.

Laga had hardly moved since he left. She was no longer retching, or convulsing. He lifted her and turned her head, hugging her to him. She was warm and quiet against his chest. It was many seconds before he realized that she was not breathing.

Even then he did not fully understand what had happened. There had been two deaths in Cloak House since Job had arrived there, but he had not seen either body. Laga was still warm, her skin was still soft, she lay just as though she were resting.

When the fact of her death at last sank in, it drained Job. He laid Laga on the floor and leaned back against the wall. He was overwhelmed with misery, but the empty feeling inside left no urge to cry. For five minutes he sat unmoving, ignoring the shouts now coming from below.

When half a dozen tough-looking men ran past him, heading for the fifth floor, Job at last stood up, gazed blankly at Laga's body for the last time, and went downstairs. He did not stop in his dormitory, or seek out any of his few possessions. He had no plan, no idea

what he was going to do. When his steps led him to the
front door of Cloak House, there was no sense of an
action taken.

The door was open. Four empty cars stood in the
alley outside, lights on and engines running.

Job stared incuriously into them, at their luxurious
black upholstery, built-in communications systems,
and tinted windows. Without slowing his step he went
on past them, to the end of the alley where the street-
lamp shone white; and on again, until he was
swallowed up in the warm dark of the city's Indian
summer night.

• Chapter Four

Bracewell Mansion

By day the city had been intimidating in its size and complexity, but never scary. Perhaps it was Father Bonifant's presence, a figure so familiar, so intense, and so obviously poor that not even the lowest *basura* in the street people thought to rob or attack him. Job had roamed the potholed roadways in his footsteps, and loved it.

But for a boy alone, and at night, the city put on a new face. Streets that he had walked a score of times became unfamiliar, filled with long, distorted shadows thrown by distant streetlights. He saw no one on sidewalk or pavement, but soft voices and strange sighs came from alleys and unlit corners. Without conscious decision Job turned his steps south and west, towards the glowing jewel of the Mall Compound. When he came within a quarter of a mile of the outer barricade, all aboveground structures ended. The Mall surround was dark, seamless concrete, unrelieved by light, tree, or blade of grass.

Job hesitated, until the far-off lights drew him forward again. He began to walk slowly towards the nearest part of the barricade. The Compound was quiet tonight, with no helicopter activity. For fifty yards he moved in an odd silence.

Suddenly a siren howled within the Compound. Twin spears of light converged and held him in a bright white focus.

ATTENTION. A great bellowing voice spoke in Job's ear, so loud that he, ignorant of focused sonics, felt sure that it was audible across the whole city.

ATTENTION. YOU ARE MOVING INTO A RESTRICTED ZONE, PROPERTY OF THE UNITED STATES GOVERNMENT. ACCESS IS STRICTLY PROHIBITED. THIS AREA IS PROTECTED BY AUTOMATED DEFENSE PROCEDURES. IF YOU DO NOT RETREAT AT ONCE TO THE BOUNDARY OF THE MALL PROTECTION ZONE, SERIOUS INJURY OR DEATH MAY RESULT. DEFENSE PROCEDURES WILL TAKE EFFECT AUTOMATICALLY IN THIRTY SECONDS. THIS IS YOUR ONLY WARNING.

While the mechanical voice was still shouting, Job turned and fled. He was desperately weary and downhearted, and he ran with failing legs directly away from the perimeter of the Mall zone and away from Cloak House. When he came to the crumbling streets of the eastern ghetto he was exhausted. He flopped down against a wall and stared around him.

The area was dimly lit, but it was as busy as the streets near Cloak House had been empty. In just a few seconds a dozen people hurried past, giving him not a second glance. One of them was carrying a basket of hot chicken, and its pungent smell made Job ready to faint with hunger. He had eaten nothing for over ten hours, and to a nine-year-old that felt like days. He sat and thought of food, of potatoes and hot meat and new bread. And with that thought the final scene at Cloak House came rushing back. He understood for the first time what had happened to Laga and what it meant. She was gone. He would never see her again. Not a day's separation, or a week, but *forever*. Job leaned forward and began to weep, silently and hopelessly.

It was ten more minutes before he lifted his head again, to become aware that not everyone had hastened past and ignored him. A stooped white-haired man was standing thirty feet away. He was gazing thoughtfully at Job.

"You are out rather late, my lean young man," he said, as Job returned the stare. "Are you a juvenile lycanthrope, or do you perhaps have no home to go to?"

Job said nothing. It was years since he had thought of the Tandyman as a real menace of the nighttime, but instinct told him that night still carried danger. And the white-haired man did not speak in the comfortable and familiar street jabber of *chachara-calle*, but in precise and carefully enunciated English.

"Are you sick?" asked the stooped man, after another quiet half-minute.

"No. I'm fine."

The man nodded, and watched Job's shadowed face as two people walked by carrying more of the spiced fried chicken. "But you are hungry?"

Job nodded.

"Very well. Then come along." And, when Job did not move, the man switched to street talk. "Do not be afraid, *chico-perdido*. If you feel leery of me, all you need to do is ask. These *basura*, they can tell you lots about Professor Buckler."

Job did not reply at once. He knew he could not stay forever on the street. Tonight was warm, but what about the coming winter? He could ask a passerby what they knew about "Professor Buckler," but could he rely on the answer? Worst of all, could he go back to Cloak House? He dreaded the thought of that, and of Colonel della Porta; but it was the smell and thought of food that finally made him wipe his eyes with his sleeve and stand up.

"I have no money," he said.

"Who does, nowadays?" said the old man, again in his refined tone. "Especially in these promiscuous parts. Let us proceed."

Without looking to see that Job was following, he strolled off along the cracked sidewalk with the air of a man out for a midday stroll.

They were approaching a part of the city that Father Bonifant had avoided and Job had never seen. It must once have been a district of substance, because the buildings were huge and the avenues between them broad and formerly tree-lined. Now the windows were broken or boarded up, and only weathered stumps remained of lofty oaks and beeches.

They walked on and on, with Job clinging closer to Professor Buckler's heels. The building that they finally came to was almost as tall as Cloak House. It was fronted by splendid stone stairs, fifty feet across, but they were littered with garbage and the lower floors behind the entrance were dark. One door was not blocked off. High above it one lit window shone out halfway up the colonnaded wall. They climbed the broad steps, and went on up unlit flights of wooden stairs inside the building. Job was at the limit of his strength. Professor Buckler seemed to know it, for he moved slowly, and waited whenever Job lagged.

On the fourth floor, at an open door leading to a lamp-lit room, he turned to Job. "There is one matter that we should resolve before we enter, if for no other reason than protocol. What is your name?"

"Job Napoleon Salk." Job could smell food again, and that was making him giddy, more than the climb or his general exhaustion.

"A name to conjure with," said Professor Buckler. And then, as they went on through into the room and approached a long red couch where a dark-haired woman was sitting, "Miss Magnolia, this is Job Napoleon Salk. I ran across him by accident on my evening stroll — although chance, of course, always favors the prepared mind. I think, my dear, that he may be exactly what we need."

She turned and gave Job a suspicious frown. He stared back. He had never seen anything remotely like her. The long, fringed dress that she wore was of a

plush crimson velvet, matching the couch, and around
her neck a string of brilliants threw off a thousand glittering reflections of the lamplight. She wore lipstick,
rouge, and eye shadow, skillfully applied. Job had seen
plenty of street tarts, but he had never before met a
woman who regarded makeup as an art. All he knew
was that her scowl drew curved black brows down over
dark-socketed eyes, and pursed the fullest, reddest lips
that he had ever seen.

"You're as big a *bobo* as ever, Prof." Her voice was deep.
"Find it on the street, no matter what it looks like, you
wanna pick it up. What you gonna do with him now?"

"He has not eaten," said Professor Buckler. "Since —
when?"

Job was staring at the woman and did not answer.

"Well, for much too long, from the look of him."
There was an old windup clock ticking away on the
wall, and the professor nodded his head towards it. "I
know that it is early, Magnolia, but is anything ready
yet?"

Early? It was nearly eleven o'clock at night — not
even Colonel della Porta's second supper had been so
late. But the woman was nodding, her dark ringlets
bobbing up and down over her forehead and by the
side of her head.

"Yeah. Lucky for him. Toria and Tracy worked
morning and afternoon, they wanted an early night.
Take him through. We'll have this out later. I have to
wait for a delivery."

The man nodded and walked on through a white
door. After a moment of hesitation, Job followed. Two
more rooms, one of them equipped with dining tables
and chairs, and they were in a kitchen. It was not of the
scale of the kitchens in Cloak House — but the food! It
was more in quantity, and as good in quality, as anything that Job had seen in Colonel della Porta's private
quarters.

The professor wandered along a line of half a dozen covered dishes, lifting the tops off and sniffing the contents. He shrugged. "Well, it is certainly not for me. I may have a little soup later. But take a plate and help yourself."

Job had seen what was in those dishes: pork and rice, thick-sliced beef, whole fish in thick yellow sauce, boiled potatoes and carrots and pasta and peas and corn. He took a plate from a warmed pile, then hesitated.

"Which one am I to eat?"

"What?" The professor shook his head vaguely, and his white hair fell forward over his forehead. "Well, I don't know. Anything you want. The fish is probably good."

Job had never tasted fish, and didn't dare to. But there were plenty of other things. He hesitated at first, but when the man did nothing to restrain him he piled his plate higher and higher. Only exhaustion kept him from eating himself sick. By the time that he had finished his second plate his eyes were closing, and he was only dimly aware of climbing more stairs and of being shown to a bed in a high-ceilinged room. He lay down (in Cloak House, day clothes and night clothes were identical) and at once fell asleep.

Job had gone to bed more tired than he had ever been. Nighttime noise did not wake him; but silence and sunshine did.

He opened his eyes to winter sunlight slanting in through the narrow window, and was convinced that he had missed breakfast. Then he remembered: Cloak House was far away.

He needed to go to the bathroom, but he was afraid to venture out of the room. There was no reason for people here to let him stay, they would turn him out onto the street. Except that there seemed to be no one in the building. This late in the morning Cloak House was bustling, with work details on every floor. Here it was totally quiet.

Job made his bed, found and used a toilet, and crept downstairs. Not until he arrived at the kitchen did he find any signs of life. Professor Buckler was sitting at one of the tables. He was alone. The morning sunlight showed every wrinkle. His jaw was withered and sunken, his hands shook, and his skin looked gray. He was sipping from a tumbler filled with clear brown liquid.

"Ah," he said wheezily, at Job's arrival. He pointed to a seat, and did not speak again until the glass was empty.

"Now," he said. His color was a touch better. "Last night I thought it better to postpone certain formalities. But it is time for them now. We know your name, and little else. You ran away from home — but what home did you run away *from*?"

Job was not sure he understood the question. Professor Buckler's voice was different, the words from his sunken mouth not so clear.

"I mean," said the professor after a few more seconds, "where did you live until last night? I know you did not survive on the streets."

"I lived at Cloak House."

"I have heard of it. Do you wish to return?"

Job thought of Colonel della Porta, and of Laga's silent face. "No, sir."

"I hear no hesitation there. And it seems unlikely that they will seek you out. However, to assure Miss Magnolia's peace of mind I must explore the circumstances of your departure from Cloak House. We would not welcome a formal search. And while I am doing that . . ." He paused, and went silent for a minute or two.

"I need someone to collect a package for me. How well do you know this region of the city?"

"Not well, sir. But I do know the part around Cloak House. I went outside every week. And I can read. I could find my way anywhere, if you tell me the names of streets."

"Excellent. And by the time that you return there will be breakfast ready." He saw Job's surprise. "We maintain rather a late household. It is the nature of our work. Here." He took Job's arm and drew him to his side. On a five-inch square of paper on the tabletop he sketched in a network of roads and names. "Follow the way that I have marked. You will know the house, it has a red door and black painted lions on the railing. Knock on the door, and wait. Be patient. If no one answers in ten minutes, simply return here, to Bracewell Mansion. If someone does answer, tell them, *Supplies for the Professor*. Got that? Supplies, for the professor. That's all. They shouldn't ask questions, and if they do, don't answer them. Don't talk to anyone on the street. Come straight back here with what they give you. Stick it inside your shirt." Professor Buckler stared seriously at Job. "You know, I told Miss Magnolia last night that I believe that you are an unusually responsible and reliable boy. She is skeptical. Do not betray my trust."

"No, sir."

Job went down to the one open door and out onto the street. By day, the spooky wide avenues and gnarled tree stumps were not scary at all. It was colder than last night, but unusually warm for the end of the year. Before he had gone a hundred yards he was beginning to enjoy himself. He didn't know this part of the city, but he was quite at home in it. He knew no one by name, but here were the same sort of vendors of street food and street goods that he had seen for years. It was a temptation to join in their calling back and forth, to share in the cheerful insults and the swapping of gossip.

He kept his mind on his job, and moved on steadily through the winter sunshine. The house when he came to it had black shuttered windows and looked deserted. He knocked on the red door. In less than thirty seconds it opened a crack and a black face peeked out. "Mmm?" The voice was a tenor hum, rising in pitch.

"Supplies for the professor." Job resisted the urge to say anything else.

"Yeah." The face vanished, and reappeared a few moments later. "Here." A skinny black arm passed a square brown package about four inches square and one inch deep to Job. "Stash that. You're new, uh? What happened to Poppy?"

Job shrugged. He stuck the packet inside his shirt and did not speak. Man, or woman? The sex of the person on the other side of the door was still not clear to him. The face wore makeup, but the arm looked like a man's arm.

The door closed, and Job turned to retrace his steps.

He felt good. He had no doubt that he could find his way back, even without the map. He had done what the professor asked him to do. He had not answered questions at the red door, or talked — the temptation was still there — to anyone on the streets. Maybe he would soon be on the street himself, with nowhere to go. But before that, he would eat breakfast.

Professor Buckler had moved into the kitchen. He had in front of him another full glass of brown fluid, and he looked quite different; pinker, younger, and mysteriously fuller-faced (in his years at Cloak House, Job had never known anyone with dentures). The professor took the brown packet and dropped it casually onto the table. He made no move to open it, but waved his hand toward the serving line. "Help yourself."

Job didn't recognize most of the food. He took bread and milk, and after burning his mouth on a hot, lumpy yellow solid he piled a plate with it and went back to the table.

"The strong appetites of childhood," said the professor. "Where do they go? *Mais où sont les neiges d'antan?*"

Job did not understand him, but he knew that he was hearing a new language, somehow like Spanish and Italian but different from them. How many were there in the world?

"You know what that means, Job Napoleon Salk?" went on the professor. And when Job shook his head, his mouth full of scrambled egg, " 'But where are the snows of yesteryear?' Where indeed?" He leaned forward, elbows on the table and chin supported in his hands. His voice changed, became harsh. "You were not honest with me last night, were you?"

Job put down his fork and gazed up at him, too afraid to eat. Father Bonifant had reserved his harshest punishment for lying. "I don't know, sir."

"You know what happened at Cloak House."

"The kids got sick. Some of them died. Laga died. I was scared, and I ran away."

"And that's all you know?"

"Yes, sir."

Professor Buckler was staring at him, seeing right inside him just as Mister Bones had done. "You didn't know that nearly two hundred children died of food poisoning, and only seven survived?"

Job could not speak. Not just Laga, but *all* his friends, the only people he knew in all the world. He shook his head.

The professor studied Job's face. After a moment he reached out to grip his hand. "I believe you. Cloak House will probably be closed. No one will make you go back there. Eat your breakfast."

But Job could not. He sat staring at the table. Across from him, Professor Buckler sat sipping bourbon.

"You are too young to remember it," the professor said

at last, "but there was a time when everyone in this city, and everyone in this country, believed that the future—"

He was interrupted by a clatter of footsteps on the tiled floor behind him. Miss Magnolia swept in, hair perfectly groomed, makeup flawless. She was wearing a fuzzy peach-colored robe, a light green scarf at her neck, and open-toed heeled sandals.

"Gabbing again," she said, addressing the professor and ignoring Job. "All talk, and we've got a busy day. Two receptions this afternoon, and three tonight. We have to get the stuff in." Her eye caught the brown package on the table. "You already did it?"

Buckler shook his head. He picked up the packet, ripped the paper open at one end, and shook the contents out onto the table. They were squares of old newspaper.

Miss Magnolia frowned down at them. "What the hell's that?"

"Trial run, my dear." The professor nodded at Job. "I could not risk a pickup with an unknown quantity. I sent him down to Sammy's, then called Sammy and said to make up a dummy test package. Job came back twenty minutes ago. Sammy told me the boy obeyed instructions exactly. Did you talk to anyone on the way there, Job, or on the way back?"

"No, sir."

Professor Buckler nodded. "How would you like to stay here?" He was speaking to Job, but his eyes remained on the woman. "Stay at Bracewell Mansion, I mean, and work for me and Miss Magnolia? We need someone reliable. Someone who is not afraid of the streets. Someone who can run errands, and pick up and deliver for us."

"I would like that, sir. Very much." Job did not hesitate.

"Then I want you to go back to the house with the red door — you remember the way? — and collect another package for me." The professor nodded at Miss Magnolia. "All right? The real thing, this time."

"Hell, I don't know." She was scowling again. "Just one test, and no background — "

"I checked background. And you were the one who insisted we had to have someone quick, to replace Poppy." He turned to Job. "Off you go now. I need to speak again to Miss Magnolia. Don't worry about your food — this is cold, anyway. There'll be plenty more when you get back, whenever you want it."

Job hurried down the stairs and headed into the street. This time on the way to the red-doored house he felt no urge to speak to any vendors. He was shaking with excitement and anticipation. Twelve hours ago he had nowhere to go, nothing to do. Now he had a place to live, and a job.

And plenty to eat. *Whenever he wanted it.*

Of all the marvels at Bracewell Mansion, the idea that food might be available whenever you chose to eat was the one that Job found most incredible.

• Chapter Five

Paradise Lost

December 31st. Darkness and snow. Falling on the last day of the year, and on Job's tenth birthday. He stood in the gentle down-drift of flakes on the front steps of Bracewell Mansion and knew he was in paradise. In the city's desert of misery, toil, and deprivation, he had stumbled on an oasis of ease and plenty.

Every morning and afternoon he ran a couple of errands, picking up small packages and occasionally delivering one. He had new shoes and warm clothes for his travels through the city, and a smog mask for bad days. The professor, and even in a grudging way Miss Magnolia, had come to trust him, so they no longer worried that he might talk to the street people; and when Professor Buckler discovered Job's command of not only *chachara-calle*, but half a dozen other languages in use around the area, he encouraged the boy to chat, to listen, to look, and to become an extension of Buckler's own inquisitive eyes and ears.

Little errands, twice a day. That was all that anyone seemed to expect of him. In return Job was allowed to eat and drink as much as he liked. He had his own bed in his own room, and the run of all the floors except the three that Miss Magnolia controlled and which Job was strictly forbidden to visit.

"Women's territory," Buckler had said to him. "Paint and powder and underwear and female intimacies. Avoid them. You wouldn't want to go there if you could."

He was wrong — Job was intrigued, by the very fact

that they *were* off-limits. But he was not about to do any-thing that might jeopardize his position at the mansion, and he was scared of Miss Magnolia.

The evening snowfall was continuing, in big, pure-white flakes. The steps of the mansion were completely covered. It was colder, but even cold was a pleasure to Job, knowing he could go in any time to closed-in warmth. Tonight was a big party night. He had been told to stay out of certain rooms while preparations were being made. But once the limousines had slid discreetly to a halt in the covered garage behind the mansion, and the passengers and cargo had been tucked away inside them, Job could go back in and do what he liked. All the same, he would like to have seen those preparations. They sounded fancy. There had been talk of tonight's party every day since the last big one on Christmas night.

" 'And now there came both mist and snow,' " said a voice behind him, " 'and it grew wondrous cold. And ice, mast-high, came drifting by, as green as emerald.' "

Job turned around, but he did not need to. Over the past month he had learned the pattern. Professor Buckler drank in the morning, every morning, "to save this crumbling corpse from rigor mortis." The prenoon liquor did not make him inebriated, but when he drank in the afternoon he became philosophical, poetic, and a little unsteady. After a lull around six o'clock, sometimes including a nap, he drank all evening, when instead of intoxication the bourbon seemed to sober him, sharpen his wits, and rejuvenate his body.

At the moment the professor was somewhere near the end of state two, with downtime due before state three.

"Magnolia told me to get out, too," Buckler went on. "All hustle and bustle, get ready for the big night — but we are not included!" The professor had a glass in each hand. He lifted his head and caught a snowflake in his open mouth. "I *created* this place, you know. Yet we have become supernumeraries, you and I, in this our own house. As the males of the company, we must revolt. It is time for us to sound the *first blast of the trumpet against the monstrous regiment of Women.*"

A red-dyed head covered in curlers poked out of the door behind the professor. It was Tracy, Job's favorite among the score of women at Bracewell Mansion. "Miss Magnolia says to come inside," she said, "before you both catch pneumonia. And you, Job, stand by. I'll probably have a special errand for you in a bit, for the boss lady. Something come up unexpected. Come on, then. Hurry hurry hurry."

She gave a shiver — real or pretended, Job could not tell — and vanished. They followed her inside. As darkness fell the temperature had fallen with it, and regardless of Miss Magnolia's order it was too cold to stand about much longer. The professor led the way up two flights of stairs and on to his own private quarters. Job had been there a few times already. His amazement at rooms with so many books and bottles was a thing of the past.

"*Hurry hurry hurry,*" said Buckler. He sat down in one brown leather armchair and gestured Job to the other. "It's always the same, and it's so wrong. Hurry, go fast, keep moving. The world today wants everything done so quick, changes so quick. All that endures is *change.*" He held his glass in front of his face and stared into it like a tawny crystal ball. "Who would have believed, seeing me six years ago, that I would have come to this? A tenured professor of sociology, in an endowed chair, at a highly regarded and well-funded university, with my emeritus on the way and full retirement benefits. And then — pffft. All gone."

"What happened to you? What did you do?" Job had not understood half the other's words, and so far as he could see the professor was the most fortunate man imaginable. But he had learned that when Buckler spoke like this, Job would often find out something new.

"I? *I* did nothing. *It* happened to me. And not only to me. To the world — the whole world. To her, too." Buckler pointed a wavering finger to the ceiling. He was drinking faster than usual, and it was beginning to have an effect. "Five years ago Miss Magnolia was selling real estate. Very successfully. When the Great Crash came she lost everything. Her job, her house, even her husband — he died of worry. He was in commercial real estate, and businesses went first. Fast. It took longer for the university. Even when our endowments weren't worth spit, we still had students. For a little while."

The Great Crash.

They were the words that Job had heard about for years from the *basura* as they talked on the street corners. *Quiebra Grande. Alboroto-oro. Dinero-fuego* — the Great Crash, the gold riot, the money fire, a dozen other terms in the *chachara-calle* that was their common language. But nothing that told him what it *was*, or what it *did*.

"Seven years ago." The professor blinked at Job. "Seven years ago I had a dozen jobs open to me, all around the world. And then, four years ago, there were none. Not here, not abroad. No more foreign visitors, no foreign conferences. That's when I knew that the economic crash and the poverty were *global*."

Job didn't argue. But it seemed to him that Professor Buckler had no idea what poverty was. Poverty was Cloak House, not Bracewell Mansion. It was walking through snow in worn-through shoes or no shoes, not riding in limousines. It was stale bread or no bread, not a choice of a dozen dishes. It was winter rooms where water froze in the jugs, not the cozy mugginess of abundant steam heat. It was cold water with no soap, not long, hot showers or the mink-oil bubble baths that the women talked about.

"Or almost global." Buckler was not talking to Job now, he was talking to himself. "The trick is to find the pockets of money. They're still there, you know, the ones that control wealth. You have to get close to them."

Wealth.

A month ago Job didn't know what that word meant, but with Buckler's informal tutelage he had been learning. Wealth was more than having enough to eat, and clothes to wear, and a place to live. Wealth was so much food that half of it was thrown away uneaten. Wealth was so many clothes that most of them you never wore at all. Wealth was — still remote and almost unimaginable for Job — helicopters and airplanes and ships, on call to take a few people wherever they needed to go.

No. Not *needed* to go. *Wanted* to go.

Job's thoughts turned to a summer night, to barricades and protection systems and watchtowers, to helicopters lifting and whirring away through the warm air.

"You mean, pockets of money like the Mall Compound?"

"My boy, the analogy is well-intended. But it is not appropriate." Buckler's lids had drooped shut. He had refilled his glass with an effort from the bottle that stood on the floor next to his armchair. "If the Mall Compound is a *pocket* of money, then the Monument that stands within it is a toothpick. For within the Mall dwell the chosen people, the five hundred and forty worthy representatives who control the expenditures of this great nation. Do not demean the Compound by calling it a 'pocket' of wealth. Call it, if you will, a vast and bloated *sack*. And be thankful for its existence, and raise your glass to it." Buckler did so as he spoke. "Your meals and mine, and the very existence of Bracewell Mansion, are owed to the Mall Compound. We are all its slaves — its *willing* slaves."

He fell silent. If the evening ran true to form he would sleep for an hour or two, to wake clear-eyed and in good humor.

Job went quietly out and up to the kitchen. Before he ran an errand tonight, in the cold and snow, he wanted warm food inside him. He helped himself from the hot buffet and was still eating when Tracy came to the door.

"Good." She stayed at the threshold. "You're here. Go get your warmest clothes, then come right back. I'll wait. I don't know what's going on, but it's hell upstairs. Miss Magnolia wants you to go the minute it's ready."

Job ran up the stairs, and back down. He was coughing and holding his chest when he returned to the kitchen. Tracy came over and put her hand on his arm. "Are you all right? You shouldn't be going out on a night like this."

"I'm fine." Job hated sympathy, even from someone as nice as Tracy. He stifled another cough and sat down. "I choke a bit, but I'm real lucky compared with other people. Professor Buckler told me all about what happened to him at the university, and about poor Miss Magnolia, and her husband."

"Told you *what*?"

"What happened to them. In the *Quiebra Grande*." He repeated all that the professor had said to him. At the end of it, Tracy burst into fits of laughter.

"Sociology? He's studied sociology all right. From the ground up. Job, we *call* him professor, because he likes that, and he's got all those books and he talks so funny. But he's no professor, never has been. Way I heard it he's been right here in the city for forty years."

"Not teaching?"

"Not teaching, 'less you count pimping as teaching. And Miss Magnolia, she only sold one thing in her whole life — and it's sure not real estate." She laughed again. "Don't you believe two words the old prof tells you, because one of 'em will be made-up. That man, he's got more imagination inside him than he's got bourbon. He just loves to talk." She shook her head. "Real estate!"

"But he didn't make up the *Quiebra Grande*."

"No, he didn't. Nobody has a mind diseased enough for that."

She went out giggling. Job sat with his face burning. He didn't so much mind what the professor had done, inventing a glorious past for himself. Job had had thoughts like that himself at Cloak House, when he imagined his real mother and father who would one day come to find him. What he hated was the idea that Tracy would tell the others how gullible he was, and they would laugh at him behind his back.

They would, too. He had heard them mocking Professor Buckler, when he came out with one of his extra-philosophical comments or poetic phrases.

Job sat with his coat and gloves on. He was too hot, but he wanted to go before anyone else came. He was not looking forward to Tracy's return. To his surprise, though, it was Miss Magnolia herself who arrived ten minutes later. Job's errands were mostly run for the professor, and for the rest it was Tracy or Rosita who brought instructions.

Miss Magnolia was frowning — nowadays she always seemed to be frowning — and she hardly looked at Job. Her attention was on the square box she was holding. "Now listen to me real careful. This isn't the typical drop-off, to the usual places. Do you know the Mall Compound?"

"I know where it is. I've never been inside."

"You won't need to go inside. Go to the northeast corner of the protection zone — that's the corner nearest here. Go in just far enough to trigger the alarm system. You know what that is? All right. You wait, until a man in a uniform comes. Don't worry about the warning message, the defense system will be turned off for you. Stay right where you are at the edge of the protection zone, let him come to you."

She paused, as Tracy came hurrying into the kitchen. "Well?"

"You were right." Tracy's manner had changed. She was pale and nervous. "It *was* Susie. Tromp saw her leave. On foot. She went east."

"With the shipment?" Miss Magnolia's face was like painted stone.

"I don't know. Tromp didn't see it, but Susie was carrying a cloth bag."

"She has it. She must have. Don't worry, I'll take care of her later. Stupid bitch. I have to get another batch over there right now, before their party starts. It won't be easy." She turned to Job. Her face frightened him. "A man in a blue uniform, with a peaked cap. Got that?"

"Will he come from inside the Compound?"

"Never you mind where he comes from. Just wait for him."

"You're sending him to the *Compound*?" Tracy's lower lip drooped in shock.

"Yeah." Miss Magnolia gave Tracy a furious glare. "Shut your yap, and stay out of things."

"But there's been patrols over there, the past week. Vince hasn't called me once, and Toria said the Compound —"

"I said, shut your big yap. Don't you know who the customer is for this one? We got clients here in fifteen minutes, every girl booked, and I'm late for this delivery. If we don't give service we'll all be out on the street. You'll be peddling your tight little ass to some rot-cock *basura*. You want that? Then shut up." She held the square box out to Job. "Here. Keep it inside your coat. It's got a waterproof cover, but don't let nobody see it. When the man in uniform comes up to you, he's going to say, 'A little something for the head honcho?' You don't say one word. You give him the box, and you come right back here, fast. I'll be waiting. All clear?"

Job had a dozen questions he would like to have asked, but not of Miss Magnolia. He nodded, stuffed the box down inside his high-collared coat next to his chest, and started off down the stairs.

"Gloves and hat!" called Tracy after him. But she did not follow to see him leave.

The snow outside lay deeper on the ground. It was still falling. As the temperature dropped, the thick, lazy flakes were changing to small icy points that stung Job's unprotected face. He pulled the brim of his hat lower, placed his hands on his chest to protect the box and hold it safe in position, and headed south and west toward the Mall Compound. The cold air was sinking to the very bottom of his lungs, producing an ache that rapidly drained his energy. He put one hand to his mouth, to filter air past his warmer glove, and trudged on.

Although it was New Year's Eve the weather was too much for most celebrants. They were still indoors, hoping that the snow would ease. Job had the sidewalks to himself. He stayed close to the walls of the buildings, sheltered from wind and safe from the occasional city patrol car purring half-blind through the snow, and crunched through the firm white layer. Even with the bright reflection of streetlights from the snow, street names were invisible. Job navigated by feel and counting, until he turned at last onto the deserted south-bound avenue that ran to the edge of the Mall Compound.

As always, the Compound was ablaze. Job stood on the perimeter, nervously watching. The searchlights on their tall towers scanned the cleared zone, ready to home in on anything that moved. Their beams made oval white circles on the untrodden snow.

Hurry hurry hurry. Job thought of Professor Buckler's

disdain for haste. Real professor or not, no other adult but Mister Bones had ever been as good to Job — and none had ever talked to him as much as an equal. But this time Job *had* to hurry, or he'd freeze on the spot. He started forward onto the unmarked surface of the protection zone, wincing in anticipation of the strident voice in his ear.

ATTENTION. It came in a few seconds. YOU ARE MOVING INTO A RESTRICTED ZONE, PROPERTY OF THE UNITED STATES GOVERNMENT . . .

Job froze, his legs telling him to run, his mind forcing him to stay. Miss Magnolia had said the defense system would be turned off. But if it wasn't . . . At the end of the message he stared around in an agony of fear. The end of the warning was ringing in his ears. RETREAT AT ONCE TO THE BOUNDARY OF THE MALL PROTECTION ZONE, SERIOUS INJURY OR DEATH MAY RESULT. DEFENSE PROCEDURES WILL TAKE EFFECT AUTOMATICALLY IN THIRTY SECONDS.

Thirty seconds. Surely it had already been more than thirty seconds.

There was sudden movement at the inner edge of the protection zone, within the Mall Compound itself. Job shielded his eyes and peered through the driving snowflakes. No man in uniform and peaked cap, but a great cloud of blown snow with a dark blob at its center. It moved through the barricade at the edge of the Compound, then turned with a scream of air-jets to head straight for him.

Job forgot Miss Magnolia's instructions. He turned and tried to run. His feet skidded and slid on the snow-covered surface. He had moved no more than a few yards when the machine reached him. He knew it was right behind him, and he tried to throw himself out of the way to one side. His feet slipped again. Before he had moved a foot he was scooped up from behind by something that lifted him and rolled him end-over-end into a dark enclosure. A clang of metal sounded around him. The machine accelerated in a turn, throwing Job's head and shoulder into a cold metal wall. He lay in total darkness, bruised along one cheek and eye socket, dizzy and disoriented.

The ride was a short one. Within a minute the machine jerked to a halt, its side opened, and Job was decanted onto a vinyl tiled floor under dazzling yellow lights.

"Stay right where you are." A hand reached down, grabbed his collar, and hoisted him to his feet. Other hands searched him. They opened his coat and pulled out the square box. Job squinted around him. Already his left eye was beginning to swell and close. He stood inside a garage with a low, paneled ceiling, beside the machine that had picked him up. The snow was melting from its windowless sides, and he could see no place for a driver.

Three men held him. Two of them wore the blue uniforms and peaked caps described to him, but Job was not naive enough to think that would help. Something had gone terribly wrong.

The younger of the two uniformed men opened the box. He unwrapped the waterproof packet inside and sniffed at the contents. "One hundred percent, for a guess," he said. "We'll know in a few minutes. God, look at him. Next thing they'll be using kids in diapers."

"They should be shot." A fat, gray-haired man who was not in uniform sat down on a workbench. "All right, let's get it over with. Who's the parcel for, boyo? Let's have a name."

"I don't know."

"Sure. You decided to wander into the protection zone in the middle of a howling snowstorm, with a million dollars worth of brain-burner on you, just for the fun of it. What made you think the defense system wouldn't fry you on the spot?"

"I thought it would."

The gray-haired man studied him. "Damned if I'm not inclined to believe you." He handed him a white cloth. "Here, kid. Wipe your face."

Job did as he was told. Until that moment he had not realized that he was crying.

"Did you know what you were carrying in the package?" said the fat man.

Job thought about that. He didn't *know*, but he had been developing his suspicions. "I wasn't sure."

"But now you are? So who sent you? Tell me that, and take us there, and you'll do yourself a favor. If we can get someone good, we won't worry much about you. Come on, now." The man could see Job's hesitation. "They dropped you in it, didn't they, without one word of warning? What do you owe them?"

Tracy hadn't done anything to him — she had done her best to protect him, even argued with Miss Magnolia. She had wanted to warn him. Job shook his head. The fat man shrugged. "If that's the way you want it. Take him away, Lou. Let him stew for a while."

The younger of the uniformed men nodded, grabbed Job by the arm, and led him through to another room. This one was warmer, not just a garage and repair shop. The man gestured Job to a chair.

"Want a drink? You must be frozen." Without waiting for an answer he filled a cup from a big metal jug and handed it to Job. It was a hot, sweet liquid that Job had never tasted before, and it burned his gullet all the way down to his stomach.

"There. Warming you up a bit?" The man had a cheerful dark face, and when he took his cap off his hair stood up in damp spikes. "Hell of a night to send a young kid out, 'specially for a drug run." He was studying Job. "Just how old are you, anyway?"

"I'm ten." Job paused, then added, "Ten today."

"God love us. What a birthday present. Did you get any presents?"

Job shook his head.

"Well, happy birthday anyway. Like your drink?"

"It's good." But it was making Job dizzy.

"More there when you want it. So what's your name, kid?"

"Job Salk. Job Napoleon Salk."

"Good. And where do you live?" The man's voice was casual. "Not out on the streets, I'll bet money on that. You'd freeze to death in this weather."

"At Bracewell Mansion." Job had answered before he thought. "And before that I was at Cloak House," he added.

"So they sent you here straight from Bracewell?" The man ignored Job's feeble attempt at misdirection.

Job knew he had been trapped; but it was too late to do anything about it. He nodded.

"Good lad." The man seemed pleased, but he wasn't gloating. "Sit there and drink as much as you like. Keep warm. I'll be back."

When he returned the other two were with him. They were wearing overcoats, and the young uniformed man was carrying Job's gloves and hat.

"Horrible night for it, but we have to take a little ride," said the fat man, his gray hair hidden now by a fur cap. He was holding the square packet in its waterproof wrapping. "Can you identify the person from Bracewell Mansion who gave you this, and sent you here?"

Job nodded unhappily.

"So you'll do that. You won't need to talk. Fasten your coat. You'll be in a car most of the time, but wrap up."

He led the way out, with the uniformed men on either side of Job. Under other circumstances, the trip back to Bracewell Mansion could have been thrilling. First they rolled nearly a quarter of a mile underground on a labyrinth of smooth transportation belts

that rose, fell, and merged with each other. Some were
deserted, some carried dozens of people. At last they
came to another garage and Job was led forward to a
long, black car. He sat in front between the driver and
the fat, gray-haired man. The dashboard was filled
with gadgets that Job didn't understand: range sensor,
radar navigator, thermal tracker. The engine was not
running, but when they were all aboard the car began
to move. It entered a tunnel, traveled for thirty seconds
in total darkness, then unexpectedly emerged at
ground level *outside* the Mall Compound and protection zone. The engine started with a low-pitched purr.
Although the night was dark and the snow drove down
harder than ever, the opaque front windscreen of the
car showed the passengers a clear, hard-edged view of
roads and buildings in black and white.

The car eased forward, lights off. As midnight
approached more people were refusing to let the
weather halt New Year party plans. They were in the
streets, many of them ignoring the sidewalk in favor of
the center of the road. Drunk or drugged, they took little
notice of the dark car sliding past them. It took almost as
long to get to Bracewell Mansion as it would have on foot.

Job stared nervously at the front steps of the mansion as the car approached, hoping to see a familiar
figure. He had been sent to do an errand, and not only
was his mission unaccomplished but he was bringing
strangers back with him. The only person who might
understand how it had happened was the professor.

The front steps were deserted. Strangely, they had
been cleared of snow. Stranger yet, the usual entrance
was closed off, while the boards in front of a great pair of
double doors in the middle of the steps had been
removed.

The gray-haired man opened the door of the car
and motioned Job to get out. "Wait here," he said to the
others. "Give me fifteen minutes. If I'm not back you

know what to do." And to Job, "All right, kid. Take me to your leader."

Job ascended the steps and paused at the top. He had never been in this way, or seen the double doors from inside the building. He had no idea where they might lead. At last he opened one of them and went in. He found himself in a tiled hallway. It led to a broad staircase carpeted in pale mauve, and at the head of that, twenty feet above them, stood Miss Magnolia in a long gown of vivid green.

"That's her," said Job in a whisper. "She gave it to me."

If Miss Magnolia heard him, she gave no sign of it. She stood unmoving and expressionless as Job led the man up the stairs towards her.

"Can I help you?" she said at last. She was looking calmly at the man and gave Job not even a glance.

"I believe you can." But there was a first note of uncertainty in his voice as he held out an oval badge. "Can we go somewhere to talk?"

"No. We can talk right here." Miss Magnolia did not even glance at the badge. She inclined her head towards the next flight of stairs. "I have important visitors tonight. I do not want them disturbed. And I would appreciate it if you would state your business promptly."

"You have important visitors. And I have important business. You sent this boy to the protection zone." The man held out the packet. "To deliver this. I don't have to tell you what it contains."

"I did *what*?" Miss Magnolia sounded more amused than afraid.

"You sent the boy — "

"You're out of your mind. I have no idea what's in that packet, or what you are talking about."

"You deny that you know this boy?"

"Oh, I know him." Miss Magnolia gave Job a brief inspection. "Slightly. He's a local street urchin. Once or twice my assistants have given him a free meal in our kitchen. A kindness that has not been returned, by the look of it."

The man turned to stare at Job.

"I live here," said Job desperately. "I have a room upstairs."

But Miss Magnolia was shaking her head. "Captain, I don't know what your game is, but I won't play it. He doesn't live here. He never has. If he says he knows his way around, then it's because when he ate here he went places he had no right to. Go get a search warrant if you like, look over the mansion top to bottom. If you find any sign that the boy lives here, or ever did, or if you find a sign of anything illegal, I'll give you free service for a month."

"Professor Buckler," said Job desperately. He turned to the fat man. "And Tracy, and Toria. They live here, too. They'll tell you about me."

"Captain, I ask you, does this *look* like the home of a professor?" There was a sound of laughter from farther up the staircase, and Miss Magnolia turned her well-groomed head to stare that way. "I don't know the boy," she went on, without looking at either Job or the captain. "There's certainly no professor who lives here. No Tracy or Toria, either. I know nothing about that package you are holding, or where it came from. What I do know is that I have very important guests, waiting for me upstairs. I always try to cooperate with officials, but if you want to detain me longer, you will have to argue with my guests, too."

"To hell with your guests — "

"Senator Nelson is here tonight. So is Senator Walsh."

The gray-haired captain said nothing, but to Job he seemed to crumple and shrink. "So we'll find nothing upstairs, eh? I hear you. And I thought I had good sources. Who told you we were on the way?"

She smiled, and Job saw a glimmer of satisfaction in her mascara-limned eyes. "Now, Captain, that's a silly thought. And it's New Year's Eve, and awful weather outside. Why don't you stop worrying, relax, and enjoy yourself here for an hour or two? I always like to make new friends."

"Yeah. I'm sure you do." The captain hefted the package he was holding. "Senator Nelson and Senator Walsh, eh? Yep. So what happens now to the kid?"

"I have no idea. But that's more your worry than mine, isn't it? You brought him, Captain. And since you will not be staying . . . " She turned in a rustle of skirts, and began to walk up the stairs to the third floor. "Close the door firmly when you leave, please. Heating this place costs a fortune."

"I wasn't lying," said Job, as she vanished around the curve in the staircase. "I do live here. Really."

"Not any more, you don't." The fat man's face was twisted with frustration. "You heard her. Senators in her pocket. We'd not get to square one. I don't know why I fucking bother." He turned, and began to walk slowly down to the double doors.

Job took a last look up the stairs, then hurried after him. "What will happen to me?"

"Possession of illegal substances. Intrusion on protected property. That's got to go in the record." The captain sighed. "I'm sorry, kid. I believe you told us the truth, and I'll put in the best word I can for you. But I don't know how much good it will do. Once I file my report, it's out of my hands." He was watching Job's face. "Cheer up. It's late, and you're tired out. Tomorrow's another day. Let's go to the Compound and have some food. Things won't seem so bad in the morning."

But in the morning, Job was sent back to Cloak House.

• Chapter Six

*Skin for skin, yea, all that a
man hath will he give for his life.*

— *The Book of Job, Chapter 2, Verse 4*

In the month that he had been away, Cloak House
had changed enormously. Job noticed some things at
once. The hundreds of dead and the handful of surviving children had disappeared, but even more new ones
had taken their place. Colonel della Porta had gone.
Father Bonifant was not even a memory. The doors of
Cloak House had been changed, replaced by strong
metal ones with double locks, and the lower floor windows were now barred.

Those were the superficial changes. It took a little
longer to discover the big one: Cloak House was no longer
a simple orphanage. It had been converted to a detention
center, and it was a center with a hidden agenda.

On the first morning, Job was taken to the first floor
apartment where the colonel used to live. He was
assigned a number. It was painlessly and sub-
cutaneously marked on his forehead and on his right
wrist in an invisible but indelible ink.

"Don't complain," said the woman who did the
marking. "That's your meal ticket. You get no food
without it. Use that number to find your assigned
duties each day. Today you're free, but you start work
tomorrow. Make sure you get a sign-off from me when
work's done. No food without that, either. Lunch at
twelve, listen for the bell."

She was muscular, short-haired, and wore a gun and a thick truncheon on her hip. She was also frighteningly casual about everything. She gave Job a chit to take out a bedroll and a blanket from stores, assigned him a dormitory, and told him to go. It took him a while to realize that this was all the indoctrination he was going to get.

Job knew his way around the building. That was just as well. The other children, all boys, showed no interest in talking to him. He spent the rest of the morning wandering around Cloak House. Although it was cleaner than it had been under Colonel della Porta, access to some floors and to all the exits was now forbidden. Not even a trickle of hot water came from the bathroom faucets, and the whole building was freezing cold.

He had been given a full breakfast in the Mall Compound, so when the bell rang at midday he was quite ready to eat but not ravenous. He wandered down to the dining room. It had not changed, but it was more crowded than it had ever been. Half a dozen adults, each one armed, stood around the walls watching. Everyone else was already seated. Job found a place, sat down, and stared around.

He was probably the youngest at his table, and certainly the smallest. The skinny boy on one side of him gazed straight ahead and ignored him completely. The boy on the other side was equally gaunt, but tall and strong-limbed, with a massive head, heavy brows, and big red ears. He returned Job's stare but did not speak.

The mutual inspection ended with the arrival and distribution of plates of food. Job hardly needed to look at what was set in front of him. The rancid smell rising from the dish was enough. A small wedge of slimy fat meat floated in thin gray gravy, surrounded by a few small lumps of soggy pasta and a spoonful of amorphous bright-orange vegetable.

Every one else was gulping down the food and spooning up the greasy gravy. Job pushed his plate way.

"Not going to eat that?" The red-eared boy spoke for the first time. "Can I have it?" Job hardly had time to nod before it was being wolfed down.

"Is it always like this?"

"Like what?" The other boy did not stop eating, and he did not seem to understand the question. Job knew he had been spoiled by the quality and choices at Bracewell Mansion, but surely Cloak House food at its worst had never been this bad?

"It's terrible," he said. "Smells rotten. And even if you could eat it, there's not enough to feed a rat."

The boy had finished, and he turned to look at Job. "You'll get used to it," he said. "My name's Skip. Skip Tolson. You don't sound like a dimmie, so you must have been jaded. What you here for?"

"Dimmie?"

"Like Guppy, on the other side of you." Tolson gestured with his spoon around Job, to where the other boy had finished eating and was impassively staring straight ahead.

"What's wrong with him?"

"Take a look in his eyes. There's nothing back of 'em. Rick Luciano — him over there — says Guppy used to be smart enough, but he got held under water too long when he was being questioned. Now he don't do nothing but eat and work and sleep. You can't get a word out of him. Lots in here like that, most of 'em born like it. Dimmies — dimwits. Not supposed to be sent here, but they are."

The plates were disappearing, every one of them wiped clean. "What's your name?" said Tolson.

"Job Salk. What did you mean about me being jaded, if I wasn't a dimmie?"

"You got labeled when you came in, right?" Tolson held up his wrist. "Know what that says, along with your number? J-D. Juvenile delinquent. You've been J-D'd, jaded, like most of us. We're too young for the Tandies. They stick us in here with the dimmies, an' hope we'll just die quiet. What did you do to get here?"

"Delivering drugs." Job did not protest his innocence. "What do you mean, die quiet?"

"All questions, aren't you?" Another bell rang, and the boys began to file out. Tolson went in his turn, and Job followed him.

"What did you mean about *dying*," he said again.

"You'd find out soon enough, so I might as well tell you. There's four hundred of us in here — "

"Cloak House only has enough space for two hundred!"

"You'd be surprised." Skip Tolson was striding upstairs, with Job panting along behind. "Four hundred. About fifty new ones come in every month, but you'll still count only four hundred at the end of it. Five or six leave because they're too old to be here — sent to the Tandies, mostly. The rest get sick and took down to the infirmary on the first floor. I've seen a couple of hundred go down, an' only half a dozen come back up. Worse than usual this last week, 'cause it's been so cold."

At the door of a dormitory he turned to face Job. His face was serious. "I'll make a deal with you."

"What sort of deal?"

"We're not allowed to steal each other's food. We get skull-cracked if we're caught, and we go without the next meal. But we can *give* each other food if we want to. So you give me half your food — not forever, 'cause you'd die, but for two weeks, 'til it starts to taste good to you and you know the ropes round here."

"Why should I?"

"Because then you get to take the empty bed next to mine, and I look after you." Skip Tolson smiled at Job's puzzled expression. "You may not think you need it, but you will. Nobody pushes me around. But you're pretty little. Did you sign out your bedroll an' blanket yet?"

"No."

"Lucky for you. If you had, and you'd left it any place, it'd have gone by now. You sleep without one when it's this cold, you shiver all night an' finish in the infirmary. I'm not making that up. You'll see it this week."

The real changes were beginning to sink in for Job. This wasn't Cloak House under Father Bonifant. It was not even Cloak House under Colonel della Porta.

"All right." But the skills developed in street forays with Father Bonifant had not been lost. "Not for two weeks, though. I'll do it for just for one week, then we'll see."

Tolson scowled, but at last nodded. "One week, then. Bet you change your mind at the end of it."

Skip Tolson had been right. Job was considering changing his mind.

When Skip had first proposed a deal, Job had been suspicious. He knew his way around Cloak House, better maybe than Tolson did. Why should he trade food for help from anyone? But at the end of a week Job was not so sure. He felt less in control of his life than he had been at four years old.

He had learned to force down the nauseous food, though there was so little of it that after sharing with Tolson he was permanently famished and light-headed. He had also, with Skip's guidance, labeled his bedroll and blanket so prominently and permanently that no one could steal it without being found out, and he carried his soap always in his pocket. Those were the easy steps to survival.

But he was smaller than average for a kid in Cloak House, and most of the time the attendants looked the other way when there was fighting. In his first few days Job saw half a dozen shivering or unconscious boys carried down to the infirmary, bones broken or bleeding from the mouth or ears. He did not see any come back. That was when he first began to appreciate Tolson's size and strength, as well as his survival skills.

He learned that the older boy took the task of Job's protector seriously. One of the few things that Job owned was the cross and chain given to him by Nurse Calder. He wore it always around his neck. On his fourth day at Cloak House a blond-haired boy with a flattened nose grabbed it from him as he was washing, and bloodied Job's mouth when he tried to get it back.

"That's Rolly Berhammar," said Skip, when Job went to him. "Where is he?"

Job led the way to the bathroom. The towheaded Berhammar and two smaller boys were still there. Skip jerked his head at them. "Out, you two. Not you, Rolly. You stay."

Berhammar ran for the door. Tolson grabbed him from behind by his hair, swung him around, and smashed his head against the wall. Berhammar sagged at the knees. While he was groggy Tolson reached into his pocket, pulled out Job's cross and chain, and flung it to the ground. Job thought that would end it, but Tolson did not release his hold. He held the other boy upright by the front of his shirt and began to punch him in the gut with his other fist. Berhammar groaned, doubled over, and gasped for breath.

Job grabbed Tolson's arm. "Skip, you're killing him."

The big lad took no notice. He went on pounding until Berhammar was making no sound at all, then let him drop headfirst to the hard floor. He nodded to Job. "All right, that should do it. Grab your stuff and let's go."

"Will he be all right?"

"Should be. Nothing's broke. But he won't try that on you again."

Job realized that Skip was right — as long as Tolson remained his protector.

Now he could see the catch. When Rolly Berhammar learned that Skip's protection of Job had ended — news traveled fast in Cloak House — he would come looking. Then Job would get what Rolly had got, maybe a lot more.

The fight with Berhammar happened on Job's fourth day. By the end of the week he had learned that Rolly's anger was not the worst that Cloak House had to offer. He saw other young boys with their protectors. The usual price of protection was not food. It was sexual tyranny. Although sex was not important to Job personally, he was beginning to realize what it meant to others. Bracewell Mansion had been an eye-opener. It had been wholly devoted to gratification, in all its hundred-headed forms. Job hadn't looked into many mirrors there, though he had surely seen plenty of them, but he had heard enough at Bracewell to understand that he was no beauty. Now he realized that might not be a bad thing.

Job looked at Skip Tolson with a new eye. He decided, to his relief, that Skip's interests did not run towards sex — yet. But Skip had his own urgent priorities. At the end of the first week he asked Job the inevitable question: Did he want to continue the food deal?

"I'll tell you later," answered Job, and headed up to the fifth floor. For the first time since his return to Cloak House he went into the dormitory where Laga used to live. It was ten minutes before dinner, and everyone else was already downstairs waiting.

The room had twice as many bunks crammed into it as the room could reasonably hold. Job sat cross-legged on the floor near where Laga's bed used to be. He leaned his head and back against the hard wall and felt the outside cold seeping through it into his bones.

He understood the logic and the statistics of Cloak House now. It was more than a detention center. One eighth of the boys went to the infirmary each month; only a handful came back. If you were strong and smart enough you might live at Cloak House until you were released at sixteen — Skip was determined to, and spent all his time and energy working on it; but you had to beat the odds to do it. The dimmies especially didn't have a chance. Rotten and insufficient food, freezing cold, lost or stolen blankets, harsh punishment, inadequate sanitation and rudimentary medical care carried them off in droves. Job had seen four dimmies, starved and shivering, collapse where they stood at the entrance to the dining room.

And it was no accident. Cloak House was *designed* to operate this way. It was a microcosm of the whole world that Professor Buckler had described since the *Quiebra Grande*. The economic crash had been like a great, global flood whose effects went on still, surging through every level of society, washing away kindness, sweeping away altruism, leaching away compassion, until all that remained was ruthless self-interest. And in that flood, God help anyone who had to rely on charity or mercy.

The dinner bell sounded below, but Job did not move. He felt doomed, devoid of choice. If he paid Skip to fight on his behalf, he would starve. Refuse the protection, and he would be pulped, robbed, and frozen.

He had pushed away thoughts of death since that dreadful day when Laga died and he fled from Cloak House. Now he could ignore them no longer. Unless he acted, he would be with her in a couple of months. But what action could possibly help him?

The answer was obvious: escape from Cloak House. Which was impossible. The doors were locked and guarded, the warders armed, the barred windows charged with stunning levels of electricity.

Job recalled Skip Tolson's ironic comment, when they had talked of getting away: "Sure, plenty of people tried. There's two ways out: sixteen years old and standing up, or through the infirmary lying down."

Job knew he could not survive to sixteen.

He stood up, went to his dormitory, and placed in Skip's bedroll his few personal possessions. The only exception was his cross and chain, which he kept around his neck. He went to the stairs and listened. He didn't have much time. Dinner was almost over. In a few more minutes the attendants would release the boys and head back for their own quarters.

The infirmary was on the first floor of Cloak House, by the loading bay at the rear of the building. Job crept downstairs, past the dining room and on to the door of the infirmary. It was closed, but not locked. It did not need to be. Except to bring sick boys under warder threat of punishment, no one would go near the place.

Job stood with his ear to the door and listened. The recent terrible cold in the dormitories had sent scores here in the past week, but he could not hear a sound. After a minute's hesitation he steeled himself, eased the door open, and stepped inside.

The freezing air in the dimly lit room hit him like a wave. After a few seconds he realized that the icy draft came from the windows on the left hand side. They had bars in them, but no glass. All along that side stood row after row of beds, and on each one, without covers, lay a boy. They were so silent and unmoving that at first Job thought they were all dead. He was about to turn and run when he saw shallow movement in the chest of the boy nearest to him. He recognized his face; it was a new arrival at Cloak House, a dimmie called Manuel Torval. Job had been there a day earlier, when Torval swung at a warder who had told him to wash a floor a second time. He had seen Torval dragged away with a broken arm, cursing and crying.

But Torval had been in good shape when he arrived, pudgy-faced and apparently well-fed. There was no reason for him to lie here, unconscious and probably freezing to death. Job walked along the lines of beds. Torval was no different from the rest. Not one boy was awake. Most were in deeply drugged sleep, and some seemed already dead. He continued to the end of the long room, where part of the floor by the loading bay was covered with a lumpy gray sheet. He bent and lifted one corner, and shuddered at what he saw. Twenty or thirty bodies lay on the icy tiles, flat on their backs. Their eyes had been closed and weighted, and around each boy's right wrist was a twist of wire holding a small square of cardboard. Job forced himself to lean close and read off a name followed by the standard three letters and five digits of a Cloak House ID.

Job was tempted to turn around and run back upstairs. He knew there would be a pickup of bodies some time during the night or the next morning, to make room for the next batch of those who no longer needed the infirmary beds. But he also knew one other thing. There was no way that he could force himself to lie down among those sheeted dead and just *wait* until the loading bay opened and the grim cargo was shipped out.

He made another circuit of the infirmary. There were drugs and hypodermic syringes, but no sign of other medical supplies. He found a box filled with wire loops, and another of cardboard squares with a pencil alongside. After a moment he picked up a square and wrote JOB NAPOLEON SALK in careful capitals. He followed that with his ID number, placed the cardboard on a wire loop, and set it tentatively around his own skinny wrist.

The act felt like death itself. He could not go on. He was removing the wire, ready to tear up the cardboard and stick it in his pocket, when he heard footsteps outside. He dropped to the floor and saw the legs of a warder as she entered the room. She muttered at the cold, rubbed her hands together, and walked briskly along the lines examining each boy. Job eased himself farther under one of the beds, wondering what the punishment would be if he were caught here.

But it was too cold for her to stay long. Another minute and she was gone. She closed the door behind her. And locked it. Job realized that she saw no danger of anyone wanting to get *into* the infirmary. She wanted to be sure that no drug-dazed but waking boy was able to get *out*.

The decision had been made for him. There was no way to go back upstairs. The question now was of surviving until the loading bay opened.

Still he could not face the idea of lying down among the corpses of the children. In any case, it would be fatal to do so. The cold air was settling into the bottom of his lungs, his half-starved body had no protective layers of fat, and Job was shivering with bone-deep spasms.

He had to find a way to get warm and stay warm.

He went back to the gray winding sheet and lifted it again from the bodies. About half of the dead boys still wore their jackets. He removed a dozen of them, trembling at the touch of icy hands and arms. When he was done he carried the jackets to an empty bed as far as possible from the open windows. He swaddled himself in the clothing, wrapping some around his head and body and some around his legs, and carefully tucking in the arms so that every inch was covered with several layers. It took half an hour and four tries before Job was satisfied that he had done everything as well as he could.

He lay down on the bed, facing the windows and staring out through a little slit in the wrapped clothing that he had left at eye level. He intended to remain awake and wait for dawn, or for the opening of the loading bay. But he was exhausted, physically and emotionally. He gradually warmed within the cocoon of layered jackets, and fell asleep without knowing it.

The sound of a diesel engine and a grinding clank of metal awakened him. He sat up, hindered by the multiple layers of clothing, and stared around. It was morning. The sliding door of the loading bay was lifting upwards.

Job jerked around to face the door of the infirmary that led into Cloak House. It was still closed tightly. Whoever picked up the bodies knew their job, and the warders were not needed to help them do it.

Job dropped to the floor and crawled over to a bed near the gray winding sheet. The biggest problem was still ahead. He could remove the jackets — he was peeling them off as he moved — and he could lie down among the dead. But he could not be cold and lifeless as they were. If anyone picked him up, or touched his hands or face, they would know at once that they were handling a living boy.

He watched as the loading bay opened fully and a truck was backed up to it. The rear door of the truck folded down to meet the edge of the loading bay. Two men rolled a big, wheeled trolley out onto the infirmary floor. They were chatting to each other as they worked, complaining as they removed the gray sheet from the silent rows of bodies. "Cold enough here to freeze your knackers off," said one man. "Sooner we get to the incinerator an' warm our hands, the better."

If they picked the corpses up one by one, and placed them in the trolley, Job was done for. He would be discovered as soon as they touched his too-warm flesh.

What he saw was worse than that. The men were *inspecting* each body before they loaded it, turning out pockets, stripping off some of the clothes, sometimes removing the shoes. By the time half the boys were in the trolley a substantial heap of clothes and trinkets stood on a brown cloth bag at the edge of the gray sheet. The men stood and looked at it.

"They're sure wiping 'em out this week," said one of them. "Hold on, we're gonna need another sack."

He went back to the loading bay and into the open rear of the truck. The other followed to the edge of the bay, clapping his gloved hands together. "Better bring a couple. We got a ton of stuff here."

Job shuffled rapidly across the floor and climbed up into the trolley. He shuddered as he lay facedown on top of those cold, half-clad bodies. There was no time to burrow down into the heap even if he had been able to force himself to do it, for seconds after he was in position the men were back. They dropped the next body on top of Job without a second look. In ten minutes he was lying beneath the weight of a dozen more corpses, nauseated and almost suffocated.

Unprotected from the cold, Job was freezing to death. He struggled to control his shivers and forced himself to lie quiet until the last body was in the trolley and it was wheeled over to the truck. The loading bay closed.

He had hoped to escape now, dropping to the ground while the two men went around to the cabin of the truck. But it took time to fight his way free of the pile of bodies, and the truck's rear door was lifting closed. He got to it too late, as the last crack of light disappeared.

Job could not bear to go back to the trolley. He sat on the floor. He was in a metal tomb, freezing cold, completely dark. He had no idea what would happen next, but it could not be worse than this.

Could it?

The man's comment about the incinerator ran again and again through his head.

• Chapter Seven

Pastorale

The exhaust manifold of the diesel truck had been poorly repaired, with replacement pipes welded along the underside of the truck itself. Job had no idea of the mechanics. All he knew was that after ten minutes of bumpy travel he felt a warmer patch on the floor. He tracked its line with his hands, lay out along the vibrating metal, and closed his eyes.

There was no hope of sleep. The floor was too hard and the ride too bumpy. The journey went on and on. The truck's compartment was almost airtight, and as the inside temperature rose Job began to smell the bodies a few feet away. He had nothing in his stomach, but he began dry heaves that lasted the rest of the trip. They continued until, after a rough patch where the trolley swayed and rolled dangerously against its retaining chocks, the truck came to a halt.

Job's stomach was knotted in cramps, but he crawled with his last strength to hide behind the wheeled trolley. When the rear part of the truck creaked down, the light that spilled in was blinding. Job lay low, squinting out past the trolley's wheels at unfamiliar terrain. Instead of roads and tall buildings he saw flat earth covered with a fine white powder. The only structure was a single tall chimney. Job moved to the side of the trolley and peered upward. The chimney rose and rose, as high as Job could see.

When voices came from around the side of the truck he retreated behind the trolley. With full daylight and bright sun, he saw no hope of remaining unseen. But not for anything would he burrow back into the middle of that tangle of warmed bodies.

The men who had loaded the truck at Cloak House were back. Job recognized their voices. They moved to pull at the front of the trolley, removing the chocks and rolling it forward to lock it into a new position. Job crept forward, flattened against its back. "That'll do," said one of the men. "She'll tilt clean from there."

"Aren't we a tad close?"

The man laughed. "You were the one looking for a bit of heat. I'll pull us away a foot or two if you like."

They disappeared, leaving the back of the truck open and the trolley locked in its grooves on the floor. Job moved to the open rear. The truck stood a few feet from a great metal plate in the ground, with the lowered rear panel extending over it.

Now or never. He eased himself off the side and down to the ground. As he did so there was a grating sound of moving metal. Job, crawling under the truck towards its front end, felt a blast of heat on his back and legs. He turned his head. The plate on the ground was sliding away, to reveal a deep, glowing pit beneath. He saw red-hot metal, and bright orange-yellow flames spurting from broad nozzles. He scrambled away. As he did so he heard the sound of another motor within the truck.

The flat interior was tilting up, the trolley turning with it. There was a moment when the angle of the floor increased and nothing seemed to happen; then all the boys' bodies were falling out at once. Job saw a moving tangle of starved white limbs and shirted bodies, until the first corpses came into contact with the flaming interior of the incinerator. Then steam and flames obscured everything. But they could not hide the sizzle and crackle of human flesh meeting red-hot metal.

Job lay flat on the ground beside the truck's rear

wheels, too weak to crawl. He had a vivid image inside his head, of thin limbs locked around him, holding him in their dead embrace as they fell together into orange flames. If he had not been too squeamish to climb back into the middle of the dead . . . he would be in that inferno now, burning alive.

The interior of the truck was tilting back into position, and the cover plate on the incinerator was closing. One of the men appeared again, checking that the trolley's load had all been delivered. His feet came within a yard of Job, but he did not see him behind the wheels.

Job did not look up. He had passed the point where he cared if he lived or died. Even when the truck's engine started and it pulled away, the wheels just missing him, he did not move. He lay facedown, feeling gritty ash on his cheek and sunlight on his back.

It was a contrast of sensation that finally roused him. His feet were freezing cold, while his head burned with radiated heat from the incinerator plate. He sat up and stared around. The truck was far away, disappearing in a cloud of blown powder. The black metal plate and tall chimney sat at the center of a featureless plain, a circle of white ash two or three hundred yards in radius. Beyond that Job saw a tangle of jagged metal, heaped into strange and contorted shapes. Farther yet was the green of growing plants and a bright blue wintery sky.

He turned to the chimney and followed its stack up and up, to twin plumes of gray and white against dark-gray overhead. The incinerator cast a pall of dense smoke over the area, blackening the sky and changing the sun to a ball of burning orange.

White ash, under menacing dark sky. *T - A - N - D.* Job was suddenly five years old, lying in the dormitory at Cloak House, shivering as the older boys told horror stories of the Tandies. The Tandyman was looking for him, coming closer, with his terrible white-hot hands.

T - A - N - D,
Toxikwace taste good to me.
Earth go white, sky go black,
You go in, you don't come back.

Job staggered to his feet and began to walk away from the incinerator and its towering chimney, towards that tangerine ball of sun. As he approached the edge of the circle of white ash he could see that the twisted metal beyond it was old trucks and automobiles, piled on top of each other in contorted heaps. The smell of charring flesh faded from his nostrils. In its place, faint and yet irresistibly powerful, he smelled food. Over beside one heap of old cars he saw an open fire, with three people sitting around it.

He had to eat, or die. He walked towards them, rubbing ash from his face. There were two men and one woman, and they were sitting on yellow plush bench seats ripped from some old luxury automobile. They were all black-faced and white-haired. They stopped talking as he approached.

"Now where'd you spring from?" The speaker was the woman. She was full-faced and strongly built. She wore a kerchief around her head, a shabby coat of black leather, and fingerless woolen gloves.

"I came on the truck." Job pointed in the direction of the vanished vehicle. "I'm terribly hungry. Can you give me food?"

It was useless to ask, but the words had come out beyond his control. The woman was standing up, frowning.

"Can you give me food?" he said again. "I'm starving."

They stared at him curiously. One of the men was holding a metal bowl full of roasted potatoes, warming his hands on it. He made no move to offer anything to Job. "That truck only brings dead ones," he said. "What's a live one doing on it?"

Job's legs were failing him. He sat down uninvited on one of the yellow car seats. "I ran away," he said. "I had to."

They looked at him without expression. He stared back, unflinching. There was no point in lying. If they returned him to Cloak House, he could starve there as well as here. He shielded aching, ash-filled eyes from the sunlight and began to talk. He told them everything; from Cloak House to Bracewell Mansion to the unsuccessful drug-running trip to the Mall Compound, from there to his return to Cloak House as a JD; of his conviction that only death waited him in the detention center, of his escape with the frozen bodies of the dead boys.

At the end the old man with the bowl of potatoes shook his head. "Damme, but you got one weird head — and I don't mean just the outside of it. Did yer make all that up?"

"It's true, every word."

"Well, I dunno. But true or made up, that story earns something." He held out a potato. Job grabbed it and burned his mouth biting into it.

"No rush," said the woman. "Take your time, boy, or you'll throw up." She nodded at the younger man. He filled a glass jar with hot sweetened tea and handed it to Job, who had wolfed the first potato and another as quickly as it was given to him.

He managed to sip now, instead of gulping. He stared at the three people, and then again all around him. "Is this place a T-T-" — he found it hard to say the word — "am I in a *Tandy*?"

They gaped at him, then looked at each other and grinned. The woman slapped fat thighs, and heavy metal bracelets jangled on her wrists. "This'n here? Well, that's the damnedest. Boy, you're at a citystate dump. Tandy! Where'd you ever get an idea like that in your head?"

T - A - N - D,
Nucleerwace taste good to me.
Face go black, hair go white,
Burn today an' die tonight.

The scary words from long ago were running in Job's head, but he pushed them away. The faces in front of him *were* black, black as soot, and their hair was white; yet these people were not terrible or terrifying.

"Listen boy, none of us ever been *near* a Tandy," the woman said. "And none of us wants to. Forget that stuff. What are *you* gonna do now? Nothing for you here."

"I know. But I don't know where to go." Job could not get over the absence of streets and buildings, and the endless green of trees and grass beyond the dump. The air he breathed was clearer, thinner, filled with strange smells of growth and decay. It was alien, and frightening. He made up his mind. He wanted concrete and asphalt and *people*, lots of people. "I've never been in a bare place like this. I want to go back to what I know. But I have no idea how to get there."

"That's easy. That way." The old man pointed away from the sun. "The big road's only a mile from here. But it's a long walk after that. Thirty mile, mebbe, if you're aiming back to the Mall. Don't know why anyone'd want to go there, though. Damned government." He leaned forward and spat into the fire. "Crooked bastards, every one of 'em, they did all this to us."

"I'd better go." Job stood up. With full sun the day was warm enough, but tonight could be as cold as last night. He was already tired, and he had no idea how far thirty miles might be. All he knew was that he needed to be back in familiar territory before it was dark.

Beyond that simple objective, he did not have the energy to force his mind.

*　　*　　*

The old man had been a poor judge.

From the dump to Bracewell Mansion it was only eighteen miles. That fact and two others saved Job: he was still wearing the solid shoes that had been provided for him in Bracewell Mansion when he was running errands for the professor; and the black-faced woman, in a final and fickle act of kindness, had filled a paper bag with molasses-dipped roast turnips before he left.

The walk was by far the longest that Job had ever made. He came to the entrance of the mansion in early dusk, swaying on blistered feet. He had slept little the previous night, and the second half of today's long trek through city outskirts had passed in a surrealist daze. He had seen strange mirages (or strange reality?) in the broad, potholed avenues, as he struggled up their long slopes and imagined Bracewell Mansion just over the brow of each hill. The parking lots of old shopping malls became rolling seas of black asphalt, dotted with shanty huts that swayed and swooped like wind-tossed paper boats. Abandoned warehouses flanked the roads, rising to cut off the dipping sun. At their broken windows he saw grinning faces, waving skeletal arms. They called and gestured, inviting him in. He shivered and looked straight ahead. Obsessively he had counted his steps, allowing himself a bite of food every thousand paces, a drink wherever he found running water. Sometimes he walked with his eyes closed. Once he had stopped to sit down for ten minutes, and knew when he continued that he must not do it again. If he did he would never get up.

Bracewell Mansion when he finally came to it was back to its old familiar appearance, with the double doors blocked off and the single entrance at the top of the broad stone steps.

And having come so far, Job did not know what to do. He was totally confused. When he was desperate and despairing in Cloak House just twenty-four hours earlier, the idea that the world was devoid of pity, mercy, and decency had hit him with the force of revelation. But the three people at the dump had shared food and drink with him, when it could not possibly benefit them. And Professor Buckler might have found Job useful to run errands, but surely there had been kindness, too, when Job had been picked starving off the street. He wanted to rely on that kindness now, but one thing held him back. Since leaving Bracewell Mansion he understood who really ran the place. And it was not the professor. No matter what Buckler might say or think, the true boss was Miss Magnolia. And Job was terrified by the idea of confronting her.

Increasing cold and the pain from his feet and chest at last forced him inside. He stole upstairs to the third floor and entered Professor Buckler's rooms. To Job's dismay there was no sign of him. This was the hour when he was normally in the brown armchair, drinking or sleeping.

He might be one floor up, in the kitchen. But Miss Magnolia might be there too, in the anteroom, and there was no way of reaching the kitchen without passing through it. Job went up the stairs step by nervous step. He peeked through the open door.

Miss Magnolia was not there. Nor was the professor. But Tracy was sitting on the plush couch of crimson velvet. She was dressed in high style, red hair up, dress low-cut, pumps so high-heeled that real walking would be impossible.

She seemed to be waiting for somebody, and she saw Job the moment that his head poked through the door.

"Job!" she gasped, and glanced all around. "You look awful. What are you doing here?"

"I came back."

"You're mad. You shouldn't be anywhere near us. Weren't you caught and jaded? That's what Miss Magnolia said."

"Yes, I was. But I escaped — "

"If Miss Magnolia sees you or finds out you were here, she'll go crazy."

"I had nowhere else to go. I wanted to see Professor Buckler."

"Oh, God." Tracy glanced over her shoulder. "Job, you can't stay, you can't. Don't you know what happens to people who harbor J-D's? You could get everyone here in trouble."

Job said nothing. He stood and stared at Tracy, eyes despairing. Another night of cold would be the finish.

"Oh, hell." She would not look at him and she was biting her lipstick, ruining its even line. "Oh, Job. Job, d'you remember Sammy?"

Job nodded. He had been to the house with the red door many times.

"Go there. Tell Sammy I sent you, for food and a place to sleep. When I get the chance I'll tell the professor, ask him to come see you, not tell Miss Magnolia. Understand?"

"Yes."

"Then for God's sake get out of here. Hurry."

Job nodded, seemed ready to speak. Tracy shook her head. "Right now. *Git*."

Job went downstairs on sore and blistered feet, out into the icy night of the city. He would try to do what Tracy ordered, but not for anything could he hurry. His lungs were beyond pain, shriveling and withering in his narrow chest. Compared to that, blisters and hunger were nothing.

Job had been to the house with the red door and black shuttered windows at least a dozen times. But the shutters were always closed, and he had never been invited inside.

After his first visit, each pickup had had the same format. He knocked on the red door. Within a few seconds it opened, and the face of the androgynous Sammy glowered out through a three-inch opening. Job gave his coded message, different for each visit. The face vanished without a word. A few minutes later a small package was thrust out for Job's acceptance. The door closed.

Now it was different. When Job knocked on the door of the four-story row house and repeated Tracy's words, Sammy for a change did not retreat. Instead there was a slow, thoughtful nodding of the head, and the door opened wide.

"Come in," said the musical tenor. "Walk careful."

The warning was unnecessary. There was enough space to walk through the long hall and up the steep stairs, but only just. On either side, built into tottering piles, were wooden and cardboard boxes. Job smelled mildew, plus a strange odor that caught at his sore throat and irritated his anguished lungs. He was so weak that he had to pull himself up the stairs using the handrail.

Sammy led the way into what had once been an elegant kitchen. The electric light was a hanging bare bulb, and the gas oven and range were not working. A portable gas stove in the middle of the room provided both cooking and heat — unnecessary, the second, because the whole house was already stifling hot.

"Food over there," said Sammy. "What time professor coming?"

"Don't know." Job's voice would produce nothing above a hoarse whisper.

"Hmph. And Trace don't want me to call, she say? OK, *hombre-delgado*. We wait. Bed for you in basement, whenever you ready."

Job was ready now. He was lightheaded and dizzy. But he could smell food, and see a pot on the stove. It might not be there later. As Sammy left he grabbed an old cane-bottom chair, hobbled with it to the table, and sat down.

The four-quart crockpot held a fish and oyster stew, thick and milky and full of bits of yellow corn. The stove was turned off, and the side of the pot was little more than blood heat. But that was good. Job's throat was so sore that hot food would have been more than he could stand. He hunted around until he found a spoon. He did not bother with a dish but ate direct from the crock, cramming solids and liquid into his mouth until his stomach bulged round below his thin ribs and refused to admit another mouthful. He put down the spoon. He could eat no more to save his life.

He felt his way downstairs, hardly knowing if lights were on or off. The basement was a junkman's dream, even more crowded than the upstairs.

Job noticed nothing, except that near the bottom of the narrow stairs was an old mattress. He collapsed onto it. His bloated stomach gave a mild twinge, and then a more painful spasm. For a few moments he thought he had eaten too much and was going to lose everything. He tried to sit up. But before he could lift his head more than a few inches he was gone, swallowed by a sleep so deep and close to death itself that Sammy, checking a few hours later, had to listen and look hard to be sure that the uninvited guest was still a living, breathing boy.

The basement of the house had no windows. It was thick-walled and quiet, holding its temperature night and day close to seventy-five degrees.

For the first twelve hours Job did not move or dream. In the next half-day he ran a temperature, tossing on the mattress in semi-delirium. Occasionally he knew where he was, lying in Sammy's cellar. But most of the time he was in Cloak House and the streets around it, with Father Bonifant and Laga and Nurse Calder and Colonel della Porta and Skip Tolson, all jumbled up together. In one terrible dream he woke inside the incinerator itself, surrounded by and tangled with dead boys. When they felt the heat they awoke to awful, twitching life. He broke loose and crawled away from them, across red-hot plates that seared his hands and made the blood boil in his veins. He screamed in agony and tried to lift smoking palms that stuck to the glowing metal.

"Hey, you," said a tenor voice. Job was being shaken, violently. "You wanna stay in my house, you don't make so mucha that damn noise."

It was Sammy, gripping him in strong, sinewy arms. Job gasped and shivered.

"Dreaming." Clotted tongue, thick head. He was still half in his dream, heart pounding wild within his chest.

"Hold quiet." Sammy had lifted Job's arm and was holding a black square instrument over his right wrist.

Job sat up, stared blank-faced at grimy walls and felt-wrapped pipes. He did not remember coming here. "Is it morning?"

"Evening. You slept round."

"Professor Buckler —"

"No professor." Sammy was peering through a glass panel in the middle of the instrument. "Sweet Jesus. You been jaded. Whyn't you tell me?" The musical voice rose an octave. "Tonight, the professor come an' explain. Or you go."

Sammy turned and ran up the steps, lithe as a snake. Job followed, slowly. On the way he took a first good look at the house. It was narrow, no more than fifteen feet from wall to papered wall. Piled boxes, high as Job's head, left a four-foot tunnel through the center. Job lifted the lid of one. It was crammed with wigs and toupees, of all colors. The next held women's hats, feathered and plumed and pom-pommed and in every style that Job could imagine. A third was filled with coat hangers.

The stairs were steep and narrow. By the time Job

reached the second floor he was breathing hard and his legs were wobbly. There was no sign of Sammy. Job went into the kitchen and found the same crockpot simmering on the portable stove. He helped himself, and ten minutes later had the strength to climb more bare wooden stairs. The third floor was like another kitchen, except that there were two stoves, half a dozen locked cupboards, and a long work-bench filled with glass beakers and measuring cups. An unfamiliar tart smell crinkled Job's nose. There was no sign of Sammy.

He kept going. The fourth floor was clearer than the rest. The walls were fresh-painted, and the landing window was free of grime. Job knew he was intruding, but he went on to the end of the landing. He found himself in a sky-lighted bedroom. Sammy was there, stretched out unconscious on a broad bed. A little twist of paper sat on the pillow beside the dark head. An urgent whisper of "Sammy" and a tug of the bare arm produced no effect. Sammy was out more deeply than Job had been, twenty-four hours earlier.

Job's first reaction was relief. Sammy was warm and breathing — and if Sammy were not awake, Job could not be cast out into the night. That thought changed quickly to alarm. This wasn't sleep; it was a coma, like Laga's coma.

He reached over and shook harder. "Sammy!"

There was no response. Job ran down the stairs to the first floor, opened the front door, and stood hesitating on the threshold. It was warmer than last night, but already quite dark. The vendors would have long since packed up their wares and gone, and any street *basura* still outside would be more likely to loot than help.

Job closed the door firmly and hurried away along the sidewalk. Bracewell Mansion would not welcome him, but people there knew Sammy. They would have to help, no matter what they did to Job afterwards.

The night was still, with a rising moon casting

shadows from tall buildings. Job steered clear of the dark areas. He had gone no more than a couple of blocks when a tall, hooded figure stepped suddenly in front of him and grabbed his arm. He gasped in terror, jerked loose, and began to run.

"Job!" An urgent hiss from behind stopped him. "It's me."

He turned. Tracy was standing on the sidewalk, the cowl pulled back onto her shoulders to reveal her coiffured hair.

"I was coming to see you." Her voice was soft, and she was staring all around her. "I've only got an hour, then I have to go back."

"The professor never came."

"I know. That's what I wanted to tell you."

"And Sammy's sick — maybe dying."

"What!" They fell into step together and hurried back towards the house. "What happened to her?"

"I don't know. Unconscious, upstairs. I thought Sammy was a man."

"She was once. Now she isn't. How long has she been sick?"

"Not long. Less than an hour. She was talking to me. She said that if the professor didn't come tonight, I have to leave."

"He won't be coming. I told him last night that you'd been at the mansion looking for him, and he fell apart. He's been drinking ever since. He's scared of Miss Magnolia. That's why I had to come."

They had reached the narrow house, and Tracy went in first. She stood staring around at the jumble of boxes and cartons.

"Straight up," said Job. "Up to the fourth floor." He led the way, wheezing, until they came to Sammy's bedside.

Tracy leaned over the silent body, feeling the reddened cheekbone with the back of her hand and rolling back Sammy's eyelid. A brown iris rolled into view, its pupil like a tiny black pinpoint.

"Is she dying?"

Tracy had picked up the twist of paper on the pillow and was sniffing it. She shook her head. "This is a case where the shoemaker *ought* to go barefoot. Sammy'll be all right. Get me cold water."

"What's wrong with her?" Job took a bowl and went through into the bathroom.

"She's been sampling her own products. I thought she'd kicked that, years ago."

"She found out I'd been jaded. I think it really frightened her."

"I bet it did. My fault, I should have told you to mention that first thing." Tracy took the bowl of water. "Get out. Come back in twenty minutes. When you do, let me handle the talking."

"Is she —"

"She'll be fine. Close the door as you leave."

Job wandered back down the stairs. He didn't know what to do. He had slept and eaten all that he could, and it was not safe to be on the streets so late. For the next quarter of an hour he rambled from room to room, lifting lids off boxes, peering into storage rooms, poking around dark closets, counting dresses and musty suits on old hangers. By the time he went back upstairs he was sneezing from dust and dazed by excess.

Sammy was sitting on the side of the bed, cheerful and dreamy-eyed. She smiled at Job.

"She's still way up there," said Tracy. "But she's coming down. And I have to get out of here in the next ten minutes, or Miss Magnolia will crucify me."

"What *is* this place?"

Tracy's stare was as blank as Sammy's.

"I mean," said Job, "there's all these old clothes and boxes and furniture . . ."

"Ah." Tracy nodded. "The house. When the owners

went broke and skipped, Sammy took it over. Used to be a theatrical costumer and supply center. All the good stuff's gone, though."

"And he gotta go, too." Sammy was more alert, and she was no longer smiling. "I can't have a J-D here. Too dangerous."

"He has nowhere to go, Sam."

"Tough. You think I run a welfare house? You shoulda told me he been jaded."

"Do you know *how* he got jaded? Trying to make a delivery of one of your packages to the Mall Compound."

"Not my business . . . *you* sent him to the Mall. You take him, if he got nowhere to go."

"I can't. Miss Magnolia was the one sent him to the Mall, but she'd turn him right in. You know Miss Magnolia."

Job was going to speak but Tracy caught his eye and shook her head.

"Hmph." Sammy's scowl said that she knew Miss Magnolia, and did not think well of her. She stood up from the bed and went into the bathroom.

"What you think, I need charity boarders?" She was at the mirror, peering at her face. "No way. I'm on the edge, Trace. Broke."

"You need somebody around here, Sammy. For yourself. He found you, and he thought you were OD-ing. He went out looking for help. How many people would do that?"

"I didn't need no help."

"This time, maybe. What about next?"

"May be no next time." Sammy was applying a new layer of makeup, and the face beneath the powder and blusher was pale. "How he gonna pay if he stay?" she said over her shoulder. "I told you, I'm broke. He can't pay, he gotta go. I don't need anyone do pickup an' drop-off for me. My business come right here."

"He has no money. You know that, Sam." Tracy shrugged at Job. *Sorry. I tried.* She stood up. "I have to get back to Bracewell."

"It's true that I have no money." Job's face was paler than Sammy's. Tracy had told him to keep quiet, but she was getting nowhere. "I might be able to make some money for you, though."

"How? You got nothing, you don't know nothing."

"I know how the street vendors work. I know how they talk, how they think, how they set prices."

"You got nothing to sell."

"I know. But you do. I don't mean the drugs." Job waved his arm around. "I mean everything else in this house, the clothes and fixtures and fake jewels."

"Is junk. All of it."

"*You* think it's junk. But people *buy* junk. I know. I bought enough, when I worked with Mister Bones. People buy *anything*, if it's cheap enough."

"That don't make sense."

"What you got to lose, Sammy?" said Tracy. "You let him try street vending, if he doesn't make enough you kick him out. If he does, you're ahead."

"He been jaded."

"So what? If there's ever a bust on this house, you think they'll bother with a jaded kid? They'll be after the real stuff."

"Still no. Too dangerous. I don't want him in the house."

"All right. So he doesn't stay here. But will you let him try being a street vendor, selling some of the stuff? You say it's junk. He says he can move it."

Sammy turned from the mirror. Her makeup was perfect again. "He can't move nothing, Trace," she said. "I'll bet on it. But you say you gotta go. So he stays one more night, we talk tomorrow morning. If you want."

"All right. That's a deal. One more night, Sammy."

One more night.

And then Job would be out on the frozen streets of the city. He had argued with Sammy, and failed to convince her. He knew it. He could see no reason for the look of sly triumph on Tracy's face.

• Chapter Eight

Basura Boy

Sammy would not let Job live inside the house. On that point she had remained adamant.

But the rear of the basement led through to a covered area that had once been a garage. Its concrete floor was sloping, and its wooden doors were broken-hinged and cracked and one of them was cemented permanently shut, but the scarred old wood kept out the worst of the cold. Job placed old mattresses upright against the doors and stuffed rags into the biggest holes. The sloping floor he ignored. He had slept in much worse places.

The mattresses had turned up in the attic when Job was making his first inventory of the house. Sammy had given him a go-ahead, but she had made it clear to Tracy that his food and lodging had to be paid for, and quickly. In two days Job identified a hundred items that should sell easily: fur hats of ancient style, mildewed but thick overcoats, solid old cooking pots, mismatched but solid boots and shoes, and fake stage jewels so big and bogus that Tracy laughed at the cheap glitter and swore that not even the street hookers would look at them.

Job ran everything out on a handcart to the nearest street corner. It was a poor location, but he had one huge advantage over all the other vendors: Sammy had set no rules on selling. Job could undercut the market by any factor he chose. And with his prices, the street hookers did more than look — they bought, and so did passersby. At the end of the first day Job took home enough money to pay Sammy for a week, along with a piece of salt pork and a five-pound bartered basket of parsnips and potatoes. Sammy grudgingly admitted that maybe he had been right, and the house junk was an unrealized asset.

"But what you gonna do *next* month, Jo-babe, when you sold everything?"

That problem had already occurred to Job. For the moment he ignored it. He had at least a year's supply of goods in the house, and three other things were more pressing. First, he had to make a full inventory and value what he had for sale. Second, he needed to nail down a good vendor location, shielded if possible from rain and the worst wind. And third — really first in his mind — he must work out a way of life that guaranteed he would never, never, *never* be caught and returned to Cloak House.

A J-D on the streets was at risk all the time. The number of policemen was never more than a handful, even in good weather, but Job set and rigorously applied his own rules. If he heard advance news of police presence, or saw any sign of it, he packed up and took his cart home at once. If there was no warning, but police appeared or were rumored to be on the way — the *basura* spread that word like the wind — Job abandoned his cart with whatever was on it, and ran. He came back when it was safe. The cart was usually picked clean, but he felt lucky when it had not been stolen.

He expected the inventory of the house to take weeks, because it seemed so cluttered and random. On the third evening he realized that the former occupants had followed their own plan. The house was organized for the production of *theatrical works*, and the boxes of clothes and furnishings were labeled. *Man and Superman, The Taming of the Shrew, Death of a Salesman, The Pirates of Penzance, The Mousetrap, Hedda Gabler, The School for Scandal, Lady Windermere's Fan, The Duchess of Malfi . . .*

Job listed every box he could find, then took the fourth day off from vending. Instead of selling he went buying, hunting through the stock of other street sellers for old books of plays while he chatted with the vendor, usually in *chachara-calle*, sometimes in other languages.

In the basement that night he started to read what he had bought, learning how to interpret the contents of hard-to-reach boxes from the words written on their sides. It was the first use he had ever found for *written* information. He was finally admitting that Mister Bones had been right, years too late to tell him.

The search for knowledge had two by-products. First, Job met dozens of other vendors and learned to his surprise that his arrival on the streets had already been noted — and disapproved. By extreme price-cutting he had been ruining the market for everyone. No one made any threats, but Job was learning. He assured them that from now on his prices would be in line (or just a tiny fraction lower).

Second, Job began to make a short list of preferred vendor sites. He wanted a place that was sheltered and yet highly public. Most of all he wanted a corner location that permitted four-way escape.

Within two weeks he had made his choice. It was a quarter of a mile east of Sammy's house, near the corner of an avenue in the doorway of an abandoned store. It had been ignored by others because it was not sunny, and because there were vendors on either side and more across the street. But by summer the shade would be a blessing, and Job was willing to give up some business for protective numbers. Before any police reached him, they would have four or five others to deal with — and street vendors did not usually go quietly.

He moved into the doorway with his cart in the fourth week. By now he was beginning to feel like an old hand. He joined in the day-long chatter of the vendors, adding to his language pool: Hungarian and Hindi, Armenian and French, Portuguese and Russian, mouthing words and phrases in silent mimicry. It was not mere entertainment. He had noticed that although all the vendors used *chachara-calle* among themselves, passersby stopped more and bought more at a vendor who spoke their own native language. Not only *written* knowledge had value.

In the seventh week, a vendor moved his stall from across the street to a location about thirty yards along from Job. The street-seller was a tall man with a big black beard, and every day at noon he strolled down past all the vendors, greeting each one. The way he looked at everything and everybody made Job very uneasy. He listened hard when the man spoke. The language was *chachara-calle*, but it lacked the easy and natural flow of someone who had been raised to the street argot. And sometimes the man brought books with him, and read when things were quiet.

Job studied the newcomer, while the man studied him and everyone else. He did not *look* like police. But ...

Spring was arriving. A great storm of wind and warm rain arrived unexpectedly one mid-morning in Job's eighth week on the street. Vendors covered their wares and fled swearing for shelter. Job's doorway was too shallow to protect him from blowing rain, but it took him a while to admit it. After five drenching minutes he gave up and scuttled along to a stone overhang halfway down the block. A dozen vendors were already there. They included black-beard.

Soaking wet and squelching in sodden shoes, Job could not be inconspicuous. His arrival was greeted by shouts of laughter from the others.

"Nice and dry, *chico*!" "Hey, *pescado*, what kept you?" "Come in, rain man, join the fun."

The blackbearded man said nothing, but he grinned

and handed Job a length of dry toweling. Job formally nodded his thanks and dried his face and hair.

"Thank you." He held out the cloth but kept his face averted.

The man nodded and took the towel back. He eyed Job with open interest. "How old are you, my friend?"

Answer, or not answer? Tell the truth, or make something up?

"I am ten years old. Why do you ask?"

"Because I see you watching me when I read. Maybe you want to learn to read books, too, as well as selling?"

"I can read."

"Can you now? I meant *real* reading, with hard words."

"Yes." Job was not surprised by the man's skeptical glance. At Cloak House, Skip Tolson and Rick Luciano and Torval Berhammar could not read, and they had not been considered dimwits. Even under Father Bonifant, readers had not been in the majority.

"All right, then." The man was holding out a book with a stiff blue cover. "Try that. Can you read the title?"

" 'Journal of a Tour to the Hebrides.' "

"Good. But that last word is not pronounced 'Heebrides,' it's pronounced 'Heb-rid-eez.' "

Job raised his eyebrows, while the other vendors standing under the overhang nudged each other.

"What's the joke?" The man had noticed the grins.

"I didn't make a joke," said Job, when no one else spoke. "It's just that maybe they think it's funny, when you start correcting the way I say things."

"Why's that funny?"

"I expect because" — Job switched to mimic the man's accent and manner of speech, with its broad, twangy tone — "because when you speak *chacharacalle*, without knowing it you say things this way."

There was a roar of approval.

"Is that me?" The black beard wagged, and the man

looked around at the other vendors. "Is that really the way I talk?"

"*Dead-on!*" "*Justo!*" "*Precisamente!*" Everyone was grinning.

"Well, I'll be damned. So I *do* sound like that. And I thought I spoke *chachara* perfectly. Nobody ever said a word to me before. But how come you can speak like me?"

Job shrugged. The rain squall was over, and he wanted to get back to his stall. He had said and done too much already, showing off — that's what it had been — how well he could read, and then showing off again to mimic the man and make the other vendors laugh. He had made himself far too conspicuous. "I just listen," he mumbled. "Then I say what I hear."

He moved away. The man followed him. Job walked faster, deserting his cart and hurrying along the rain-drenched avenue until he could turn onto another street. He waited. When no one appeared after five minutes he peeked around the corner. The stalls were occupied again, with everything back to normal. The black-bearded man was sitting at his stall and reading his book.

But Job went back, grabbed the handles of his cart, and left. *Don't get caught again. Never, never, never.* That was the Golden Rule, the only important rule.

He headed for home and the safety of his garage. Although it was not yet noon, he felt he had been exposed to too much risk for one day.

Job spent an uncomfortable night. The next morning he decided that while running away had not been wrong, it had solved nothing. Today he again had to sell his goods, or he would soon be out on the streets; which meant that either he went back to sell at the usual place (which he now thought of as *his*), or else he had to find a new spot.

But if he did move, and the man was police, it would be little trouble to track Job down. It was not practical to push the cart more than a mile each way. All that black-beard would have to do was walk the streets systematically, and he would find Job again in a day or two.

In the end Job went to the usual spot with his hand-cart, but he piled on it only a quarter of its usual load. If he had to abandon it, the loss would be small.

The rain had blown through and away, but instead of carrying dirty air with it the changed weather had brought an inversion layer. The air sat thick and heavy over the whole city. Even with his mask in place, Job felt the yellow fumes crawling to the bottom of his lungs. He walked slower and slower. One thing was sure, if he wanted to escape from someone today he'd be in trouble. He could not run more than a few yards without choking. He paused on the final corner. The avenue was filled with the morning crush of pedestrians and crawling vehicles. All the vendors were in position, including black-beard.

Job trundled his cart the last fifty yards and set up shop in the usual doorway. The man had seen him arrive. Job was convinced of that, even though there had been no movement of the dark head in his direction.

After half an hour Job's suspicion was confirmed. The man stood up from his stall, stretched, and wandered casually in Job's direction. He nodded when he was a few paces away and turned to walk directly towards Job. The hair on the back of Job's neck seemed to crawl. The man's nose and mouth were hidden behind his smog mask, but his dark eyes were visible. He was pretending to be relaxed, but he really wasn't. He was as tense as Job.

It was already too late to run away. Job sat dead still and waited.

The man flopped down uninvited on the little stool that Job brought with him for customers who wanted to haggle before they bought. It was a breach of vendor protocol, to do anything that might interfere with another vendor's sale, but Job sat uncomplaining.

"What you did yesterday," said the man at last. "That was pretty impressive. Imitating the way I speak. I was thinking about it all last night."

Which makes two of us. Job just nodded.

"I was thinking," the man continued, "if I sound different from all the people around here, I bet I lose a lot of sales. And I was wondering if you could help me do better — you know, catch me when I say something wrong, and tell me how to do it right."

Was that it? No more than a desire by the black-bearded man to fit in? It was tempting to believe that; but Job couldn't take the risk. The other man was just too intense. "I don't know. Some people can hear and say, others never do it right no matter how hard they try."

"Tin ear, you mean? Maybe that's my problem. But I'd like to solve it if I can." The man was smiling behind the mask, but it didn't reach to the eyes. "Look, please don't misunderstand me. I'm not asking something for nothing. I can pay, if that's what you want. Or maybe you can teach me, and maybe in return I can teach you."

"Teach me what?"

"I'm not sure. I'd have to give you a few tests first."

"I had plenty of tests when I was little. They were stupid. All they showed was what I knew, that I have bad lungs and bad teeth and a funny jaw."

"I don't mean medical tests." Now the eyes *were* smiling. "I mean *mental* tests. Did you ever have one?"

"I don't know. I don't think so." In spite of himself, Job was interested. The man talked differently from everyone he had ever met. "What are the tests for?"

"They tell you what you're good at — to be more accurate, they tell you what you *might* be good at. Take you, for instance. Everyone around here says you talk to them in their own languages, without being taught. That sort of thing can be tested for."

"I already know I can learn languages."

"Sure. But there could be things you might be even *better* at, only you've never run into them. That's what these tests do — tell how good you might be at something, before you ever try it."

He saw Job's hesitation. "Look, this isn't an urgent thing. Think about it, see if it appeals to you. Most people like to know what they'd be good at if they had a chance." He stood up. "Maybe we can talk about it more tomorrow. By the way, my name is Alan Singh. What's yours?"

"Job Salk."

Mistake! His brain shouted the word at him. He had given his real name. It was on file at Cloak House and with the J-D center, more than likely it was on file in the Mall Compound.

But Singh was nodding and turning away, as though asking Job's name was no more than courtesy.

Maybe it was just that.

But Job was trembling. How much was due to fear, and how much to a perverse excitement, he could not say.

Chapter Nine

Escapegoat

Job had never taken a formal test in his life. The very idea of sitting at a table for three hours, just reading and writing, was peculiar — even without other distractions.

He fidgeted in his chair and looked around the room. He had thought that Professor Buckler's living quarters were full of books. But this place *was* books. From floor to ceiling every wall was covered with them. Bookshelves broke into the living space, so that just to move around the room you had to walk along long, narrow book-lined aisles. In fact — he stared around again — there *was* no living space. He could see no bed, no kitchen or bathroom.

Alan Singh was sitting at another little table about ten feet away. He saw Job's head movements and laid down the book he was reading.

"Look, when you are all through I'll give you a full tour if you want it." His accent in *chachara-calle* was improving, but Job thought that he would never fully lose his foreign twang. And when it came to difficult subjects or fast talking, Singh still preferred to switch to standard English.

"But those are *timed* tests you're doing," Singh went on. "If you don't start promptly, you'll never finish. I'm going to re-set the clock. Then I want you to stop gawking and begin reading and thinking." He pressed a button on the top of a curious round-faced clock that had been distracting Job with its loud ticking sound. "You're starting again — now. Get to it."

Job bent his head and began to read. Regardless of books and clocks he found it hard to concentrate. The journey here with Singh had been disturbing, and he was still not sure why he had agreed to come. He had told Sammy what he was going to do, and she had stared at him and told him he was mad. Singh was surely going to kill him or rob him.

It still seemed to Job that she might be right. They had meandered for miles through a warren of littered streets, to a totally unfamiliar part of town and a matched group of buildings of gray stone. Someone clearly lived in them, because the grass between some of the buildings was well tramped down, and anyway, someone lived *everywhere* in the city that a person could live. But Job saw no sign of people. And although Singh seemed to know his way around the place, he did not act as though this was his home.

Anything could happen to Job here, and no one would ever know it. He forced thoughts like that out of his head, and stared at the page.

A man is traveling in a country where there are only two sorts of people: those who always lie, and those who always tell the truth. The man meets a native at a crossroads, and wonders how to get to the next town. He is allowed to ask the native just one question to find out the right way to go. What does he say to the native?

After the first set of easy questions they were all like this. Weird. What sort of country had two such odd sorts of people? *Nobody* told the truth all the time, and probably nobody lied all the time. And *why* could the man ask only one question? What happened to him if he asked another one?

Some of the problems weren't questions at all. They were funny little drawings that you had to turn around or back to front or inside out, and then say which one was different from the others. Others asked about wood and metal balls dropped from the top of buildings, or weights placed into buckets of water.

The final set was strangest of all.

Three men are placed in a room with stickers on their foreheads. They are told that the stickers are either red or black, and that there is at least one red sticker. The first man who can say correctly what color the sticker is on his own forehead will be the winner . . .

Anyone in his right mind would peel off the sticker and look at it. But Singh said that sort of answer was not permitted. The men had to *reason* the color of the stickers.

Job frowned and puzzled and chewed at the end of the pen. He was amazed when the clock gave a loud pinging sound, and Singh said, "All right. Time's up. Don't write any more."

"I haven't finished all the questions."

"That's all right. Hardly anybody does. Hand it over."

It was Singh's turn to frown and concentrate, while Job wandered around and stared at books. Some of the titles made no sense. He found a whole section of books filled with nothing but numbers, strange symbols, and a few lines of writing between them. He stared at other shelves for a long time before he realized that they held books in other languages, some that he already spoke but had never seen written down. The spelling was often confusing, and didn't match the way that the words were pronounced.

"Well, that's one theory disposed of." Singh had finished his pondering, and was leaning back in his chair. "Damnation."

Job came to sit next to him.

"You've certainly got a talent," Singh continued. "But it's not what I hoped it might be." He was flipping through the pages that Job had filled out in his careful printing. "You answered correctly every question about words and language. How long did that part take you?"

Job looked at the pages. Singh was pointing to the easy questions at the beginning. "Not long. No time at all, I just filled them in."

"Most people can't get them right, even if they take their time doing it. You've got a first-rate memory and a pretty good grasp of logic and spatial relations. But I don't see any sign of unusual mathematical talent, or physical intuition."

Singh laid down the pages. "Probably just as well, from your point of view." He leaned back and rubbed at his black beard. "Did you ever have any courses in science or math?"

"Father Bonifant used to teach them at Cloak House. But when Colonel della Porta came he stopped that. He said the courses were 'useless and seditious.'"

"He was following the party line." Singh stood up. "Come on, let's go. I want to show you something."

He led the way from the book-lined chamber and out of the building. "This place used to be a university," he said. "Before the *Quiebra Grande*, when there was money for things like education, people a few years older than you would come here for four or five years."

They were cutting across a big square of ground covered with long grass, following a well-walked path. Job stared around, and saw no sign of stores or workshops. "What did they do here?"

"They learned — at least, some of them did. And I taught. In this building." They were entering a massive stone edifice that looked to Job like one of the old churches that still scattered the city. He thought of Professor Buckler, and his talk of being at a rich university. Maybe Alan Singh maintained the same delusion.

"This building, and this lab," said Singh. They had walked up two flights of littered and filthy stairs to an open door. The room beyond was long and wide. Within it were rows of benches covered with dusty equipment. It had all been cannibalized. Job saw broken lenses, ripped-out wiring, and smashed glass jars. At the front of the room stood a platform, and behind it was a set of three wide blackboards. Singh went forward and mounted the dais. He turned to Job. His face had become wistful, lacking its usual energy. "Three thousand mornings, I stood up here and talked. Now I wonder where all my words went. And where my students went."

Job was becoming uneasy again. Singh was full of some obsession with the past. It had been a mistake to come here. But as though reading that thought, the man on the dais suddenly smiled.

"You know, this is something I always wanted to do here, and I was never allowed to. Against university regulations." He pulled a black cigar from his pocket, lit it carefully, and leaned forward with his elbows on the podium. He blew a smoke ring towards Job. "So, Job Salk. You're not a scientist. Well, lucky for you. You won't become a scapegoat, the way we did."

"What's a scapegoat?" Singh had switched to standard English, and Job had never heard that word before.

"I don't know how to say it in *chachara-calle*. A scapegoat is someone who gets blamed for something."

"That's a *pagano*. Same as a fall guy. Why are you one?"

"Me, and science too. You know how the word 'scapegoat' came to be used? Thousands of years ago, the high priest would take a goat, and lay on it all the sins of all the people in a big ceremony. And then the goat was sent off to the wilderness. All the sins were supposed to go away with it. Just the way it happened to us."

"I don't understand."

"That's because you're only ten. You're too young to remember what it was like before the *Quiebra Grande*. Science used to be *respectable*. Twenty years ago it was all right to call yourself a scientist. But bit by bit there was more garbage, and more acid rain, and toxic wastes, and runaway reactors, and the air got worse and the water got worse. And there were more and more people, and the cities began to fall apart. The sewage and transportation systems overloaded. And all that was *before* the big financial crash and the beginning of the real troubles. Governments all over the world were in deep *guano*. They didn't know how to solve any of the problems, but they needed their scapegoat. When the *Quiebra Grande* came and the population was up to nine billion, they picked their *pagano*: science. Scientists made technology possible. Technology produced wastes and pollution. Ergo, scientists were to blame for everything.

"Your colonel knew the party line. Science courses are seditious. *Science* is seditious. If you are a scientist, you have a choice: go into hiding, do something else for a living, study in secret, and hope you don't get caught. Or be sent to the wilderness. That's what happened to most of my colleagues. All that remains is the network. And even that . . . "

As Singh spoke, Job was becoming steadily more uneasy. The man was rambling on and on, apparently talking to himself more than to Job.

Job had known him for a couple of months, and in that time he had checked him out with the other street vendors. No one had anything bad to say, but when Job had agreed to come with him and try the tests he knew he had taken a risk, drawn by the strangeness of what Singh was proposing.

But the process could be looked at the other way round. Job had never talked of his own background to the other street vendors, so Singh knew less about him than he knew about Singh. What risk had *Singh* taken, bringing Job here? For all the man knew Job could be an informer, paid by the government to collect information on the streets. If Job had not been jaded, he could have made money by revealing what Singh had just told him.

For the man was talking freely — much too freely. Far older than Job, he was still hopelessly naive. And anyone who lacked the right survival instincts was too dangerous to be around. Unless Singh were *himself* working for the police, and testing Job. In which case . . .

Or if he were *not* working for the police, but somehow interested in *recruiting* Job. In which case . . .

There were as many involutions as in one of Singh's contorted test problems.

Job cut through the logical twists with a single stroke. *The Golden Rule: Don't get caught again. Never, never, never.* Even if nothing happened to him, this trip with Singh was violating the principle.

"I have to get back home. My people will wonder where I am."

That was complete fabrication, and if Singh had done his homework he would know it. Job had no people. Sammy would miss his money if he didn't come back, and she would wonder what had happened to him, but she would never dream of reporting the disappearance of a jaded person.

Job's words interrupted Singh in full flow. He frowned down at Job, then glanced around the room as though expecting to see rows of attentive faces staring up at him. His cigar was in his hand, but it had long since gone out.

"Those were good times, the old days," he said abruptly. He stared down at the dusty surface of the podium. "You know, sometimes I wish that I was in the wilderness, too. At least I would be with my friends."

After the trip to the university, Singh's interest in Job faded. Job had failed the test. He knew it; he was not what Singh had thought he might be. That was fine with Job. He still corrected the man's speech now and again, but he gradually and deliberately reduced the extent of their interaction. By the time that spring turned to summer and Job's shaded doorway had become a coveted prize, he thought that he was safe.

And doing well. The treasures from Sammy's house were vanishing, but Job had learned other vendor tricks of the trade. If you were willing to push a bigger cart, or better still could barter for the use of a small truck for a day and went far south and east of the city, you would find country places where goods were still available for trading. The first trip brought back terrible memories of the incinerator and of burning bodies, but after that Job began to enjoy the startling green of plants, horizon to horizon, and a brighter, haze-free sun.

In early July he made a trip many miles to the southeast, almost as far as the shore of the great bay, and returned late in the afternoon of the second day. The truck driver had no other business that night. He agreed to save Job the trouble of multiple cart trips to where the truck was garaged, by driving to the rear of Sammy's house and allowing Job to unload directly from there.

On the way they passed along the avenue where Job had his stand. Alan Singh's stall was set up with goods, but there was no sign of the familiar black beard. Job saw the other vendors clustered around, talking and ignoring potential customers. Three strangers stood in Job's own doorway.

He hunched low in the truck. "I've changed my mind. Don't go to my house. I'd rather unload at your place later tonight, and pick my stuff up tomorrow. Can you drop me round the next corner? I'll come by to do the unloading in a couple of hours."

The driver stared at him. "Sure you want to do that?" He was a brawny thirty-year-old, and he had seen Job struggling to lift loads that he would have thrown into the truck one-handed.

"I'm sure. I've got other things I need to do."

"All right." The truck turned the corner and stopped. The driver leaned over as Job climbed down. "You don't need to come and unload, I'll do that for you. Pick up your stuff from the garage whenever you're ready."

He waved his hand and pulled away. Job waited until he was out of sight. He had made the decision not to take the truck to Sammy's garage on instinct. Now he was not sure what he ought to do. Check the stalls, and try to find out what was happening there? Or make a discreet trip to Sammy's house, and see if it was still safe to go back? Both alternatives were risky.

Job realized with dismay that he had been getting sloppy. He had told the truck driver how to get to his place. Singh knew it, too. And Singh talked too much. He could have told one of the other vendors.

Or anyone.

It was almost five o'clock. Job retreated to the shelter of a doorway. He waited.

It was a little after six o'clock when a vendor appeared. She was Missie Chang, queen of the early risers. Usually in position before six o'clock in the morning, she was also first to leave at night. Now she pushed her iron-wheeled food cart along wearily.

Job knew she had five children to feed and a second job that would keep her working until midnight. He watched to make sure that no one was trailing her, then fell into step alongside and began to push her cart.

She turned to nod thanks. "You were not there today." She spoke in Mandarin, knowing that Job was at home in it. "But I saw you drive by in the truck. I think it was as well that you did not stop."

" 'The cautious seldom err.' " Job waited for her smile at his use of the Confucian proverb that she had once quoted to him, then went on, "I saw the signs of excitement. What happened?"

"Your friend the blackbearded one was taken."

Your friend. So much for the attempt to distance himself from Singh. "Who took him, and why?"

"I do not know. No one knows, except that it was the government. But there was screaming and shouting and beating, and he did not go easily. They sought you also. No one knew where you were."

The decision to extend the foraging trip to a second day had been made on the spur of the moment. Job shivered when he thought how close he had come to being trapped in his doorway when they arrived for Alan Singh.

"I said nothing when I saw you in the truck," went on Missie Chang. "They made big speeches, and told us that it was our duty to the country to tell them anything we knew. But as our ancient friend also says 'Fine words and an insinuating appearance are seldom associated with true virtue.' "

They had reached the corner where Job normally turned off to go home.

Except that tonight he dared not do it. And if he was being hunted, he should not be seen with Chang.

He released his hold on the cart. "Thank you, Missie. I will not forget what you did for me."

She nodded quietly and trudged off west. He watched her out of sight, then eyed the setting sun. It would be light for less than one more hour. The dark streets of the city were dangerous, and usually he avoided them.

But tonight was not usual. He walked to an old shelter for a long-gone bus route and sat down to wait.

Dangerous or not, tonight he needed darkness.

There were two ways to the garage of Sammy's house: through the basement, or down the alley at the back and in through the old wooden doors. They both had dangers too big for Job to live with. He started towards the front of the house, hesitated, and turned back. Before he could reach the red door he would be completely exposed, on a street with no bolt holes. And anyone could be *inside* the house.

He went along the side street that led to the alley, and halted before he was halfway there. This was even worse. The alley didn't even have two entrances.

But he *had* to go home.

Didn't he?

Job sat on the curb in the darkness and rested his head on his folded arms. If "home" meant possible capture, and a return to Cloak House, did he have to go there?

He stood up and set off through the streets for Bracewell Mansion. When he got there he did not go in. He lurked in the shadows and waited.

The evening wore on. Job was tired and hungry, but he had no thought of leaving. When after three hours the familiar stooped figure of Professor Buckler came creaking down the steps, Job waited until he could move to place himself between the professor and Bracewell Mansion.

He tiptoed forward until he was almost on Buckler's heels.

"Professor."

No one more than twenty feet away would hear that hiss. But Buckler certainly heard it.

And knew who it was. He jerked forward as though Job were a cobra at his heels.

"What do you want?" His back was rigid.

"I want a favor."

"I can't give you one. If Miss Magnolia finds out I've been talking to you, or even seen you —"

"One small favor, with no risk to you. And then I swear I'll never come here again, or try to reach you. Ever."

Buckler turned warily and stood looking down at Job's skinny figure. "What do you want?"

"When you brought me to Bracewell Mansion, you sent me on my first errand, to Sammy's house. Remember?"

"Naturally. As you well know, my memory is excellent." The professor was recovering a little of his poise.

"When I got back, you told Miss Magnolia that you had checked with Sammy, and that I had followed your instructions exactly. But I came back so quickly, you couldn't have *met* with Sammy. So although I've never seen a telephone in her house, and I've never heard one ring, there must be one. And you must have a way of calling her when you want to, from Bracewell Mansion."

"What if we do?"

"I want you to call Sammy for me. Ask if everything is normal there, and ask if it's safe for me to go back to the garage."

Buckler was stooping, staring into Job's face. "That's all you want? Just the phone call, and that question?"

"Just that, and I'll go."

"Wait here." The professor took a couple of paces towards the mansion, then turned back to Job. "If I'm not here in ten minutes, it means there's a problem. Don't come inside, whatever you do."

"I won't. But I'll stay all night long if I have to."

Buckler nodded. He went up the stairs, turning at the top to make sure that Job was not following. Job nodded to reassure him.

In less than five minutes the stooped form was back, hurrying down the stone steps as fast as Job had ever seen him move. "Sammy's there," he said. "And she thought *you* were there, too. Someone has been banging around in the garage for the past hour. When I called she was thinking of going down there and telling you not to make so much noise. Now she's going to lock off the basement access. Who is it, Job?"

"I'm not sure, but I think —"

"No." Buckler held his hands out to ward off words. "Don't tell me. The less I know about this, the happier I'll be. Remember what you promised. I did what you asked me. Now go."

"I'm going." Job turned and began to walk away into the darkness. When he had gone ten steps he spoke over his shoulder. "I won't pester you any more, Professor, but I want you to know one thing. I appreciate what you did for me tonight, and I appreciate what you did when you first brought me to Bracewell Mansion. If there's ever anything you want, and you know how to reach me, just ask."

He turned his head. It must have been the wrong thing to say. Professor Buckler was standing motionless, face turned sideways and down as though he had been struck. He muttered something under his breath and hurried away along the sidewalk.

As soon as the professor was out of sight Job stopped walking.

Where was he going? It could not be to Bracewell Mansion, or Sammy's house, or to his old vending stall. In a few hours he had become a true street *basura*, part of the homeless human rubbish that shared the city with the wild dogs and cats and rats.

And it was all his own fault. He had allowed himself to dabble in matters of no importance, just to satisfy his curiosity.

If he could learn that one lesson from this experience, he would be ahead. And tomorrow he would be ready to start over. From scratch.

Except that it didn't have to be from scratch! Job remembered the goods waiting for him at the truck drop-off point. At least four cartloads, probably more. He didn't have a cart — that was in Sammy's garage — but he had taken most of his valuables with him for his trading trip to the country, and he had a fair amount left. More than enough for a new cart.

But his new home must be far from here. In the city, surely, because that's what he knew, yet far enough away that none of his old acquaintances was in a position to see him and point him out.

Job strolled through the warm night, making his plans. Leaving Sammy's house and the final meeting with Professor Buckler was like severing another umbilical. He had learned a lot in the past half year. He could survive on the streets. And he was determined to do so. As determined as Skip Tolson had been to make it all the way through Cloak House.

But he must remember the rule, the Golden Rule, the only rule. He had forgotten it for a little while, and it had almost been his downfall.

He chanted it to himself as he walked. *Don't get caught again. Never, never, never.*

Chapter Ten

Le coeur a ses raisons . . .

Don't get caught again.

If Job could have remained at ten and a half forever, more than likely he would have followed his Golden Rule and lived uncaptured in the city for the rest of his life. But while weakness and malnutrition may delay puberty, they do not prevent it. Between fourteen and fifteen Job added five inches to his height and matured sexually. And with those physical changes came emotional ones.

Their effects were not obvious at once. Job continued life according to the rigid procedures he had adopted after leaving Sammy's house.

Stay with what you know. He had to move from the area near Bracewell Mansion to a place where he was unknown, so some change was inevitable. But he should stay within the city, where he knew the geography and understood the languages and customs.

First he made a deal with the truck driver. He could leave his country purchases there as long as he liked for a tiny storage fee. Then he started to wander. Finally he chose an area south of the Mall Compound, not far from the river. He had not been there since his shopping trips with Mister Bones, but unless things had changed a lot the mile-long forbidden rectangle of the Compound would serve as a barrier. People who lived to the north rarely went around to the south side.

Don't live anywhere with only one entrance. The place he picked out was on the ground floor of an old factory. There were four doors to the rambling building, each leading to a different street, and upstairs the sealed door that led to an outside fire escape could be broken open in an emergency. The Brazilian family who occupied the rest of the ground floor were the "owners," who kept squatters out and would sell Job meals if he wanted them and oil for the stove. They extolled the virtues of the place and quoted a price. He pointed out that there was no heat and no running water, and made them a counteroffer.

But the oil stove keeps the room warm, and there is a faucet in the alley, just outside the back entrance . . .

Sure. But in the middle of winter, when the faucet freezes . . .

After fifteen minutes of happy haggling in Portuguese, the owners produced a bottle of wine to seal the deal. Job tried a glass and nearly choked. Sammy was right, alcohol was worse than brain-burner.

He bought a small cart and spent four days transferring his goods from storage to his new home. He took the long way round, heading far north and east before he came south again. Those journeys confirmed his first impression. His new home was in an area even more run down than the one he was used to. It sat at the edge of one of the city's big red-light districts, but one that catered to the poor. There was nothing with the grandeur, good-looking girls, and upscale clientele of Bracewell Mansion. However, there was plenty of business. And it was needed. Any money that Job's landlords and neighbors possessed came somehow spilling out from the bordellos, a by-product of prostitution.

Don't meet more people than you have to. A street vendor had to interact with strangers, it was the nature of the business. But Job could set up his stand right outside the factory where he lived. He no longer roamed the streets, by day or night. His monthly foraging expeditions to the country were a necessity, but the people there hated or despised the city and the government. He felt safer there than anywhere, and sometimes thought he should leave the city. But if he did, how would he survive? He lacked the skills and strength to be a farmer.

Job settled in and settled down. Life was good. He had food, a place to live, a job that he understood. It produced more than enough money for his simple needs. For entertainment he had reading. Once a week he went to the area's magazine vendor, bought a copy of each polyglot news-sheet on the stand, and pored over them when it was quiet at his stall. If that ever became boring he had the passing drama of the streets. He saw argument, murder, lovemaking, despair, greed, sickness and cruelty. He watched them all with interest, but always as a part of the audience, standing apart and never becoming involved in the action. As time went by he understood better the emotions and motives that drove the players. But they were not *his* emotions.

By the time he was eighteen he had reached his full height, a skinny, alert six-footer who believed that he had seen everything and was touched by nothing.

He had no friends. He felt no need for them. Since Laga's death, he had never had friends. He would have sworn, quite honestly, that he needed nothing. Until one October morning, three months before his nineteenth birthday, when he woke with a throbbing pain in his jaw and a left cheek so swollen that his eye could not open.

The Brazilian wife took one look at him and crowed with satisfaction. "Teeth! I knew with those teeth you would have problems one day. There is only one man in this whole town I would trust." She gave him an old bill, with an address scribbled on it. "Say that I sent you."

It was pelting with rain, but the torment was too bad

to bear. Job took a waterproof coat and hood and left at once, hurrying along through deserted streets. He found that the address was right in the middle of the red-light district.

"Wisdom tooth," said the dentist. He was a frowning forty-year-old Mexican with monstrous, black-haired forearms. "Impacted, and abscessed. You're lucky you found me on a quiet day. No point in messing about. It has to go. I'm going to give you a shot, but this may still hurt."

It did. Ninety minutes later, Job was helped pale and groggy from the chair. He put on his coat and hat, went to the doorway, and stood there.

"You all right?" The dentist held up the bloodied and fanged wisdom tooth for Job to admire it. "You're still feeling the anesthetic. Want to sit down for a while?"

Job shook his head. He didn't want to sit down for a while. He wanted to lie down for a week. He went out into the sodden street.

Although it was not yet midday a few of the hookers were already on the streets. They were overpainted and underdressed, making sure that no one could miss the message. He walked slowly through them, ignoring their come-ons. Once they took a good look at him they didn't try very hard.

He was a couple of blocks from the edge of the bordello district when dizziness and nausea caught him. He lurched away from the gutter and leaned his head against the side of a house. With his open hands flat on the wall he struggled to remain upright. As the world steadied, he closed his eyes.

When he opened them he found that he was standing just a foot from a ground floor window. He could see in. And someone in there was gazing right out at him. Even in his dazed condition he realized that she was very different from the *puta* women he had just passed.

She wore little makeup, delicately applied. Her figure seemed to be excellent, but it was concealed by clothes that were sedate, almost prim, with a gray skirt that ended below the knee and a high-collared blue blouse. The blouse material was fine and unfamiliar, and threw off every gleam of light. Her hair was styled as he had never seen hair, straight and dark and skirting a broad forehead to end at mid-cheek. Her skin was that of a thirty-year-old; but her gray eyes had the clarity of a young child's.

She was opening the window, sliding it up in its wooden frame. "Are you all right?"

The voice held the same contradiction, deep as a woman's, with a childlike intonation.

"Not too good." The words came out as a mumble. Job pointed to his jaw. "Tooth. Just out."

"You have to sit down." The woman disappeared, and a moment later the door of the house opened. She came into the street, helped Job inside, and sat him on a little chair near the entrance where he could catch the breeze from the street. "You're not Matt, are you, the one that Daniello said would come to see me?"

He shook his head. "I am not Matt." As the anesthetic began to wear off, the left side of his face was sending pulses of pain up to the top of his skull. But at her last words, his muddled brain began to work.

It was English that she was speaking, standard English. But what was her accent? It was nothing he had heard before. Its strangeness was totally different from the Texokie twang he had learned from Alan Singh. The woman's vowels were broad and open-mouthed, while her consonants were clipped and precise. He had already decided that she could not be one of the standard city hookers. Her voice confirmed it. But if she was not, then what was she? All the houses in this street were for the business. Someone's wife, then, or a sister?

She went to bring him a glass of cold water. He sipped it one-sided, keeping it away from the left side of his mouth. She was staring at him, her head on one side.

"It's not just a tooth, is it?" she said. "You have a swelling, but there's something wrong with your chin, too." And then, with no pause. "My name is Stella Michelson. I am visiting my cousin. What's your name?"

"I was born with my chin like this." Job did not give his name. He never gave his name, not to anyone. But the sound of her voice produced a flash of memory. He had heard that tone during his last days at Cloak House. The woman spoke almost as the dimmies spoke, flat and factual. And she was not wary of a stranger, as any woman in this part of the city would be wary. He stared again at the calm eyes. "What do you mean, you are visiting?"

"The Capitol, and the Mall Compound. This is my first time."

"But where do you come from? And why did you come here?"

She seemed to find nothing odd in his questioning. In twenty minutes Job knew more about Stella Michelson than anyone in the whole world knew about him. She was from the far northeast, hundreds of miles away. This morning she had flown to the airport just across the river and was supposed to be picked up there and go to the Mall Compound. But there had been a hitch. The woman who was supposed to accompany her had not been on the airplane. Her luggage had been collected and taken to the Mall Compound, but her cousin had not met her. Instead, Daniello had found her wandering the airport and brought her here. He had promised to go to the Mall Compound later, and come back with her cousin.

"Who is your cousin?" Job was beginning to have suspicions about Daniello.

"Reginald. Reginald Brook."

"Does he live here?"

"He lives for part of the year in the Mall Compound. And then at Recess he flies home."

Job stood up. Daniello, whoever he was, didn't realize what he had got himself into. He had been prowling the airport and found a woman, confused and alone, without luggage. He had picked her up and brought her here.

Job could write the rest of the story for himself. Stella Michelson was attractive. A valuable property. She would go through a breaking-in period, and then she would be added to Daniello's stable and made to work the streets. Matt would be part of her sexual submission, helping Daniello. Either of them might be here any time.

It was an old and familiar scene. Except that Daniello had jumped to a wrong conclusion, and it could be his downfall. Stella Michelson was not what she appeared to be, a runaway woman without possessions and friends. She had connections within the Mall Compound. The Compound was the center of the country's wealth and power. Daniello was about to find himself in deep trouble.

Along with anyone else who happened to be too close to Stella Michelson. "I have to go now, Stella. Thank you for the water."

"Not at all. It was very nice to meet you." She smiled, and her conventional words became full of meaning. Her face was like an opening flower.

The memory of that smile stayed with Job as he hurried home. He decided to go nowhere today. The rain had returned, business would be poor, and although his head had stopped spinning he could use a day of rest and sleep.

Except that he could neither sleep nor rest. He lay on his narrow bed, stared at the ceiling, and saw images. Of the arrival of Matt, of the return of Daniello.

The doors and windows of the house would be shuttered and locked. The two men would strip her naked. Then they would beat her. One or both would have sex with her. Stella Michelson's "education" would begin.

It was sad, but it was none of his business. He owed her nothing but a glass of water. It was not something for which Job should risk comfort or security.

That's what he told himself as he put on his coat and hood, and hurried out into the hissing rain.

The house was still unshuttered. He peered in through the window. She was there, alone. The street was empty. He went around and knocked on the door.

"Stella." He pushed his way in and was speaking before the door was fully open. "Get your coat. Daniello isn't coming here. We have to leave and meet him."

Job had already decided that there would be no time for true explanations. In any case, she might not believe him. He would take her from the house to the edge of the Mall Compound, and tell her to stand there for a few minutes and wait for Daniello. Job would leave at once. The surveillance system would home in on her, as it did anyone on the Compound perimeter, and it would pass on her picture. By now her cousin would have alerted the Mall police, and they would be searching. She ought to be safe inside and back with her family in less than an hour.

What the devil was she doing?

"Stella!"

She turned from the mirror. "If we're going outside, I have to check my hair and do my makeup."

He glanced at the closed door. "Do it when we get there. We have to hurry."

She nodded, and walked calmly across the room to put on her coat and hat. "I wish we had an umbrella. It's raining terribly hard out there. Maybe there is one in the cupboard." She opened a closet between the door and window and began to rummage around inside.

For God's sake! Job stepped to her side. He was reaching down to take her arm when the outside door opened.

The man who came in was bareheaded. His dark hair was slicked down over his forehead and dripping with rain. He was a couple of inches shorter than Job, but a lot more heavily built. In one hand he carried a coil of rope, in the other a two-foot length of thick rubber hose. He hardly had the door open before the rope was on the floor and the hose was lifting.

"Who the hell are you?" The voice was a wolf's growl.

"Daniello!"

Job did not need her cry of greeting. The man was blocking the doorway. If there was another way out, Job did not know it. And he would be allowed no time to seek. The man was moving forward, ready to hit first and then ask questions.

Job had not wanted violence. But he could not have survived eight years in the city without being prepared for it. He reached inside his coat to his belt. As Daniello brought his arm down, Job felt for the narrow-bladed knife and threw up his other arm protectively. The blow took him on his raised left elbow, and the pain was astonishing. His arm fell numb to his side. He nearly dropped the knife from his other hand. One more hit like that, and Daniello would be able to do what he liked with him. As the bludgeon was raised again Job thrust forward and up, under the other man's ribs.

He had never stabbed anyone before, and he was surprised at the force that it needed to push through fat and muscle. The knife blade stopped after it had penetrated just a few inches.

But it was enough. The hose came down on the side of Job's head with no force to the blow. The man was grunting, doubling over, reaching for his midriff with both hands.

Job pulled the knife out and stepped clear. It was not a killing stroke. He had seen men with worse wounds rise and clear the street. In a couple of minutes, when the first shock was over, Daniello might come at him again. Job had to be out in the next few seconds; or he had to finish the job and kill the man.

As he hesitated, Stella began to scream. She was retreating from Job, staring at the knife. He stuck it back in his belt. He had to shut her up, or the whole street would be alerted.

"He's not badly hurt." (But he looks like he is, grovelling on the floor grabbing at his guts.) "Stella, *shut up*. We have to get out of here *now*. I'll explain later."

She stopped screaming at once. Not probably because she believed him, but maybe because she was scared. Well, for the moment that would have to do. He could use her fear. He took her arm. "We're leaving. Daniello will be all right. But don't say one word when we are out on the street. Understand?"

She nodded, staring wide-eyed at the bloody knife at his belt. Her expression was more curiosity than fear.

"That's good. Button your coat." He hurried her outside. At the door he took a last look. "Is there anything else of yours in there?"

She shook her head. Job was certain that there was no evidence that he had ever been in the house. He looked both ways along the wet street. There were only two men in sight, both far-off and walking away from them. Job pulled his hat low over his face and reached across to do the same for Stella. She shied away from his hand for a moment, then stood still and allowed him to adjust her hat brim.

"Come on." He took her arm again.

"Where are you taking me?" She had been told not to speak on the street, but there was no way to keep her silent.

"Where you will be safe." He headed for home.

*   *   *

Job Salk at nineteen was bigger, smarter, more learned and more experienced than Job at fourteen. But he was making mistakes that the fourteen-year-old would never have made.

First of all, the younger Job would never have gone back to the house to find Stella Michelson. And if by some chance he had found himself there, and been forced to rescue her, he would not have taken her with him to his own den. Never, never, never. He would have pointed her towards the Mall Compound, hurried home, and hidden for at least three days. And if somehow Stella had found her way into his home, he would have got rid of her at once and abandoned his hiding place without looking back.

Le coeur a ses raisons que la raison ne connâit point. The heart has its reasons . . . At thirteen, Job had read Pascal as he learned French and wandered randomly through its literature, but he had not known what those reasons were. At nineteen he knew, but at nineteen he could not deny.

Job had gone back for Stella. He had rescued her. He had taken her home. And now he explained what he had done.

She listened gravely, sitting on the bed and drying her dark hair as he talked of the area where he had found her, about the meaning of her pickup at the airport, of what Daniello did for a living, and what Daniello and Matt had had in mind for her.

He explained slowly and carefully, as to a child. After ten minutes she hung the towel on the line, turned, and said, "You think I'm an idiot, don't you? I'm not. I may not be smart, but I'm not an idiot."

While Job stared, she went on, "I believe what you are telling me, even though I shouldn't, because you're nice and I *want* to believe you."

Job believed her, for the same bad reason.

"You are right about some things," she went on. "I *was* silly to believe Daniello, when he said he would go and bring my cousin for me. But where I live, there is no danger. I have never been in any danger, ever." She sat on the narrow bed again. "Are you going to feed me now? I have had nothing since the flight down this morning."

Was there ever such a place, where it could be safe to trust a complete stranger? Job could not imagine it. He went to his food cupboard and examined what he had stored away there. It was more than good enough for him, but not for her.

"Wait a minute." He went out, and returned with a long loaf of bread, a *bouillabaisse* that was his Brazilian landlord's masterpiece, and two bottles of wine. It had cost him more than he usually spent on food in a month.

Stella accepted it all casually, pulled a face at the wine, and drank it anyway. They had a long, leisurely meal, talking mainly about her home and her life-style. Airplanes, ocean cruises, a house with a hundred rooms. Dogs and horses — but as pets, and not to eat. Parties and waterskiing and powerboats and luxury cars. To Job it all had the unreality of elf-land; yet somehow he believed her. When they had finished eating she watched as Job cleared up, washed and dried the dishes, and put things away.

"Do you often do this *yourself*?" she said. She had made no offer to help.

He stared at her. She wasn't joking. "I do. Who does your work for *you*? When it's not me, I mean."

"People." She missed the irony, and waved her hand vaguely. "You know. There's always people around for that sort of thing."

In Job's mind the gulf between them widened still further. He put the last dish in the drawer and went across to feel the hanging coats. They were dry. "Come on."

"Come on where?"

"Home. Where you ought to have been hours ago. It's getting dark. Your cousin will be worried sick."

She put on her coat and hat while he stood and waited, and went with Job through the corridor and as far as the outside door. As he opened it, cold rain came blowing in. It was pelting down harder than ever. She grimaced and pulled back. "I'm not going out in *that*. Why don't we just call my cousin?"

"I don't have a phone." Calls from any telephone could be traced. He had decided long ago that he would never own one. But he was sure that he could get her to the Mall Compound in such a roundabout way that she would never find her way back here.

"Then my cousin can wait a while longer. This won't let up tonight." She closed the door and went back along the corridor toward Job's room. "I'll go in the morning."

He followed her, indecisive. She had to go, that was clear. But how was he supposed to make her? She sounded firm, while he was finding it harder and harder to summon the energy to do anything. He had drunk only one glass of wine, to keep Stella company, but it had followed a bad night, a painful tooth extraction, and plenty of stress and physical violence. His left cheek still ached, and so did his bruised elbow. All he really wanted to do was flop down somewhere and postpone worry about Stella's problems until tomorrow. And it was not as though she was in any danger. She was as safe with him as she could be anywhere in the city.

It did not occur to Job, then or ever, that there was another and simpler reason: he did not want her to leave.

He took off his coat without speaking and placed it again on its hook. For his trading expeditions into the countryside he took with him a roll mattress. Now he pulled it out from under his bed and spread it on the floor. It was frayed at the edges, with bits of dried grass still stuck to it.

Stella stared. "What's that for?"

"Sleeping on. Maybe you. More likely me."

She snorted at some secret joke. She was opening the second bottle of wine and pouring. Job took a glass and leaned back in his chair.

Stella was talking, to him or at him. He must have been answering, but his own words vanished from his mind a moment after he spoke them. At last she came over and touched his face, and then his neck and chest.

"You're a sweet man, you are. What's your name, sweet man?"

"Job Salk. Job *Napoleon* Salk." Eight years of self-discipline, dissolving into the night.

"Well, then." Her face was an inch away from his. "Where are we, Job Salk? Not *there*, for sure."

She was laughing at him as he failed to remove clothing, either hers or his own. She had to do it for both of them. He felt huge satisfaction when he saw her body naked. He had been quite right; the clothes she wore had been designed to conceal beauty, but beauty was there in abundance.

He forgot his aching arms and face. He felt wonderful. *She* felt wonderful.

And as she lay down beside him and took him in her arms, everything felt wonderful.

From their languorous awakening the next morning until almost midday, it was a contest with lovemaking as the prize: Who could think of the best new reason why Stella should not leave yet, or contact her cousin?

After noon neither mentioned it. Job watched Stella, touched her, and listened to her, and was watched and fondled in return.

Everything about her pleased him. She yawned, and he admired the strong and regular white teeth. She scratched her thigh, and he watched an after-blush of pink blooming on her fair skin. She ate, with an appetite three times Job's, and he touched her face, feeling the contraction of strong muscles in her upper jaw as she bit and chewed and swallowed.

In the late afternoon Job began to wonder what they would eat for dinner. Stella had exhausted the best of his own and his Brazilian landlady's food supplies, and he wanted to give her something special.

He took his jacket. There was a street market a mile away, and a liquor store in the same direction.

"Wait here."

"But I want to come with you."

"I'd like you to. But they're bound to be looking for you. Once you're seen, they won't let you stay any longer. I'll only be a couple of hours. Maybe less."

"But there's nothing to *do* here."

"Read a book." Job glanced at the shelved walls of his room as he left. Books were like thoughts, they crept up on you. When he looked with a stranger's eye, he saw a room where books were as numerous as in Professor Buckler's study.

"Read!" Stella grimaced at him and flopped down in a chair. "Who reads?"

"I'll be back as soon as I can. Less than two hours."

But it was closer to four. The nearest food market was already closed. After grocery shopping, and a long wait at a beer and wine store, he had continued to the magazine shop. He wanted to buy the government daily broadsheet, and see if it said anything about Stella. And she had been complaining about the awful quality of the soap he gave her (the very best he had), so he needed to buy something out of his usual interest or price range. After the second food market that meant another long walk.

It was almost dark by the time he reached home. He was loaded with groceries and supplies, enough to eat for a week without ever going out. It was a struggle to open the door while balancing bags, and then to turn and close it the same way.

Stella had not come out to help him, although she must have heard him fumbling around in the doorway. She had not even thought to put the light on, even though the room was now dark. That no longer surprised him. She was used to having things done for her. It never occurred to her that others might need help.

But she was wonderful, all the same. He turned around, arms still full of bags and boxes. "I'm back, love."

"So you are, love," said a man's voice in the darkness. "And not before time. You said two hours. What kept you, Job Salk?"

• Chapter Eleven

> *"So twice ten miles of sterile ground,*
> *With walls and towers were girdled round."*

Matt and Daniello. Hunting him down and looking for revenge.

Before that thought was fully formed, Job was hit by another. His name! The man, whoever he was, *knew his name*. So it couldn't be Daniello and friends.

The light went on as Job flattened against the wall. The intruder was sitting at ease in Job's only good chair, hands folded in his lap. Before Job could move, one hand lifted to show the tiny gun it was holding. There was a soft popping sound and the wall a couple of feet from Job's head began to smoke and crumble.

"That is to discourage action, not to suggest it." The man let his hands fold again into his lap. "Before you are tempted to folly, let me assure you that whether or not I could kill you before you reached me — and I would bet heavily in my favor — there are men guarding each exit. You would never make it out of this building."

"Stella," said Job, glaring around the room.

"Is not here. Obviously." The man smiled. He had a fair-skinned and cherubic face, and was almost totally bald. With his short stubby arms and legs, and a belly that protruded far out over his belt, he gave the impression of a huge and good-natured dwarf. "You don't know our Stella very well, do you? Telling her to sit down and read a book! Might as well ask her to grow wings and fly. You hadn't been gone more than fifteen minutes before she got bored and decided to take a look around outside. We had five hundred people searching for her. She was spotted in half an hour."

"You're her cousin, Reginald Brook?"

"Good lord, no." The fat man laughed. "My name is Wilfred Dell. Reginald Brook would be truly appalled at the idea that I might be mistaken for him. But don't just stand there — take a seat."

The tone was joking, but it was an order. Job sat down on the edge of the bed.

"Before we begin," went on Dell, "let me tell you some ground rules. I don't want you to have the wrong idea about your own situation. Stella Michelson belongs to a very old and wealthy family. Should a street *basura* like you even try to touch her hand, the men of the family would want him castrated or executed. What they want, they usually get."

Job was making his automatic assessment of the man's voice. It was standard English, with the open vowels and clipped consonants that he had noticed in Stella. But there was a subtle difference, a suggestion that this was not Wilfred Dell's first language.

"What makes you think that I would ever try to touch her hand?" Job threw the question in rapid *chachara-calle*.

Dell pursed rosebud lips. "Mmm. Very good." He replied in the same argot of the central city. "And quick. It's nice to know that not everything in the data banks is rubbish. We'll get to that later. How do I know about you and Stella? I don't *know*, in the sense of absolute proof. I cannot ask her, and if I could she would not tell me. But I do my homework, and I make good guesses. When Stella arrived at the Mall Compound she went to the bathroom. By that time the central data bank had turned up some interesting material about you, so I made sure that we obtained a urine sample as the toilet she used was flushed. And what do you know? There was semen in it. Now, I've known Stella for a long time, and I'd be the first to admit that if you put her lovers in line, you'd have enough men to fight a fair-sized war . . . "

Wilfred Dell shook his head at Job's expression. "I'm sorry if I'm upsetting you. But I must go on. If I were to take a specimen of *your* semen and do a DNA mapping, I *might* find that it was nothing like the sperm sample we took from Stella's wee-wee. Or I just might find that you and Stella have been playing rub-the-rhubarb. That's my guess. Stella's not above plucking a wildflower, even if it happens to be growing in a dung-heap.

"So let's take the next step. Reginald Brook is delighted that Stella has been found. He knows that she has no idea of danger. He's not surprised to learn that she wandered off through the city and stayed away overnight; it's just the sort of thing she would do. End of episode. The matter goes no further. *Unless* someone were to put the evidence of what *really* happened right under poor Reggie's nose. Now, it's not my job to cause Reginald pain or discomfort. I wouldn't dream of showing him what you did . . . if your name was not Job Napoleon Salk, and if I did not have other needs."

"How do you know my name?"

"From Stella. No, don't have any silly thoughts that she 'betrayed' you. If you don't want something passed on to others, you don't tell it. You know that rule as well as I do. But once I had your name, I thought I'd run it through the data banks, just for the fun of it. From your address I didn't expect much. Maybe a little petty theft, or an addiction or two. But instead I got this."

Wilfred Dell reached into his jacket pocket and pulled out a sheaf of paper. "Job Napoleon Salk, aged eighteen. Born in the *Aeterna Lux* charity ward of the L Street hospital. Should have been stillborn, and nearly was. Birth report shows numerous physical problems."

Dell looked up. "You seem to be managing them pretty well, but they'll cause trouble later. If you have a later. Let's continue: Raised in Cloak House until age ten. One of just a handful of children who did not die in a contaminated food incident there." Dell raised his fair eyebrows. "Smart?"

"Lucky. They wanted to starve me, not poison me."

"We all need luck. But then you escaped, and the record is blank for a month or so until you were caught running drugs to the Mall Compound. Taking a bit of a chance, weren't you?"

"I was. But I didn't know it."

"Just like today. Were you a virgin, by the way, until the fair Stella came along?" Wilfred Dell nodded at Job's sick look. "Well, never mind. One consolation, virginity is a one-off deal. You can't get fooled again that way. Let's go on. J-D'd, and sent back to the Cloak House detention center. But you escaped *again*." Dell laid the papers in his lap. "No one ever escaped from the Cloak House detention center before, and they couldn't figure out how you did it. Like to give me a hint?"

Job shook his head.

"Well, no matter. You can tell me later. But at the next point in your record I became very interested. After Cloak House there's another gap, almost nine months. Then your name appears in a roundup of dissident scientists. One of them had tested you as a possible recruit. So far as he was concerned, you failed. But the results of the test are in the files, and it's obvious that your scientist friend must be a bit of a moron. He was so busy looking for what he wanted to see, he missed the most important point: you were only ten years old, with next to no education, but you spoke seven languages fluently. More than that, the tests showed you had absolute pitch, a near-perfect word memory, and an amazing ear for language." He looked up at Job. "You still have that, I assume?"

Job had nothing to lose. "I think that would be a fairly safe assumption." He spoke as Wilfred Dell spoke, the same broad vowels overlaid on the faint residue of a street accent. "I also do my homework. And in the area of language, at least, it is not necessary for me to make many guesses."

The other man listened closely. "Do it again. Some more." And then, after another few sentences from Job, "I've heard enough recordings of myself to know how accurate that is. Do you realize how useful you could be in the right situation?"

"I'm in the wrong situation."

"We'll see. How many languages do you speak now?"

"I'm not sure." Job frowned. "I'd have to sit down and count."

"Some other time. Let me continue. There was a scientist roundup — but no sign of little Job Salk. Where did he go? How did he know to run for it, when the others didn't? How could he disappear so cleanly? None of the prisoners could tell, even when they'd been dosed with drugs that squeeze your memory like a wet sponge. So. Job Salk disappears *again*. And this time he stays vanished. For nearly nine years. Until this afternoon."

"I was a fool. I deserved to be caught."

"Perhaps. But you would prefer not to be killed? Or even castrated? Then let me spell it out for you. You can assist me with one of my current little problems. Or I can give these records" — Wilfred Dell tapped the papers resting on his paunch — "to Reginald Brook, together with the results of a comparison between your semen and that taken from Stella's pee. And then I can walk away and busy myself on other matters."

Job stepped closer, peering into Dell's eyes. "Who are you?"

"I am Wilfred —"

"No. You know what I mean." Job studied the

chubby face, in repose like a Buddha in meditation. "Who are you?"

Wilfred Dell stood up. "I will give you an answer. But not here and now. Come on."

"Where are you going to take me?"

"To a place where our conversations can have more meat. And where you can see how the other half lives — or rather, one-tenth of one percent." Wilfred Dell was smiling his half-smile. "We are going to the Mall Compound."

One persistent rumor of the city concerned the true size of the Mall Compound. The aboveground area, with its barricades and watchtowers and searchlights, was little more than a mile long and less than half of that wide. But the Compound was said to continue underground, stretching its tentacles out through subterranean tunnels of unknown extent.

Job had seen the evidence long ago, when he was taken from inside the compound to Bracewell Mansion. But he had been too young and too overwhelmed to note much of what he saw or where he went, and his underground journey had been mainly in darkness.

This time he was in a better position to observe, but again he was distracted. His mind ran far afield. He noted that he and his guards walked eight long blocks to the gaudy heart of the bordello district, entered a red brick building, and descended for many seconds in an elevator before emerging in a brightly lit tunnel. He climbed into the car that waited there, sitting silent next to Wilfred Dell. The man did not try conversation. He sensed that Job needed time for his own thoughts.

The sheer *stupidity* of it, that was what Job could not get over. It seemed that the moment he had set eyes on Stella Michelson, every thinking part of his brain had turned to mush. He had lived totally in the present, like an animal, with no thought of future consequences.

And the idiocy had not finished yet. He knew that Stella had behaved without a shred of responsibility, doing exactly the opposite of what he had asked her, and leading Wilfred Dell and his assistants straight to Job's home.

But with all that, he could not feel angry with her. He felt anger at *himself*, for forgetting the lessons that had shaped his whole life. She had never pretended that Job was her first or her only lover. He had just invented the idea that he was and acted as though wishing made it so.

Job's brooding ended when they left the car and began a journey through the labyrinth of the Mall Compound's interconnected buildings. Useless as it might be, he began to study the path they were taking, counting turnings and noting coded wall colors. The buildings had once been discrete units, each with its own external wall. There must still be doors that led to the outside.

Wilfred Dell watched Job with that little smile on his face. "Never say die, eh? I like that. But this is not Cloak House. The chance of escape from the Compound is quite negligible." He glanced at the guards and switched to *chachara-calle*. "Negligible, *chico-terco*, without my help. Believe me."

They entered a glass-sided elevator and went slowly up, higher and higher in a tall, square-sided tower that rose above all other structures of the Mall Compound. Job had seen it many times from far away, wondering what it was and how it came to be there. He had never in his life expected to be inside it. The windows that they passed in their ascent faced southwest. As the car rose, Job saw the dark and quiet river, then the lights of airport runways. Beyond that, the dimly lit city went on forever.

"After you." The elevator finally stopped. Wilfred Dell had the gun in his hand again. He gestured to his armed assistants to descend in the elevator, and directed Job forward through a heavy wooden door. "You will sleep up here tonight, in guest quarters. Turn around." He watched closely as Job turned to face him. "How are you? Exhausted?"

"I've felt better. But I'm all right."

"Lively enough to absorb information? If not, we'll postpone this until morning."

"Try me." Job was tired, but he was taking in everything around him. Dell's office was furnished with a luxury that Job had never seen, not even in the most opulent chambers of Bracewell Mansion where only senators and congressmen were received. This room reeked of wealth: massive wooden desk, discreet recessed ceiling lights, coffee tables with delicate cups and saucers and glasses upon them, oil paintings on the walls that subtly enhanced the rest of the furnishings . . .

"You can look around some other time." Dell seemed to see and understand everything. "I brought you here," he went on, "because I want you to do a job for me. To be specific, I want to send you into the Nebraska Tandy." He smiled. "There. Now you're awake, right?"

Job was very much awake.

"The Nebraska Tandy," repeated Wilfred Dell. "You know the jingle?"

"T-A-N-D—"

"Not that one. That's the kiddy version. This one's a bit more grown up:

"So twice ten miles of sterile ground,

"With walls and towers were girdled round.

"In Xanadu, the sky burns black.

"If you go in, you don't come back.

"How much do you know about the Great Nebraska Tandy?"

"Enough. I'd be better off handed over to Reginald Brook, right now."

"He might send you there anyway. And if he sentenced you, you *wouldn't* come back. Whereas if you go for me, the whole point of your trip is that you *will* come back, or it's not worth your going." Dell gestured to a white chair built of strips of stout cloth and metal bars. "Sit down. It's a lot more comfortable than it looks. I can see you're baffled, and you should be. Why would anyone care what's happening inside a Tandy?" He sat down behind the desk, opened a carved jade box that sat on the corner, and pushed it towards Job. "Help yourself."

Job glanced at the assortment inside and shook his head. "I don't use any of those."

"Good," Dell closed the lid. "Do you use alcohol?"

"Not normally. I did with Stella."

"I'll bet you did. But you're sober now? I have to tell you a few things. You may think you know them already, but you don't. While I was waiting for you I took a look around your place. Lots of books. Have you read any of them?"

"Some. Most."

"So you read about the Great Crash — the *Quiebra Grande*?"

"A bit."

"Then don't believe a word of it. What the books say caused the crash, that's pure fiction. They follow the official line, what the government wants you to believe. I'm going to tell you the truth."

Dell paused. The lights in the room were unobtrusive, but they were four times as powerful as the bare bulbs in Job's room. Job could see the lines around Wilfred Dell's eyes, and furrows in the high brow. The baby face was deceptive. The man behind the desk was in his forties, perhaps in his fifties. And he was an enigma, a type of personality that Job had never met before.

"I thought that you *were* the government," he said.

"The *Quiebra Grande*." Dell ignored the implied

question. "I still lived in the city in those days, not too far from where we found you. And not much richer." He flashed Job a look. "There *are* ways out, you know, just a few. I used to read the papers, too. I remember when it began.

"It was like a smelly fart at the duchess's tea party. At first, all the governments ignored it. They pretended that it didn't exist, that nothing had happened.

"Then things got worse. The stink became terrible, too bad to ignore. And all the governments turned and accused each other. *You* did it, one said, when you cut down all your forests. No, it's *your* fault, said the next one, you spent more money than you had, and you pulled down all the world's financial markets. But *you* were burning the high-sulfur coal, ruining the air. And *you* were fouling the oceans with your wastes. And *you* had the bad reactor meltdown, and quadrupled the background radioactivity.

"Everything was going to hell. But there's one other thing to remember about a high-class tea party: no matter what happens, the Duchess won't be blamed for the fart. And no matter who gets hurt, the Duchess herself won't suffer. In our case, the Michelsons and the Brooks and the big land-owning families were the Duchess. They were not about to lower their living standards. Other people could do that.

"But the *Quiebra Grande* was too bad to ignore. So the powers in this country and elsewhere did what rulers in trouble have done for centuries: they looked for a group to *blame*.

"And they found one, people easy to identify and too naive to defend themselves. The air was dirty and radioactive, the water was foul, the topsoil was blowing off the land. There was no money to repair roads or runways or cities, and the transportation system was collapsing. What was the common denominator of all the problems?"

"Technology," said Job quietly. "And behind the technology, science."

Wilfred Dell had not been expecting an answer. He stared at Job. "You really *did* read those books, didn't you?"

It was nice to know that Dell's records were not perfect. "I did, but not until I was sixteen years old. I knew the official position long before that. A scientist told me about it when I was ten. Alan Singh. He was one of those they rounded up. I've often wondered what happened to him."

"I could find out. But I hardly need to look. The Toxic And Nuclear Disposal sites started growing before the turn of the century. By the time of the *Quiebra Grande* there were hundreds of Tandies, all around the world. The biggest in this country is Xanadu, out in Nebraska — over twenty miles square. It holds the most toxic chemical wastes, the highest radioactivity levels. And when the scientist pogrom began, Reginald Brook and friends decided that the punishment must fit the crime. Scientists should go to the Tandies. The vast majority of them were sent to the Nebraska Tandy." Wilfred Dell smiled pleasantly at Job. "So your friend Singh probably landed in Xanadu. And he is certainly long-dead."

That was where Father Bonifant had been sent, uncomplaining. *The assignment to the Nebraska Tandy thus carries a great responsibility, and I choose to regard it as an equally great honor.* Job recalled the calm face of Mister Bones. There was no hint in his expression that he had just been sentenced to a terrible death.

Dell had seen Job's expression, and misunderstood it. "I know what you are thinking: if Xanadu is fatal to Singh and anyone who goes there, why should it be any different for Job Salk? If you were to stay for a long time in the Nebraska Tandy, or any other — I'm told that the Mongolian Tandy makes Xanadu look like a pleasure palace — you would be right. But that's not what I'm proposing. You will make a short trip. How short? Depends on how efficient you are at collecting information. As soon as you have what you need, you come out."

"And as soon as you have what *you* need, you kill me?"

"Now then! Such an idea." Wilfred Dell clucked his tongue. "I don't mind your suggestion, it shows that you think along the appropriate lines. But you happen to be quite wrong. I always need first-rate people, as many of them as I can get. And my staff are well-treated. Don't take my word, ask any of my assistants. All I require in return is loyalty. Of course, this will help." He picked up Job's folder from the desk. "Little things like this are held in a safe place. If anything happens to me, they will be delivered to where they will do the most good. Like, to Reginald Brook."

"You might as well give it to him now. I can't do your job. You must have people better suited for it than I am."

"Three months ago I might have agreed with you. Four of my staff went into Xanadu. Two men, two women. None came out, or sent messages. Our spaceborne imaging systems remain in position, of course, but — now what's the matter?"

"Spaceborne systems. I thought nothing had gone into space since 2003."

"That was just the dissolution of NASA. There are other programs, always have been. The remote collection systems keep on looking; but there is a limit to what spaceborne or airborne observing systems can hope to see. A person with the right contacts on the ground, *inside* Xanadu, can be far more flexible."

"I don't know anything about the inside of the Nebraska Tandy. And I don't know anyone there."

"That's not necessary. You have *this* going for you."

Dell tapped Job's folder. "Before you get there, we'll make sure that the people who run Xanadu have your records. The place wasn't intended to have *anyone* running it when it started out. Criminals were supposed to go there and just die, nice and quiet. But once people began to be sent in they set up their own internal power structure within a few months." He sighed. "Sometimes I think about dying. And then I wonder about going to hell. And then I think that if and when I go there, the place will be completely organized and run by lost souls, with a council and a works committee and an ethics panel, and I'll feel right at home. Anyway, you have impeccable credentials for Xanadu. J-D marks still on your wrist and forehead, drug-running conviction, high scores on the science aptitude test."

"Why bother? Why don't you go in openly, in force, and see what's happening?"

"Because I'm not willing to admit — officially — that anything at all is happening. Remember, a trip to a Tandy is supposed to be a one-way ticket. To change that policy for more than a few people would cost me too much equity. In any case, collecting information is a tricky business. Access is the first requirement. Your record will help you gain that access, to criminals or to scientists. And the *second* requirement of information collection is to understand what you hear. No one on my roster is as well qualified as you are. The leaders can use any language they like, but you will be able to follow it. And speak it, too — though that might be unwise."

Behind Wilfred Dell, a carved clock hanging on the wall began a strange buzzing. A door opened in its front, and a little painted skeleton emerged. Job heard an unfamiliar C-minor dirge on musical bells, and a rattling of bones.

"Midnight already. Where does the time go?" Dell smiled, a brief gleam of teeth. "We must wrap this up. I have other obligations."

He turned to stare at and through the white wall to the left of him. In the bright light the pupils of his eyes seemed to vanish, while their irises passed though a color shift to paler blue. He was still wearing his half-smile. Job suddenly saw before him a grinning gnome of lust, straight from a five hundred-year-old woodcut.

"I'm sure that you will have more questions," went on Dell. "But is there anything that cannot wait for tomorrow?"

"You haven't told me what you want me to do."

"True. But does it matter, beyond the fact that you will seek information? The main thing is to know where you are going, and why you were chosen. Tomorrow will do for the rest of it."

"Do I have any choices?"

"Ah, that is a nice question." Dell leaned back in his chair. "Technically, you do. You can go to Xanadu on my behalf, find what I need, and come back. Or you could go into the Tandy and loaf about until you die there. Or, if you were really a masochist, you could encourage me to present your entire folder to Reginald Brook. I would not deny such a request, but I hope you will not consider such a foolish action. I like you, Job. Now, is there any final question?"

"You promised to tell me who *you* are."

"So I did. Hmm. I assume from your dossier that you never attended school after your first flight from Cloak House?"

"I never did."

"You were lucky. But it means that you will have to take my next statement on faith. Although the schoolchildren of this country emerge from our institutions of supposed learning ninety percent illiterate, knowing nothing of science, nothing of technology, little geography, and less history, every one of them will tell you who rules the country. We are governed by the interaction of a President, learned judges, and our peoples' representatives.

"Every child knows this; and every child is wrong. Perhaps it was once that way, but today the Court and President and Congress are either members of the old and wealthiest families, like the Michelsons and Brooks; or they have been bought and controlled by them. The sprawl of government passes and implements policies. But far fewer people, about a hundred in number, *set* policies.

"I, and a handful like me, serve the interests of what we term the Royal Hundred. Our job is to make sure that their families, people like Stella, can live lives of perfect irresponsibility in the midst of global chaos. She must never have to worry about a thing. Others will take care of her food, her travel plans, all her material needs. She must be able to walk out into the most dangerous city on Earth, with not a thought for her personal safety. It is my job to guarantee that safety. Sometimes — like yesterday — I can come close to failure. But usually I do very well. I feel sorry for the failures, because Reginald and friends are not tolerant people. But as you see, success has its perquisites."

Wilfred Dell glanced smugly around his office, and again stared at the wall next to him.

Sorry for the failures? There was no trace of compassion in Wilfred Dell's face. Job recalled one of Father Bonifant's warnings, when he reminded Job to be careful of possible thieves and murderers on the streets of the city: "There is no end to Our Lord's mercy and compassion, and there is no one so bad that he or she *cannot* be saved. But there are those who *will* not be saved. The world contains people who are truly evil."

There was a dreadful plausibility and friendliness to Wilfred Dell, but his smile seemed to Job to be truly evil. Whatever he did, whatever he made Job do, it would be only to serve his own purposes. He would allow nothing to jeopardize his own position. He appeared quite invulnerable.

But perhaps there were chinks in even that armor of self-confidence.

"And one day," said Job innocently, "I suppose that you will be one of the Royal Hundred."

Dell scowled. "One is born to that status, one does not ascend to it. The hundred are drawn only from the Brooks and Michelsons, and families like them."

He stood up abruptly and turned away. In the instant before the cherub's face became hidden, Job saw that all satisfaction had vanished from it. He understood, and was perversely pleased.

Wilfred Dell claimed that he liked Job. Perhaps he did, a little. Perhaps he even liked Job as much as he liked anyone. He probably had no one that he *loved*, as others used the word love.

But he did have someone that he hated.

What would please Wilfred Dell more than anything would be to send Reginald Brook and the rest of the Royal Hundred on a one-way trip to the Great Nebraska Tandy.

● Chapter Twelve

*I go whence I shall not return, even to the
land of darkness and the shadow of death.*

— The Book of Job, Chapter 10, Verse 21

Job had seen maps of the country. He knew that the
Nebraska Tandy lay more than a thousand miles west,
fifty times as far from the city as he had ever been,
halfway to the western ocean. But maps were one
thing. Physical experience was another.

Thirteen hundred miles by aircraft, eighteen
hundred by road: it meant eternity, seven bruising
days sitting in a hard seat on a stinking, broken-
springed bus, with no chance to wash or change
clothes. As they came closer to their destination, Job
yearned for the sight of the Nebraska Tandy. Anything
was better than another day of travel.

Outside it had been snowing for forty-eight hours.
Inside it was hot and stifling, with the stench of sick and
pent-up humans growing steadily worse. The bus
rumbled on at a steady thirty miles an hour, over ruler-
straight roads whose surface was cracked and broken.
On either side, the white plain ran from horizon to
horizon. Xanadu should be only a couple of hours
ahead. Job stared out through the forward window.

Now and again they hit a real break in the roadbed,
one that jolted every passenger and threw them from
side to side. No one but Job seemed to notice. They
slumped on the frayed seats, eyes open and placid.
Back in the city, Job had been the first to board. He had

watched in horror as the bus made its stops and the other prisoners appeared. They were all men, and every one was pleasure-drugged to the point where no physical discomfort would rouse them. At four-hour intervals during the journey, the two drivers moved around the bus and stuck a little patch onto each prisoner's neck. Job had ripped his off before there could be any effect, but the pads proved to be no more than skin-penetrating stimulants. Within thirty seconds the others were sitting up and taking notice. They were fed a packaged meal and permitted to use the roadside as a toilet. In five more minutes the jolt from the stick-on patch wore off. The prisoners returned to their usual blissful apathy. Sores from the seats were ignored. As the days wore on, the trance deepened. Some of the prisoners began to foul themselves where they sat.

Seeing them at the beginning of the journey, Job had appreciated the favor that Wilfred Dell had done in decreeing that Job did not need to be sedated, and that his drip-I/V could contain not drugs but water. By the third day he was not so sure. The other prisoners could not talk to him, or he to them. He could not speak to the driver or his assistant, without revealing his own unique situation. And the ride was too bumpy to let him sleep for more than a few hours a night. All he could do was ride the jolts, stare out at the dreary landscape, and worry.

Their destination lay almost exactly due west. But they had angled at first to the north, into colder weather and forlorn countryside. Mile after mile, their route passed old and derelict wayside structures, motels and repair shops and restaurants and gas stations and food stands. In front of them, squatting at the roadside, sat newer and smaller buildings of wood and sheet metal. Behind everything, fading off to wooded hills and bare fields, were family vegetable plots.

Were there thousands after countless thousands of them, or was there just one, endlessly repeated? Job saw in each field the same stooped elders and the same tiny children, scrabbling in wet dirt.

During the second day the country changed. The bus chugged through a sterile, deep-scarred terrain of pits and quarries. Beside the old strip mines, scrawny yellow-flowered plants struggled to find a hold in steep-sided slag heaps, more harsh and inhospitable than fresh volcanic lava. Nothing else grew, from horizon to horizon. But still there were people, patiently sifting the rubble.

Job had no idea what they were seeking. There was no one that he could ask. He leaned his forehead on the seat in front and closed his eyes. Still he saw the array of slag heaps and quarries, marching off to infinity.

Could the Nebraska Tandy be worse than this? It was hard to see how. The pictures that Wilfred Dell had shown suggested pleasant and peaceful communities, not a hell on Earth . . .

"Two years ago." Dell tapped the table-sized color print. "This is what the spacebirds sent back from a routine scan of Xanadu. There was nothing interesting, except that right here"— he touched the place with the end of a pencil — *"an area was being cleared around one of the towns. This is Techville, where most of the scientists sent to the Tandy live."*

Job leaned over the table. The image was an oblique shot, taken in full sunlight and with excellent detail. The prospect was pleasant. He saw nothing but a well-organized town, laid out as rings of buildings around a central cleared area.

"Now, look at a year and a half ago." Dell slid another print partly over the first. "A fence has gone up, all the way around the town. And another fence is being built here." He ran his pencil point over a rectangular region close to the town center. "So, you tell me. Why would anyone build fences like that inside a Tandy? Are they there to keep something out, or to keep something in?

"Every space image receives its own analysis. The fences were noted, but no action was taken. No one brought this to my attention. Even if they had, I'd have thought nothing of it. So now we come to this, one year ago."

The new print on the table was at a finer scale than the earlier two. The small rectangular region filled the whole scene.

"See the people outside that small building," said Wilfred Dell. *"Mostly they work inside, but on this shot our viewing system got lucky. The analysts zoomed in to the highest resolution available. They could see enough to pick out faces, and ask the computers to enhance them and look for matches in the main data bank. That's when they made an identification of one of the people outside the building."* Dell slid a full-face ID photograph in front of Job. *"Dr. Hanna Kronberg. That's when I was called in. I've been tracking Hanna for over seven years...."*

Since that first sight Job had spent a lot of time studying the subject of that photograph, in every light and from every angle. As he leaned with eyes closed on the bus seat in front of him, he could see Hanna Kronberg now in his mind's eye. If ever they met he would recognize her at once. But he was less confident than Wilfred Dell that the meeting would ever take place.

If Dr. Kronberg were inside that fenced area, Job would have to find a way to be invited in. That seemed an impossible task. Even if she were outside Techville, the chance of a random meeting was slight. The population of Xanadu was a hundred thousand, maybe more as new prisoners were poured in. No one on the outside was sure of the present number, and if the people inside took a census they kept it to themselves. Job was beginning to think of the Tandy as a separate nation. Nothing was sent in but toxic wastes, radioactive material, and condemned criminals. Nothing came out. Mean life expectancy within Xanadu: one and a half years.

He shifted on his uncomfortable seat and stared

around at the others in the bus. Everyone here was doomed, except — just possibly — Job. He wondered at his companions' offenses. If one happened to be another Hanna Kronberg, a condemned scientist of great brilliance and reputation, he would not know it. Every face on the bus was pleasure-sated and lethargic.

But someone might not be what they seemed. Job recalled Wilfred Dell's words: "It is not a matter of trust. It is that more than one point of view is valuable. So there will be others in my employ, seeking to crack the secret of the Nebraska Tandy. You will not know their identity, as they do not know yours. You will each serve as an independent check on the others. I hope that at least one of you succeeds."

There was no reason for Job to assume that another agent in Dell's service would be on this same bus; but there was no reason to assume that he or she was *not*. . . .

After the gouged landscape of the strip mines finally ended, the highway improved. The bus picked up speed to nearly fifty. On their right lay a vast lake, on the left an unbroken vista of buildings was coming into view.

It had to be Lake Michigan, the second of the Great Lakes on their route west. They had already skirted Lake Erie from Cleveland to Toledo, but that had happened in the middle of the night. Job knew of it only because he had heard the night shift driver talking the next morning, complaining about the smell that came off the water.

Job studied the wind-ruffled waters off to his right. Lake Michigan was just as acid and necrotic as the other lakes; yet there were people all the way along the shore. Ignoring a cold rain they were paddling in the chill lake water, probing at the bottom with sticks.

What could they be doing? The last fish had vanished from the lakes a generation ago, well before the *Quiebra Grande*. Phosphate runoff had filled the lake with the green slime of algal bloom, but that was not edible. Maybe the people had come from the sprawl of Greater Chicago, simply because there was no place left in the whole city where they could live. More and more cities were ridding themselves of the homeless and the indigent, trucking them far beyond city limits and dropping them off to fend for themselves. How long before the countryside itself was full, and everyplace was chock-a-block? According to Wilfred Dell, that lay a long time in the future.

"Four hundred million sounds like a lot of people to you, but it isn't. We've not doubled in a generation; some countries in Africa have tripled in that time. China tops one and a half billion, India's the same, Brazil and Mexico and Indonesia and the old Soviet states push six hundred million each. The thing that hurt us the worst was when the economic collapse pulled the rug from industrial development. We could have lived with everything else. You won't believe this until you've seen other places, but this is still a rich country."

Job didn't believe it. Unless it were possible to have a rich country filled with poor people. But hadn't the last Depression, ninety years ago, been exactly that? Starving people, and abundant resources all around. Maybe Wilfred Dell was right. So far he had been right about everything else.

Job leaned back in his seat and closed his eyes. *Right about everything, including his assessment of Hanna Kronberg?*

"They kept the watch going, but there's been no more sightings of Kronberg. It would be blind luck if there were one — naturally, she'll mostly stay inside the buildings because that's where her work is. I wouldn't have sent her to the Tandy at all. Damned do-gooder, ready to change the world — I would have had her killed, the moment I caught her." The cherub's face still wore its half-smile. *"But unfortunately she was caught out on the West Coast, and shipped before I could have a say in it."*

Job studied the pictures of Hanna Kronberg. She was a short, gray-haired woman of casual dress. He knew that physical appearance told little of a person's mind, but the face was good-humored and relaxed, with twinkling blue eyes. And this was supposed to be the most dangerous woman in the country?

"You're like everyone else," said Dell. "You look at her, and you think, that's just a harmless little lady. But I've been on to her for over six years. You have to know about her work to know her. I don't pretend to understand the technical material, but I do understand her aims.

"She's a brilliant biologist who became a fanatic on the subject of world hunger. She was once married to Raoul Kronberg, another biologist. When the Quiebra Grande hit he was on a field trip in South America, in the high Andes. The funds for his project were cut off overnight. The helicopter that was supposed to bring him and the rest of his party out was never sent, and finally they had to trek down on foot over a hundred and fifty miles of rough terrain. One of them made it — not Raoul Kronberg. The others were found later. They starved to death.

"That's when Hanna got the bee in her bonnet. She learned that Raoul had starved and died, in a place where lots of animals survive very well. They do it because they can digest cellulose, the woody material in stems and leaves. Hanna was a specialist in recombinant DNA technology, splicing genetic material to make new living organisms that do things no natural organism has ever done. She decided to make a hybrid that would live in the human gut and let people digest cellulose."

"It doesn't sound dangerous. It sounds useful." There had been many times when Job wished that he could eat grass and leaves.

"Depends how you define danger. Do you want to see the world population double — again? That's what it might do, if we could all eat cellulose. It's nice to have plenty of young and poor, to look after the needs of the old and wealthy, but the biggest threat to the Royal Hundred, and therefore to me, is change. Any major change is bad. We control food and fuel and dope and land and almost everything else. But could we

*stay in control if the demand side on food went haywire? No
one is sure. No one would want to try. That's why Hanna
Kronberg is so dangerous. If she's still working on her project,
inside the Tandy . . . "*

Except that she was surely not. Job had become convinced of it as the bus toiled on over the Great Plains
like a snail, hardly seeming to move in a whole day. He
had been filled with a sense of paradox as they passed
through the barren lands of Iowa, where topsoil had
vanished and only a gray and sterile substrate was left
for crops. The Nebraska Tandy was supposed to be a
place of ultimate punishment. Yet every space image
suggested a land more fertile than anything Job was
seeing on the way. In Xanadu, Hanna Kronberg would
not *need* to pursue her dream of humans who could eat
twigs and leaves. And it made no sense for her to do so,
for another reason: no matter what she developed, it
could never be exported from the Tandy.

If you go in, you don't come back. Hanna Kronberg
might be brilliant, but the one-way nature of the Tandy
was as true for her as for anyone.

A clatter of metal a few seats in front woke him from
his reverie. Feet drummed on the bare floor of the bus,
rhythmic at first, then random and convulsive. Job
heard a strangled cry and smelled a terrible stench of
evacuated body fluids. The driver stopped the bus. He
and his co-driver walked back to the seat where the
noise had come from and bent over the prisoner there.

Job knew that it was too late. The same thing had
happened five times in the past twenty-four hours.
The pattern was clear now. The drug that kept the
prisoners sedated had a cumulative effect, or it was
being fed intravenously at higher and higher doses.
First a prisoner showed little interest in food and
relieved himself at less frequent intervals. Then the
stimulant patches lost effectiveness. The prisoner
would remain slumped in one place, unaware of

anything. At last he went into periodic convulsions of increasing severity. If the first fit did not kill, the second or third would always do the trick.

The drivers finished their examination. They pulled the body into the aisle and dragged it away to the door of the bus. It would be stowed with the other five, in the empty luggage compartment. The task of the two drivers was to deliver a shipment of prisoners to the Nebraska Tandy. Dead or alive, that made no difference.

They left the door wide open. The wind that blew in was icy enough to make Job shiver in his thin shirt and pants, but he welcomed it. He could stand cold, but the smell of sweat and urine and excrement inside the bus made him gag. He had been unable to force down the last two food packages. He peered at the road ahead, wondering when he would catch a first glimpse of Xanadu.

The drivers returned rubbing chilled hands and cursing the snow, and slid the door closed at once. They were impervious to the stench. From their point of view it was part of a trade-off. Job had seen them eating the extra food packages left by the dead prisoners. The bus started on its way again.

Fifteen minutes later Job heard a change in the note of the engine. He thought at first that it was a mechanical problem, something that had held them up twice already on the trip. Then he realized that they were ascending an incline, so long and uniform that the ground ahead looked flat.

Over the brow of that long hill, according to everything that Job had been told in his briefings, lay the only entrance to the Nebraska Tandy. Already the sky ahead was a darker shade of gray.

In Xanadu, the sky burns black.
If you go in, you don't come back.
History recorded no exception to that rule.

• Chapter Thirteen

Xanadu

The bus grumbled to a halt on a long, flat stretch of road. The nearest buildings were still a quarter of a mile ahead, half-hidden by a flurry of snowflakes. Just fifty yards in front of the bus stood a flimsy wire fence with huge red signs set along it at regular intervals:

T. A. N. D. I.
TOXIC AND NUCLEAR DISPOSAL INSTALLATION
ENTER AT YOUR OWN RISK

NO EXIT PERMITTED BEYOND THIS POINT

The bus drivers were suddenly busy. One of them was tinkering with the dashboard, while the other went down the aisle. Job, halfway back, saw that the man had a hypodermic and a big bottle of milky liquid. At each prisoner he stopped, filled the syringe, and gave the man a shot in the thigh.

No pretense here of clean needles. But as the prisoners at the front of the bus began to stir, Job had a frightening thought. A stimulant that would bring a heavily drugged man to consciousness might blow an undrugged man's brain right out of the top of his head.

When the driver came to him Job put out a hand, restraining the syringe. "Not for me, I'm all right without it."

The man stared, at Job and then at the bottle he was holding. "You can't possibly be all right. You have to have this."

He moved the needle closer. Again Job pushed him away. "I'm fine." He spoke loudly and clearly.

"But—"

"Rafael!" The voice of the other driver came from the front of the bus. "Don't dawdle around. If he says he's awake, he must be awake."

The man with the syringe straightened, gave Job another puzzled look, and moved on. He was still injecting the last prisoners when the second driver left the bus, went around to its side, and pulled a flat runabout vehicle from the luggage compartment. Job heard the whine of an electric motor, and the shout, "All set. Come on!"

The second driver finished the last shots in record time and ran for the front of the bus. He moved a lever on the dashboard and at once jumped out, falling down in the snow. The other man helped him to his feet. They were both climbing onto the runabout when the engine of Job's bus roared to life. There was a jerk of meshing gears and skidding wheels. The driverless vehicle began to move along the road at a steady five miles an hour.

Job's first urge was to follow the drivers into the snowy road, but the bus was already rolling past the fence with its warning signs. Job moved to stand at the open door, peering through the front window. And then another vehicle was moving up alongside, paralleling theirs. As Job fell back into the vacant seat of one of the dead prisoners, a bearded man leapt across to the steps of the bus and ran lightly up them. In a couple of seconds he had control of the vehicle. He drove it to the nearest buildings and brought it to a careful halt.

A small group of people was waiting in the snow. They came forward as the bus stopped.

"All right." A squat man wearing a sleeveless shirt to show off massive arm muscles put his foot on the lowest step. "Let's see what pile of crap they've left with us this time. Digger and Sim, you get the live ones. Looks like they're pretty far gone. Smells like it, too."

The prisoners had been returning to dazed life. Judging from their groans and shudders, they felt terrible. The crew from Xanadu shepherded them from the bus and placed them shivering in a line in the snow. The cold wind sliced through the thin shirts, providing the last step of uncomfortable revival.

"Right then." The muscle man stepped in front of them. "In a few minutes Digger'll take you inside. You'll get warmed up, and a bath, and food if you feel up to it. But first things first. You made it. You're inside Xanadu now, the Great Nebraska Tandy. And you're going to stay here. There's the way out—but it's closed."

He pointed back up the road. There was a long stunned silence, while the prisoners scanned the empty waste of snow. At last one of them gave a warbling cry of fear. He started running towards the fence.

Job knew how he felt. He had the urge to run himself, but he noticed that the Xanadu guards made no move to pursue. They were watching, waiting.

The fleeing man's condition was no better than Job's. As he ran his legs became wobbly and he moved with more and more effort. He slowed to a walk, until right at the fence line he gave a shout of triumph, raised his arms like a runner breaking the winners' tape, and rushed forward. As though that were a signal, a series of whiplash cracks sounded from beyond the fence. Beams of blinding blue flashed out from three small cones and converged on the escaping prisoner.

He exploded at the middle. The head, chest, and raised arms were blown high in the air, up and away from the running legs. While the half-torso was still rising, the three beams hit again and again. There was a series of secondary explosions. Head, arms, and chest spattered into bloody mists, the hips and legs formed another.

The whip cracks ended. A strange and absolute silence fell on the snowscape. The flakes still drifted down. Where they touched the road through the fence, a lurid splotch of crimson and black slowly began to fade to pink and gray.

Job shuddered. Wilfred Dell had told him that if and when Job gave the signal, the boundary security system would be switched off on this same road so that Job could escape. But Job would not *know* that the signal had been received and it was safe to pass through, until he was actually outside the Tandy. Did he have the nerve to try, after what he had just seen?

"That was lesson number one," the squat man was saying. He looked along the line of stunned prisoners. "Anyone else want to try? Guess not. We never have more than one in a busload. For your general information, your buddy there just used the only practical spin-off of the old SDI program. You saw it at low power. It steps up the energy if it doesn't wipe out a target first time. People here found out — the hard way — that it can vaporize a full-size battle tank if it has to." He turned away. "All right, Digger, get 'em in now, before we all freeze our nuts off."

The prisoners were steered to a long, low building of sheet metal and ushered inside. It was even hotter than the bus, and the sudden changes of temperature were too much for a couple of the men. They doubled over, clutching at their middles. The bearded guard, Digger, walked to stand by them.

"Wait it out." His voice was oddly gentle. "It's the drugs, you see, just the drugs. Once you sweat 'em through your system you'll feel better." He helped one of the prisoners to his feet. "There we go. Clothes off now, all of you. It's bath time. Smell yourselves, an' you'll know why."

Job was soon naked except for the crucifix around his neck. He was issued a square cake of gray and grainy soap. He sniffed it, and wondered what Stella would have made of *this*. Its stink rivalled what it was supposed to wash off. He followed the other prisoners through a long continuous shower of hot water, soaping as he went. They were partially dried by hot air at the other end, and emerged to find Digger waiting with piles of clothes.

"Help yourselves, and get a move on," he said. "Paley will be along in a minute, an' he'll expect you dressed. There's all sizes, an' all clean."

Digger was an optimist. Job could find no shoes as good as the ones that he had abandoned, and all the clean clothes hung loose on his frame. He was not alone in that — half the new arrivals were as badly off. And now that he could take a good look at his fellow arrivals he noticed that he was not conspicuous in another way, too: they all seemed close to his age. That lessened the chance that someone else from Dell's organization was on the bus, because the schemer in the Mall Compound had told Job that all his people were a lot older than Job.

But how much could anyone rely on the word of Wilfred Dell?

Job allowed himself to be lined up again. In a few minutes the gorilla-armed Paley was back, walking along the file and examining every man critically.

"Not bad," he said. "Considering where you come from, and the condition of that bus. You had a rough trip. If you don't like the set of your clothes you can have a go at 'em later. You'll be fed in a few minutes, but before that here's lesson number two. You've arrived, and maybe you've heard that arrivals in Xanadu live only a year or two. That's true enough, so maybe you think you're dead already. You're not. Those numbers are *averages*. They include people like your buddy back there, who lasted all of two minutes. An' they include me, I've been here eight years going on nine, and I'm not planning on leaving any time soon. You'll get rotten jobs, first few months, all new arrivals do. You'll work Tandy Center, where it's hottest and you can average thirty rads a week. That's no picnic. You'll feel bad, just like I did. But if you're careful, you'll survive. And after the first months you can get work in places like this, where it's not much different from outside. Got any questions, before we go on?"

Job had plenty, but he was not about to ask them. A corollary of the Golden Rule (for whatever that was worth now): *Don't make yourself conspicuous*.

A youth a few positions along took a step forward and half raised his hand. He was about Job's age, thin-faced and brush-haired, and he seemed less battered than most of the others.

"Sir. What's a *rad*?"

"You come here and you don't know what a rad is?" Paley studied him, poker-faced. "I can see you're going to do great in Xanadu. I bet you'll look real good with no hair."

He turned to glance along the line. "Any other questions?"

The youth looked puzzled, but there were no more takers.

"Right," said Paley. "Food now. All you can eat, then you get to sack out an' live like kings — 'til the day after tomorrow. One thing, though. Just don't think it's going to be soft like this all the time."

Job lay in darkness, wondering where he was and how long he had been there. Had he been drugged? His head felt muzzy, his eyelids too heavy to lift.

The arrival at the Tandy. Then the bath, and the briefing. Then the warm dining room and food that was hot, plentiful, and bland. And then?

Then, nothing.

There had been no need for drugs. The long journey west had pushed him and the other prisoners to the limit. He had the feeling that he had slept the clock round, and more.

He opened his eyes and struggled to his feet. A thin line of light marked the door of the room. He went to it and tugged it open. There was a mutter of protest from occupied beds behind him as bright light spilled into the dormitory.

"Well, at last." A brisk voice greeted him. "You're the first, an' it's about time."

Job squinted into bright morning light and saw Paley, Digger, and Sim sitting across from each other at a square table. Paley was drinking from a metal mug. He gestured with it to a door on his right, as soon as he saw Job stop blinking. "Pee through there, if you need to. Then come right back here."

Job went through a second door and found himself outside the building. It was still cold. He found that his clothes might be ill-fitting, but at least they were warm. The snow had ended, leaving a three-inch blanket that felt soggy under his feet. To the east a ghostly sun shone through morning mist. The clouds overhead were thinning, rapidly burning off.

He used the outside toilet, but before he went back in he took the time to stare all around him. He had been well-briefed on the geography of the Nebraska Tandy, and could orient himself from the sun and the line of the outside fence. The hot, lethal heart of Xanadu lay about ten miles west. The fenced town where Hanna Kronberg had been sighted was beyond that, nearly to the western Tandy boundary. It was a long day's walk, if the temperature continued to rise and there was no more snow. But it would be futile to think of trying such a thing until he knew a lot more about Xanadu, and how it worked. He went back inside the building.

They had moved the table since he left. One chair, heavier than the rest, was against the wall. Paley gestured Job to sit down on it.

"Hungry?" And, at Job's shake of the head, "All right, let's get this over with. Don't worry, this is all pretty standard."

Before Job could move Digger had gripped his arm and was applying a spray hypo to his shoulder. The room spun and turned black, and then as rapidly steadied. Job was still sitting in the chair, but his mind went zooming up through the metal ceiling and hovered far above in the clouds.

"What's your full name?" Paley's voice came from miles away.

"Job Napoleon Salk."

"Check. How old are you?"

"Eighteen years and ten months."

"Check. Does he have J-D marks, Sim? His record shows it." There was a hand on his arm. Something was pressing at his wrist, then at his forehead.

"Check."

"Tell us where you were born, Job Salk, and where you grew up."

Job began to talk, without concern or reservation, about Cloak House and Bracewell Mansion. He told of his arrest trying to deliver a package of drugs to the Mall Compound, and of his return to Cloak House. He described his escape, and his life as a street *basura* and vendor. He left nothing out, and answered any question asked along the way.

"Check. How did you get caught, and sent to Xanadu?"

Job told of meeting Stella Michelson, of taking her away from Daniello and back to his home, of making love to her, of her return to the Mall Compound and of his own rapid arrest.

He was totally calm, although he knew that the very next question would lead to his death. When they asked *who* had sent him here, and *why* Wilfred Dell had sent him, he would tell them without hesitation.

"Christ." Paley had turned to Digger. "Did you hear him? He says this Stella Michelson is a Rep's cousin, an' he screwed her! It doesn't have *that* in his record. I guess her family hushed it up. Did they have him castrated before they sent him here?"

"He looked all there coming out of the bath."

"Then he's one lucky *hombre*."

Paley was staring at him. Job knew that this would be it, the key and fatal question. He waited peacefully.

But Paley's expression was more like admiration. "You're a nervy bugger, aren't you? You're plenty ugly, but you sure nabbed some high-class tail."

He added a note to the file in front of him. "All right, Digger, give him his shot. Anyone with his record has earned his way in here."

The second shot took Job down and almost out. He vaguely knew he was being led through into another room. He felt something rough and hard on his forehead, but it was a few minutes before he realized that he was sitting slumped over a wooden table, and that he was in the same dining room where he had eaten his last meal.

He was alone, with no sign of jailers. As he realized that, he understood something new about the Tandies: the men were criminals, but they were *not* jailers. If there seemed to be minimal supervision, it was because there was no need for supervision. *Everyone* was a prisoner, everyone had been condemned. If he wanted to run away, where would he go? Out through the boundary fence, to be blown apart in a hot spray of blood and tissue? Or on to the heart of Xanadu, to be poisoned by toxins or cooked in a lethal oven of radiation?

He did not feel like eating, but long self-discipline took over. He poured a cup of hot, sweet liquid that was someone's attempt to mimic tea, and forced it down. A plate of greasy vegetables and fried rice followed. He sat quietly until he was sure that his stomach was not going to reject everything, and at last went back to the room where Paley and the others were sitting. They gestured to Job to keep quiet. Another man from the bus sat in the chair, eyes glazed. He was describing the rape of a small boy in calm and chilling detail. The listeners showed equal lack of emotion.

"He checks," said Paley. "All right, give him the Number Two shot and get him out of here." He turned to Job. "You seem in pretty good shape so there's no need for you to hang around any more. I got another busload coming in at midday, an' we need the space. Here's your ID. Look for a blue van outside. Tell the driver — name's Ormond — that you're ready for assignment. You get no choice for the first three months, but you should start thinking about what you want to do after that."

Job stood for a few seconds before he realized that Paley was finished with him. There would be no more instructions. He wandered out into the sunshine and around the building, seeking Ormond and the blue van. He saw a couple of people, but neither took any notice of him. Everything was oddly casual in Xanadu. If general movement within the Tandy was going to be this easy, maybe Job's task was not impossible after all.

Start thinking about what you want to do. That was the most surprising statement of all. The very idea that you had a real *choice* as to what happened was a new one. Every decision that Job had made since he was eight years old had been dictated by necessity. (Except, maybe for Stella — and what a hash he had made of *that*.)

The blue van was parked about thirty yards from the building with the engine running. Job approached the tinted windshield and held the little yellow ID card that Paley had given him towards the driver's window. "I'm looking for Ormond."

"I know you are. I'm Ormond. Stop gawping and get in."

Job could finally see inside. The driver was an attractive blond-haired woman in her late twenties.

He felt like an idiot. He *had* been staring. The people he had met so far at the reception building had happened to be men, like the busload he arrived with. But equally many woman were sent to the Tandies, with no attempt to keep the sexes separate. Anyone delivered to a Tandy was already officially dead. The Reginald Brooks of the world did not care if the residents chose to mingle and to mate — or even, against all logic, to breed.

There were eight people in the van, three women and five men, and with Job's arrival it was overfull. He squeezed in next to Ormond as she turned the wheel to take them west. Job could not examine the others in the bus without turning around and making it obvious, but from his first glance they were all at least ten years older than him. One was a woman in her sixties. No one spoke, but Ormond whistled as she drove, so off-key that it was pain to Job's sensitive ear. She was obviously cheerful. The residents of Xanadu appeared at least as happy as people outside. Job decided that misery must have little to do with life expectancy.

"They got a drop coming in at noon," said Ormond, after they had driven for ten minutes and Job estimated that they were within a couple of miles of the center of the Tandy. "You'll be able to see it easy from here. Over thataway."

They followed the line of her well-muscled arm, to where the gently rolling horizon was broken by a sequence of steep, snow-covered ridges. Job heard a faint rumble of engines. Four dark specks appeared over the horizon and grew rapidly in size.

"Drones," said Ormond. "Pilotless." She was still driving, but with little attention on the road. "Five-hundred-ton capacity. Hope they get the release right this time. Last year they missed the target area and dumped two thousand tons right on a bunch of our buildings. Hell of a mess."

The specks had grown to giant winged planes,

bee-lining for the snowy ridges that marked the middle
of the Tandy. They were a few thousand feet up when
they leveled off over their target zone, but so big that
Job could see the bays beneath them opening. Scattered masses of objects fell out.

Ormond was watching with a critical eye. "Close to
center," she said. "I'd say within a few hundred yards,
every one of them. That makes the cleanup and sal-
vage job a lot easier."

The last of the drones had delivered its load, and the
ridged snow hills had become a jumble of dark debris.
The planes turned in a wide circle. As they did so, a
louder sound of motors arose from behind the van. A
convoy of a dozen bizarre objects appeared, moving in
line across country and heading for the middle of the
Tandy. They ignored the roads. Job could see that
although they held to a rigid line they were not con-
nected to each other.

Black against the snow, each member of the convoy
possessed a long, broad body flanked by tracked wheels
like a tank. Beside each wheel were three leglike pillars,
and rising from the forward end of that broad gray base
was a tall cylindrical body with two pairs of jointed arms,
each red-painted and ending in black pincers. On top of
the body, ten feet above the ground, was a small, nar-
rower cylinder that swivelled constantly from side to side,
like a watchful, flat-topped head. The strange centaur-
like vehicles — they *were* vehicles, whatever else they
might be — trundled along surprisingly fast, leaving
straight grooves in the unmarked snow.

"What the hell are *they*?" The speaker was a middle-
aged woman. It was the first word that Job had heard
from any prisoner in the van.

"Cleanup squad." Ormond had driven far from the line
of approach of the tracked vehicles and allowed the van to
coast to a halt. "They go into the drop zone first, check out
what's there, maybe move it around and start sorting."

"There are people in those things?"

"Maybe. Maybe not. Each one can operate in two modes, either with somebody inside — in a lead-lined chamber, of course; radiation levels from new waste get pretty extreme — or remote controlled. We try to use remote control for the hottest material, old reactor fuel rods, broken isotope ampoules, stuff like that, but it's more flexible when you have a human controlling. Better at picking up odd shapes, more stable on hills. There's plenty of big heaps of old trash to be climbed. That's why they need those legs." Ormond stared at the questioner. "I'm surprised you don't know all this. I'd heard of Tandymen long before I was sent here."

Tandyman! The childhood chant rolled into Job's head:

T - A - N - D,
Nuclear waste taste good to me.
Nuclear core she drive me wild,
Pull the rods and spoil the child.

Just machines. But how easily imagination could transform giant cleanup vehicles into terrifying bogeymen, prowling the night, seeking out a sleeping child. The grimy, battered bodies. The wicked-looking pincers and shears, clever enough to tease apart whole reactors and strong enough to slice through the hardened metal cans of nuclear fuel rods. The questing cylindrical head with its red-lensed eyes, never ceasing in their survey.

Ormond might not share Job's fancies, but she certainly gave the Tandymen plenty of space. Only when the great robots were half a mile in front of the van did she again move into gear.

"I'm going to follow, so you can get a look at Tandy Center. But don't worry, I won't take us too close." She gestured at the dashboard. "See the monitor? That's the ambient radiation level. You must always keep your eye on that. You don't want the reading to go above twenty if you can help it — that's two rads a day for received dose. In the first couple of months you won't have much choice, but it's good to get careful early."

Everyone in the van craned to see the monitor. "It's reading down below one," said a man at the back.

"It is now. But keep watching."

The little van eased forward along the deserted road, parallelling the path of the vanished Tandymen. On the dashboard the monitor drifted higher, to two, to three, to five. They were still a mile from Tandy Center. Job stared out of the forward windshield, seeking twisted, misshapen vegetation or monstrous animal life. He looked, even though he knew that the idea was nonsense, part of the folklore of the Tandies. Mutated plants and animals born in the toxins and the radiation would be sickly and defective, unable to compete with the robust natural forms of the region. But still he stared and stared.

Everything seemed normal. Beneath the thin blanket of snow Xanadu lay peaceful under a bright blue sky. Except . . .

Job peered at the broken ridges ahead. It was not imagination. The snow was melting faster there than anywhere else. The released radioactivity of long half-life isotopes was heating the ground, and the monitor had crept up past six. The air around Job was filled with a silent sleet of radiation. Forget the effects on plants and wild animals. Every person in the van was burning, slowly cooking from within.

They were hardly moving forward now, with Ormond keeping a careful eye on the monitor and the road ahead.

"See that?" she pointed to a blue sign by the roadside. "That marks the official limit of Tandy Center. As you'll find out, it's not an absolute boundary like the outer edge of Xanadu. You don't die automatically if you go inside — lucky for you, because you'll be doing that when you get your first assignments. And you're not safe just because you're *outside* it. Some days, like today, there's new high-radioactive materials been dumped, and you don't want to go even as far as the marker unless you have to."

She brought the van to a halt.

"We don't have to, so we won't. But I wanted you to know that you can come to Tandy Center, and survive. Some people get too scared to think straight here, and that's a fatal mistake. Remember, the Tandymen handle the hottest stuff. Before you're done you'll have to pilot one. But they're real well-shielded. Tuck away inside one of them, you'll get less dose than sitting out at the edge of Xanadu."

"Why does anybody go in right away?" asked a voice from the back of the little bus. "Why not wait a while, until the short-lived radioactives get less hot?"

"Because the bad stuff can spoil the good — half the containers split when they land, so unless we go in real quick the leakage gets to everything." Ormond turned to glance back along the bus. "Any more questions? If not, we'll head back."

There was a movement from the people in the van, like the release of long-held breath. The dashboard monitor had edged its way up past twelve. As the van turned, Job took a last look at Tandy Center. One of the Tandymen was climbing down the side of a steep ridge, black legs pumping and sturdy tracks digging in for a grip. The bright-red arms were clutching a roll of wire to the barrel chest, and the lenses of the red-eyed head glittered in the sunlight.

Job watched until the Tandyman had trundled around the base of the ridge and out of sight, then did his own exhaling of breath. He leaned back in his seat. It was not every day that a long-feared demon was so cleanly exorcised.

● Chapter Fourteen

> *. . . and it shall bring him to the king of terrors.*
>
> — *The Book of Job, Chapter 18, Verse 14*

Again, the informality came as a surprise.

Ormond drove to a fair-sized town eight miles from the center of Xanadu, where she assigned each person a dormitory and a room. They were fed in a dining room big enough to hold four or five hundred. One hour later they were assembled in the main square, along with fifty other newcomers who had arrived at the Tandy during the past week. Only then did Job learn that Ormond was not merely their driver of the day. She would be their watchdog, tutor, and absolute boss until the end of their three-month training period. After that they would be assigned to other duties and become someone else's worry.

"Always assuming that you make it," explained Ormond. "You probably want to know what the odds are. There are sixty-four of you. A month from now that will be fifty-one, in two months you'll be down to forty-four, and by the time training's over I expect to shake hands with thirty-nine. Sixty-one percent training survival. If you don't like the sound of that, check around. My figures are as good as anyone's.

"Study those numbers, fix 'em in your head. They're only averages, naturally, but they ought to tell you one thing: *the first month is the worst.* And the second month is the *next* most dangerous. If you make it through them and the rest of training and don't get sloppy after that, you can live here for years and years. Like me."

Job was reevaluating Ormond. The young face and casual manner disguised a lot of self-confidence.

"When in doubt," she went on, "*ask questions*. Xanadu charges a high price for ignorance. So who's going to start, and ask me something useful?"

The new arrivals stared at each other and at their surroundings. The square they stood in was broad and open, flanked by big brick buildings intended to house a hundred people or more. Beyond the town were cultivated fields, empty of crops and fast losing their snow cover in the late afternoon sunshine. It would be dark in another hour. The group stood cold-footed in melting slush.

A tentative hand went up near the back.

"Why do new people like us have to work near the middle of the Tandy, where the hot drops are made? Why not fence that part off, and just leave it?"

"Good question. Anyone like to answer for me?"

Job had been absorbing her intonations and speech patterns. Xanadu was a melting pot for people from all over the country, but it also seemed to have developed its own characteristic accent. Job had noticed it in Paley, and now he was tracing it in Ormond. He needed to hear as much as possible, and he needed to *speak* it. He could not do that following his usual rule of remaining silent and inconspicuous.

He raised his hand. "Because you need what's dropped at the center of Xanadu."

That brought a flash from Ormond's gray eyes. "All right, so far so good. Go on."

"People come in from outside, but they don't bring supplies. Even if you are self-sufficient for food and fuel, you need finished products. The buses we came in stay here, but that's not much. You need the things that are dropped off by air, whatever happens to be mixed in with the toxic wastes and nuclear by-products.

They're your only source of outside materials."

"Right answer. There's just one thing wrong with it. Anyone know what it is?" She was cocking her head at Job.

Challenging me, he thought. Testing me. But he could find nothing wrong with his answer. He shook his head.

Ormond grinned. "Just a detail — but an important one. Think of the way you gave your answer. *You* need finished products, you said, and *you* need what's dumped at Tandy Center. What you should have said is that *we* need those things. You're part of Xanadu now. Don't forget it.

"All right. Any more questions?"

Before the group could respond a growing rumble sounded from behind. They all turned. One of the Tandymen was chugging along the road that led to the square. As it neared it suddenly accelerated. In a few seconds the mechanical robot was traveling at top speed, fast as a running horse.

"Wild Tandyman! Scatter!" Ormond was off like a rabbit, racing for the nearest building. After a confused pause, everyone followed.

The long journey west to the Nebraska Tandy had stiffened Job's legs. They had not yet recovered, and he was slower off the mark than the others. Lagging the field, he heard the clatter of Tandyman tracks behind him. The thick concrete of the square was shaking under his feet. He ran on. Already he could imagine metal treads on his back, snapping his spine, flattening his rib cage, squirting the lifeblood from his open mouth.

And then the Tandyman was *past* him. It had singled out one man from the group, a balding forty-year-old, and it was ignoring everyone else. Twenty yards short of the building the Tandyman caught its prey. Four pincered arms reached out and down, seized the man at waist and shoulders, and lifted him into the air. He screamed in wordless terror, wriggling and twisting in the metallic grip. The Tandyman brought him up to touch its broad chest, then lifted him higher on telescoping arms. In a few seconds he was dangling upside down, bald head fifteen feet above the concrete of the square.

Everyone else had reached the safety of the building. They turned and looked. Job, with the Tandyman between him and safety, did not know what to do. He backed away, while the man hung suspended in midair, shouting and writhing.

And then, inexplicably, the metal arms shortened and swung down. The man was rotated in midair and placed lightly on the ground. His legs buckled beneath him and he sank sobbing to the concrete.

The Tandyman's pincers released their hold and rubbed slowly up the man's body from knees to neck. At the head they paused for a few seconds longer, running pocked metal claws around the naked scalp. The man shivered and began to crawl away through the slush. The Tandyman retracted its pincered arms. It turned and rolled quietly away, the questing head rotating back and forth on its smooth bearings.

Job started to walk forward. The man had risen to his knees and was rocking backwards and forwards, eyes wide open and staring.

"Are you all right?" asked Job.

"I thought I was dead." The man brought his soaked hands up to his face and gave a shuddering laugh. "God in Heaven, I *knew* I was dead. I was sure it was going to tear me apart."

"Stand back!" Ormond hurried forward and pushed Job away from the kneeling man.

"But he needs — "

"He needs nothing you can give him. Wait here, don't go nearer — any of you! That's an order. Give him at least twenty feet clearance. I'll be right back."

She ran into the building and was gone for a couple of minutes. In that time the Tandyman's victim managed to stand up. He stared around in confusion. The others were watching sympathetically, but they left a wide circle of space about him. When Ormond emerged she was wearing a gray suit complete with a glass helmet and was carrying another suit under her arm. "Here." She thrust it at Job. "You're skinny, you ought to be able to get into that with no trouble. Do it. The rest of you, inside."

The gray suits had their own shoes. Job was forced to remove his and stand barefoot in freezing slush before he could climb into the legs and pull the suit up over his body. He clamped the helmet closed.

"Take his other arm." Ormond was running a device the size of a small calculator over the man's body and peering at its display.

"I don't need help." The man tried to shake off Job's hand. "I'm fine. It didn't hurt me."

"It didn't *hurt* you. It killed you." Ormond held out the little sensor. "See this? That Tandyman came right from the middle of Tandy Center. Its pincers have been soaking in the hottest nuclear material. You just got four thousand rads. You're a goner. All we can do is try to make you comfortable."

"Four thousand rads! But I'm . . . I'm . . . " The man opened and closed his mouth, then turned away and vomited into the slush.

Ormond eyed him with disgust. "That's not radiation sickness, friend, that's funk. You won't start to feel real symptoms for hours." She nodded to Job. "There's no danger now to anyone else, but I'm going to put him in separate quarters. And I'm detailing you to stay with him. Ever see anybody die of radiation sickness?"

Job shook his head.

"Well, now's your chance. Got his arm? Let's go."

Between them they walked the baldheaded man across the square. He had started to shiver.

Job felt like shivering, too. How much dose had *he*

received, when the Tandyman ran past him, or when he had stood close to the doomed man?

"*Why*?" he asked. "Why did it pick him out, and not me or somebody else?"

"I don't know yet," said Ormond. "But *he* knows. Don't you? You can tell us."

The man did not seem to hear. He was staring straight ahead.

"He failed the test," Ormond went on, "the same one you got when you came into Xanadu. Either he's some kind of spy sent in from outside, or else he's an old enemy of one of the Xanadu bosses from their days outside. Either way, it makes no difference. He's a goner."

"I thought *I* was a goner when I heard the Tandyman right behind me."

"I believe it." Ormond nodded. "Takes everybody that way. Using Tandymen to punish people is a great method to scare everybody and keep things under tight control. But I wish they'd either find another way, or at least let me know in advance when it's going to happen. Every time I see a Tandyman running loose it gives me the willies. I guess it's supposed to. Come on, let's get him into the house."

The building that Ormond led them to was a small wooden structure set apart from the rest. She placed the stricken man inside, then made Job strip in the cold Nebraska twilight while she went over him with the radiation monitor.

"Couple of rads," she said. "Nothing to worry about. You don't need the suit, but I wasn't sure how big a dose we might get. I'm going to take your clothes and bring you new ones. Maybe I can find something that actually fits."

Job was left alone and naked with the silent stranger. The hut had a stove inside, but it had only just been lit. The room was freezing. Job hunted around until he found a closet full of blankets and helped himself to a couple. He went back to the main room and found the man crouched by the stove. "Want to talk about it?"

The man shook his bald head. "Go fuck yourself."

Job was already seeing the skull beneath the skin. Four thousand rads. Ormond was right, the man was a goner. An average lethal dose of radiation was only a tenth of that.

He retreated to the far side of the room, wrapped himself in blankets, and stretched out on the couch. How long before Ormond came back? She had made no promises. The man was beginning to shiver, bone-deep tremors that had nothing to do with cold.

If Paley had asked one more question . . . Job might be sitting there by that stove, too, deep in shared despair.

And the danger was not over. There could be random truth tests at any time, a convenient way for the leaders of Xanadu to keep abreast of what was happening inside the Tandy. The idea that the people in Techville might be doing something that the Tandy bosses did not know about and approve of became less plausible.

Job drifted off into sleep. After midnight, for the first time in a decade, he dreamed of the Tandyman. A huge golem, half man, half machine, was pursuing him through the labyrinth of the Mall Compound. Its red eyes were gleaming, its hands blazed white-hot. As it reached down for Job and the burning hands seized him, the face changed to become the grinning gnome mask of Wilfred Dell.

Across the room, the real Tandyman's victim had begun to groan. Job awoke, drenched in sweat. He listened, and found reality worse than nightmare. For the first time he understood fully where he was: inside the Nebraska Tandy, with a minuscule chance of ever getting out.

Chapter Fifteen

My breath is corrupt,
my days are extinct,
the graves are ready for me.

— *The Book of Job, Chapter 17, Verse 1*

Two rads of absorbed radioactivity produces no immediate effect on a human. Nor does twenty rads. A hundred rads will lead within thirty days to loss of hair, loss of appetite, and a feeling of malaise. Four hundred rads will kill half the people who receive it. Four *thousand* will kill with a hundred percent fatality rate, and the afflicted person will die within seven days.

Job had learned the arithmetic of radiation sickness quickly, but without facilities for treatment the facts were useless to him. By the second day Untermeyer — the man had finally told Job his name — was nauseated and vomiting. He could eat nothing. By the third day ulceration of his whole digestive tract had begun and any hope of obtaining information from him was abandoned. Untermeyer's throat had become too painful to permit speech. By the fifth day edema of his body and limbs made it impossible for him to move.

At midday on the sixth day, Untermeyer died. Job assisted with the burial. Two hours later he received his own assignment: Tandy Center. He would work there for two months before reassignment could be considered.

Ormond was apologetic. "I told my boyfriend that you're prime material. After the way you've looked after Untermeyer, I said you shouldn't be wasted. Mannie works in Headquarters. But he says there's no exceptions for anyone. New arrivals have to work the hot spots."

"Thanks for trying." Job followed her to the blue van. He was already mimicking Ormond's accent, although she did not seem to notice.

"I found out more about Untermeyer." Ormond started the engine and headed in the direction of Tandy Center. "They didn't catch him on the entrance test. Mannie says that Untermeyer worked for Gormish — she's one of the top three in Xanadu — on the outside. It was his evidence that put Gormish here. When Untermeyer was sent here too, he bought a false ID. He must have hoped that Gormish was dead. But somebody recognized him and went to her. She set the Tandyman onto him. She was controlling it herself."

Job registered the new information: he had the name of one of the three people who ran Xanadu, Ormond had a friend in Headquarters, and the entrance test had its problems. Both he and Untermeyer had passed it. So the chance of continuing tests and checks was increased.

But none of that information was going to be much use. Job became convinced of that after they arrived at the Xanadu cleanup and maintenance center. It was a long, low building, with a score of trucks and bulldozers parked in front of it. Off to one side loomed dozens of the giant Tandymen. As Job stepped out of the blue van, one of the robots jerked to life and rumbled away down the road that led to Tandy Center. Job could not take his eyes off it until it was right out of sight. After it vanished he went inside and was placed with twenty other newcomers in a cold, low-ceilinged classroom.

"You'll work in and around the center, all of you," said Ormond. She was standing in front of a wall-sized map of Xanadu. "But of course you won't sleep there.

No point in absorbing more toxins and radiation than you have to. You'll do a nine-hour shift, six days a week, and come back here at night.

"The first trick to working cleanup is easy: *Know your geography*. There's runoff from the center whenever it rains, and the flow directions are well known." She turned and tapped the map. "The main runoff and seepage paths are marked. Spend as much time as you can in here, learn the black areas of the map by heart. If you avoid them and stay on areas marked in green, you'll halve the poisons you pick up.

"I said the *main* runoff patterns are marked. But there's hundreds of minor toxin pools and radiation hot spots, and a lot of them aren't plotted anywhere. So you have to learn to use your eyes." She picked up two flowering twigs from the table. "Some plants have high tolerance for certain toxins, others can't stand them. This one thrives in soil full of poisons that will corpse you. Long spiky leaves, yellow flowers — you see them and you stay clear. This one, flat leaves, hairy on their underside, needs pure, clean soil. If you see it, you can go there safely. *Except* that the same plant has a high radiation tolerance, so you need to keep an eye on your personal monitor. You need to do that anyway wherever you are. Make it second nature."

Job could see that some of the others in the room were hardly listening. When at the end of the session Ormond offered sheets describing plants that flagged safe or dangerous areas, only half the class bothered to take one. Job took two. Illiteracy in Xanadu carried a higher penalty than it did outside.

So did many other things. On the second day, when the group made its first trip into Tandy Center, Ormond drove a different route. She took the van past a line of scaffolds, where bodies hung eyeless, blackened and rotting in the freezing air.

"Nasty, eh?" she said. "I think so, too. But don't

blame the Xanadu authorities. The recruits do that, to
people in their own group who try to avoid handling
radioactives, or put others in danger. You have the
same right." She smiled around at them as she headed
the van directly to Tandy Center. "So work hard, boys
and girls, and help each other. If you don't, you might
find you've earned a *long* vacation."

Without a shielding cover of snow the Center was
revealed as a wilderness, an amazing jumble of barrels
and carboys and boxes and storage tanks, some still
intact, others shattered by the air drop and spilling
solids and liquids onto the ground. The Tandymen
had already made a first cut at sorting the debris into
useful or lethal heaps. It was the cleanup squad's job to
refine that and bring the most valuable and least
dangerous finds out of Tandy Center, to the manufac-
turing and storage facilities.

Each new recruit was left in a different place and
given an individual task. Job was told to seek out and
collect cubical containers from the most recent airdrop.
"Not dangerous in themselves," said Ormond. "They
contain waste products with a high selenium content.
We can use the selenium, but more than that we don't
want it in the aquifers. It's teratogenic, and people
inside Xanadu are having babies."

Not dangerous in themselves. Maybe. But the blue-and-
gray half-meter cubes were scattered over an area with
a quarter-mile radius, and some of them sat on the side
of steep mountains of trash and were the devil to reach.
Job struggled up and down jagged ridges, trying to
tread carefully and still keep one eye on his radiation
monitor; but by the end of his shift he had a long skin
wound in his left calf and his monitor showed that he
had received nearly ten rads. Two months like that and
he would be dead.

He was ashamed of himself until he reached the bus
that would take them back to the dormitories, and

found that the *average* dose of the group for a single day's work was fifteen rads, not counting one unfortunate who had absorbed an incredible six hundred. Ignoring warning signs and her own radiation monitor, she had sought a dropped package in the glowing heart of Xanadu, where only the Tandymen could go, and had stayed there for most of the shift.

Ormond said nothing, but the next morning the woman had vanished from the group. She never returned.

On the first day of the second week, when Job's cumulative dose had already climbed to twenty-two rads, Ormond introduced him to the Tandymen.

"Suits on before we start," she said. "Most of the radioactivity is in the chest and arms and pincers, but even around the back you can get a pretty stiff dose."

Suited, she led him into the heart of Tandy Center, to where a couple of dozen Tandymen stood in random array. Pausing by the nearest of them, Ormond showed Job how the back of each had a door that could be pulled open. Inside was enough room for one gray-suited person to sit down. Ormond pushed Job through the narrow opening. "Not enough room for two," she said. "I'm going to be out here, remote controlling. Let me do most of the work. You can always override me manually if you want to, but you don't need to. You're in a lead-lined enclosure, and you could roll or walk right through the hottest spot in Xanadu and not get hurt. If you want to be logical, the inside of a Tandyman is the *safest* place you can be in the whole of this Tandy."

The door closed. Job was sitting in claustrophobic darkness. And then the displays came on suddenly, and he was seeing the terrain from ten feet up, rolling across the flat surface of Xanadu. The controls were in front of him. If he chose he could make the Tandyman roll faster, walk, run, or pick up any object that weighed a ton or less. Ormond was in control as they headed for Tandy Center, but after a while Job took over. He soon realized the problem with automatic and remote-controlled modes. Ormond could see an object as small as a pin, but she lacked the coordination to pick it up. Job could do that, easily, with his own direct control. For two hours he forgot Ormond and established the full range of his skills. On level ground the Tandyman was superb; only on the steepest trash-heaped ridges did control and stability become a question.

"Well," said Ormond, when he finally relinquished command and let her steer him back towards the dormitories. "You certainly got off on *that*, didn't you?"

Job grinned. He had. The speed, power, and precision of a Tandyman were overwhelming. After nineteen years of being a weed it was nice to be able to throw quarter-ton packages around like pillows.

"You won't get more Tandyman rides until training is over," Ormond went on. "You're real good at it, but tomorrow it's back to pick and shovel for you."

Pick, shovel, and higher radiation and toxin doses. Job had noticed inside the Tandyman that his cumulative dose did not increase at all. But that was an anomaly, a day of special dispensation arranged by Ormond because she had been able to do nothing for Job earlier.

His total dose crept up, to thirty rads and then to forty. He began to feel queasy when he ate certain foods, his mouth was plagued by little ulcers, and when he showered his hair came out in handfuls. His only consolation was that others of his group seemed worse. Ormond's grim statistics were accurate. At this rate they would lose over a third of the new recruits by the time training ended.

Work took on a pattern. Job thought about it, and created a new Golden Rule: *Do your work if you can, during the shift, but if you get behind, don't compromise on safety. Never, never, never. And never ignore your radiation monitor.* By the end of the sixth week he felt that he had been doing this kind of job all his life. Wilfred Dell was a million miles and a thousand years away, almost forgotten until one bright mid-December morning when Job was sorting through a pile of short steel bars. He noticed a stranger standing thirty yards away and staring at him intently.

Job froze. Had they seen through his test, or was he betrayed by some other word or action?

The man was coming forward. He was tall and burly, with a full brown beard and long swept-back brown hair. Job gave up the pretense of work, straightened, and returned the stare.

"Yes?"

The tall man snorted. "I knew it! When Mannie said skinny brute, with a receding chin and a face like a fish, I was sure there couldn't be another in the whole world. You made it out! I always swore you had."

The voice had given Job all that he needed in the first few words. "Skip Tolson!"

"Who else? I told you I'd last through Cloak House, and I did."

"You don't look like Skip. You used to have curly hair!"

"Yeah." Tolson swept a hand through his mop "Funny thing, that, I lost it in the first few months here, and when it come back it grew straight."

"You were sent right from Cloak House?"

"Well, not quite right here." Tolson was grinning down at Job. "I had a few years out and free. But then me and a friend knocked off a car, an' it turned out it belonged to a Representative who was out slumming. Our fault, we shoulda' checked it out. Time we did, it was too late. How did you get out of Cloak House? There were fifty theories — none of them any good."

"Through the infirmary. In with the dead boys."

"That was *my* suggestion. Some of the others got pretty wild. A lot of the kids said you went off the roof. They said that if you jumped at just the right place and the right time, the updrafts around the building would float you down gentle. They had fun with that one. Teeter on the edge, screw up your courage, then jump and *whomp!* For a coupla' weeks they were sweepin' up splattered messes every morning in the road outside. Dangerous place, Cloak House — if you didn't know what you were doing."

"Not as bad as Tandy Center. Do you work at Headquarters?"

"I do, matter of fact." Tolson stared hard at Job. "What difference it make?"

"I thought you might know a way to get me out of this, to somewhere safer." Job held out his radiation-dose meter.

Tolson hardly looked at it. "Forty rads. That's nothing. I had near twice that when I finished training, and look at me now — fine. You'll be fine, too. Remember, it's radiation gets the publicity, but it's toxins does you in."

"But can you get me out?"

"Doubt it. Why should I?"

"I gave you everything I had when I escaped from Cloak House."

"True. But what you done for me *recently*?"

"Same old Skip."

"Hey, be reasonable. *Nobody* gets another job 'til they done hot service. Not Pyle, not Gormish, not Bonvissuto. They done theirs, I done mine, you do yours."

"How about after that, then? You must know where the good jobs are."

"Well, what sort of thing you want to do? What you good at?"

There was a dreadful temptation to say biology, and hope that would lead to Hanna Kronberg, but the first question from an expert would show that Job knew hardly more science than Skip Tolson.

"You know what I'm good at, Skip. Languages, same as always. With people coming here from all over the country, there must be a need for somebody who can talk to all of them."

"I'll see what I can do. Don't get your hopes up. An' I'm getting out of here now — too hot for my taste." Tolson was turning away when he had another thought. "Hey, I met an old buddy of yours when I first come here."

"Alan Singh?"

"Never heard of him. I meant Father Bonifant."

Job found himself unable to breathe. "Mister Bones is *alive* — here in Xanadu?"

"Nah. Not any more. He died a few years back."

The new bright warmth in Job's heart faded. "How did he die?"

"Went near the hot spots once too often. Helping recruits."

"Yes. He would have. That was Mister Bones." But Job spoke under his breath.

Tolson nodded. "I'm goin'. This place got too much burn in it for me."

He strode away. Job watched him out of sight, and was smiling by the time that Tolson vanished behind a ridge of trash. Skip hadn't changed. The ultimate pragmatist, but you couldn't dislike him for that. It was good to see him again. And he was quite right; Job had nothing to trade.

For the next forty-eight hours Job thought about Skip in every spare moment. How had he survived at Cloak House? How was he surviving *now*? One thing was guaranteed, if there were a safe burrow in Xanadu old Skip would have found it and crawled inside. The Tandy might be a death sentence, but it was a slow one. Ormond and Skip and Paley had lived here for years; Father Bonifant had survived for over a decade, and he had surely not taken good care of himself. He never did.

Job relived his years at Cloak House under the benign rule of Mister Bones and felt curiously comforted, until the third morning after Tolson's visit brought a major airdrop and the threat of a winter blizzard. Then there was no time for reminiscence.

The temperature across the Nebraska Tandy had been dropping steadily as the New Year approached. While long-time residents could batten down against the cold and go outside as little as possible, for the new recruits there was no such relief. The airdrops would go on in any clear weather and the cleanup work had to begin at once, before rain or snow turned the dropped materials into a coalesced mass, impossible to work with and hopelessly contaminated. Job and his companions were sent out in all weathers, until the cold became so intense that lubricants in the Tandymen congealed to a viscous solid, and the gears of the giant robots froze into place. Then the Tandymen could not make their first sorting of the most dangerous dropped materials, and all work halted.

Ormond had been watching today's weather closely. "Cold, but still clear," she said from the driver's seat of the truck. "They'll make the drop. The schedulers outside don't give a damn what happens here afterwards. The Tandymen will have time to take their cut, too. Then it gets tricky. You'll have to move *fast*. There's a winter storm sweeping down through Canada and Montana, and it's a bugger. Gale-force winds, foot or more of snow by tonight."

The recruits, bundled in multiple layers of warm clothing, waited tensely. There was already six inches of snow over Tandy Center. That would make the darker mass of the new drop easy to distinguish from the rest, but harder to handle and move around.

At noon half a dozen of the great pilotless drone aircraft came winging from the east through a sky of deep and flawless blue. The drop was made to perfection, masses of dark material falling to stain the snowy ridges of Tandy Center. A score of Tandymen went rumbling by the truck where the recruits were waiting, raising every pulse rate until the giant robots were safely inside Tandy Center and the danger of a wild Tandyman was past.

And then it was another agonizing wait, while the sky slowly clouded over and a north wind began to pick up strength. No one would risk going into Tandy Center before the Tandymen had done their work and left, but at the same time everyone dreaded the idea of scaling the snow-crusted and treacherous ridges of compacted trash in high winds and poor light. With just two days to go to winter solstice, dusk would arrive by five o'clock. Most of the training course casualties had made their fatal mistakes in failing light, at the very end of the shift when fatigue affected judgment and concentration.

At three o'clock the first tentative snowflakes drifted down. The wind began to gust more strongly. Ormond swore, and spoke into the van's two-way radio. "Just a few more minutes," she said at last. "Then they promise the Tandymen will be out and we can go in. You'll have two hours. Better be ready to hop."

It was more like half an hour before the last Tandyman beelined away across the flat plain of Xanadu. The workers jumped down from the truck and hurried into the wilderness of Tandy Center. It was familiar ground now, and they had well-defined tasks. The group of three that Job was assigned to advanced along a series of broad, cleared corridors that had been swept through the mountains of trash. They held their monitors and counters before them as they went. All the prisoners had become old hands at the job, and they swapped information and snap judgments as they went: " . . . real scorcher here, iodine-130." "No problem, half-life is only twelve hours. Leave it, and we'll handle it next time when it's not so hot. . . . " "This box has a high beryllium content, and it's leaking." "Poisonous as hell! Grab it *now*."

The snow was falling faster, driving along close to horizontal in the rising wind. The moving air produced eerie screams and howls as it passed through struts and open-ended boxes at the summit of the garbage mounds, interfering with conversation and slowing progress. It was clear that there would not be time for half the job that Ormond was demanding. She must have known it, too, because instead of sitting in the truck as she usually did she was walking through Tandy Center and urging the teams on to greater effort.

"You can't afford to leave that up there!" She stood splay-legged at the foot of one of the giant heaps of trash, while Job and his two companions perched precariously halfway up the side of it. They had been pulling futilely at a huge cylindrical container, slightly cracked along one side, and had just agreed that with the icy condition of the steep slope there was no way to obtain the necessary leverage. The cylinder seemed to be stuck immovably, buried deep by the force of its fall from the drones. They started to slide back down towards Ormond.

"Look at the sign on the side of it!" She was shouting through cupped hands, but the wind snatched her words away. "You could poison half a square mile if that got loose. Get back up there, and go *above* it, for God's sake. *Push* it down!"

Job and the other two hesitated. Ormond did not know it from where she was standing, but there was a second hazard on the mound. Farther up, close to the summit, lay another item from the recent drop. It was a great tangled bundle of thin metal tubes, probably cans from reactor fuel rods, and the counters showed that it was highly radioactive. If the team ascended to a point where they could shove at the big container of toxins, they would be dangerously close to the bundle of radioactive tubes. And at every gust of wind that bundle lifted and turned, as though ready to tumble and roll down the side of the ridge.

While they hesitated, Ormond started to scramble up the heap towards them. The wind had become so strong that she assumed they could not hear her. "Higher!" She was waving her arms as she shouted. "Go higher."

She was halfway to them, crabbing along the side of the mound to avoid slipping, and when she was still five yards away the wind struck the heap with new violence. Job heard a warning shout from one of his companions and turned to see the whole top of the ridge, lifted by the wind, rolling in an avalanche of trash down towards them. It was too late to run. Job and his two companions did the only thing they could do. They dived for the shelter of the big cylinder, hoping that it was so firmly planted in the side of the ridge that it would not move. The dislodged top of the mountain rolled and crumbled past them in a mix of old trash and new loose snow. Job, head down, felt small fragments fall harmlessly on his thickly dressed body. He heard a cry from Ormond. When he was sure that the wave had passed he looked out cautiously from the shelter of the container. The whole side of the mound where Ormond had been standing was swept clear. At its foot stood a jumbled heap of snow and rubbish, but of Ormond there was no sign.

"Come on." Job shouted to his team and started down. As he left the protection of the great cylinder the wind tugged at him, almost knocking him over.

He went wallowing into the new, soft heap before he

realized that no one had followed. They were still standing by the cylinder, pointing past Job. Ten feet away from him the tangle of lethal fuel cans was visible half-buried in snow. Midway between that and where he stood was the sole of a booted human foot.

He had left his pick and lever up on the side of the mound. He dived for the exposed foot and began to push snow and garbage out of the way with his bare hands. In a few seconds he could see the waist and the trousered thighs. He began to pull, desperately, repressing the warnings and the urge to run that bubbled up in his terrified mind.

His thoughts became totally focused. *Radioactive dose is proportional to time of exposure.* Speed was the thing, the main thing, the only thing. She had been in for only a couple of minutes. If he was quick enough, he could save Ormond.

The legs were free and feebly waving, but still there was something holding her. Job burrowed deeper, head down in a tangle of metal, plastic, and fabric. He pushed a tow-bar from some wrecked vehicle out of the way, and felt Ormond's whole body move when he lifted. He cursed his own feeble frame and weakness, cursed Ormond, and finally toppled over backwards as her body came free and tumbled with him down the last few feet of the mountain of trash.

She was out of the pile, alive but unconscious. But Job could do no more. She probably outweighed him by thirty pounds. He turned and screamed at the other two standing halfway up the mound. "Come and help. You stupid assholes, she's not dangerous *now*! You know you can't get a bad dose, just from a person who got one. Get down here!"

With the howling wind it was unlikely that they heard a word, but they were coming, scrambling down the slope and over to Job. Other teams must have seen the top of the trash mountain blow over, for people were appearing around the end of the ridge. Job could hardly move or speak. He pointed to Ormond, and then back towards the truck. The others lifted her and he followed, bowing low to lessen the murderous force of the wind and staggering as he went. The icy blast cut through to the very bottom of his aching lungs.

Ormond was dropped into the back of the truck. While the rest of the group stood wondering what came next, Job climbed into the driver's seat, turned the key, and was off without another word.

"Hey!" The answer came faintly from behind. Two people were chasing, floundering through deepening snow. "Stop. How will we get home? Come back!"

Job heard, but he did not comprehend or care. All his energy had to go to driving the truck, something he had observed many times but never done. While the wind howled outside and struck at the side of the vehicle like an angry elemental, he steered a veering, drunken path south across the open plain of Xanadu. In that direction, according to everything that he had heard and conjectured, lay Headquarters, and within Headquarters was the only place that could help Ormond: Decon Center.

He tried the two-way radio, but either he was using it wrong or no one was listening at the other end. It remained dead. The snow fell harder, reducing visibility to a few yards. The road itself was vanishing, forcing Job to drive blind and across country. As the world closed in and became nothing but swirling white, he finally allowed the thought that he had vetoed when he was pulling the supervisor free: *Radiation does not distinguish between rescuer and rescued.* Job's actions had placed him in as much danger as Ormond.

He pressed harder on the accelerator. The world was darkening, the windshield wipers had given up the effort, and the window in front of him had become a snowy mirror. Reflected in the glass Job saw the ghost of Skip Tolson. "Idiot," it said. "Didn't you ever learn *anything* from me? Ormond got *herself* in trouble, you don't have to lift one finger to save her. It's a dog-eat-dog world. You're getting yourself eaten."

Skip was right. Job could feel the truth of that, burning in every cell of his body. But behind Skip, diminished by distance, stood the frail specter of Father Bonifant.

Job pressed the accelerator to the floor and drove into the storm.

• Chapter Sixteen

> *I am a brother to dragons,*
> *and a companion to owls.*
> *My skin is black upon me,*
> *and my bones are burned with heat.*

— *The Book of Job, Chapter 30, Verses 28 and 29*

Except for a brief spell of groaning wakefulness in the truck, Ormond remained unconscious. Job stayed awake throughout. By the end of the first night in the Decon Center he was convinced that she had the better deal.

His knowledge of the location of Headquarters had been all hearsay. *Go south,* said the rumors, *as far as you can travel in Xanadu, to the place where the radiation is lowest, the water is purest, and you are farthest from the approach paths of airborne toxic drops. There you will find Headquarters, the operations center for the Nebraska Tandy.*

And there you would also, according to training center rumors, find Decon Center. Untermeyer and others like him had been given no treatment, but that was only because they were already sentenced to death. Xanadu had as much experience as any place in the world at radiative and toxic decontamination.

Job had no choice but to rely on hearsay. He drove south. Normally the road would have guided him, but he was driving blind and in heavy snow. He plowed on across the slow-rolling, featureless plains of the Tandy. There were no landmarks, no signposts to guide his path.

Two things saved him, from fire and then from ice. He ran into a five-foot drift of snow which stalled the truck's engine just a few hundred yards short of the Tandy's outer boundary. One more minute of forward progress and the guardian ring of power lasers would have vaporized the vehicle. Clogged with snow, the truck's engine then refused to start. The heater was useless. With the outside temperature dipping below zero, Job began to shiver. He prepared to leave the truck for a surely doomed trek on foot. But the truck's blundering run south had intersected the eastern edge of a guarding ring of watchdog sensors around Xanadu Headquarters. The presence of an unauthorized vehicle had been noted. Alarms sounded. Security forces set out through the driving snow and reached the stalled intruder within twenty minutes.

They dragged Job out and flattened him face-up in the snow, guns ready to shoot him at the first sign of resistance. Who was he, and why had he violated the secured perimeter?

Job was past worrying about details. He ignored the guns, sat up, and pointed to the truck. "In there. Ormond. Training course supervisor. Radiation overdose. Pretty bad."

How bad?

Job shrugged. "Don't know." When he had last looked at her monitor it showed three hundred rads; borderline for a lethal dose.

No one asked if Job had been affected too. He was swept into a security snowmobile and whisked away. Within five minutes they were inside Decon Center. Four gray-suited technicians stripped him and Ormond without a word, pushed them into a sealed bath that squirted and scrubbed hot water and detergent over every square millimeter of body skin, and then submitted Job to an exquisitely painful and lengthy process of deep lavage. They irrigated his alimentary canal from both ends, penetrating deeper and deeper until he was convinced that the enema tubes and stomach pump were going to meet in the middle. They simultaneously catheterized his penis and flushed his bladder, inserted tubes up his nose to wash out his sinuses, and did the same for his ears.

That was the beginning. While one technician hooked the pair of patients to intravenous nutrient drips, another was systematically shaving every hair from their bodies.

"You're going to lose it anyway," she said, at Job's feeble protest. It was the only words spoken to him until a grinning ape of a technician approached with a syringe big enough to knock out a horse and injected the whole thing into Job's left buttock. "There," he said. "You'll piss green for a week, but it's all in a good cause."

The technicians left. Job had assumed that the last injection was some sort of sedative. He was wrong. It was a strong sudorific, designed to make him perspire. Within two minutes the sweat was pouring off him, his head swam, and he wanted to vomit but could not — he had nothing in his stomach. He shivered and writhed on the hard bed, sure he was dying, wondering how long it would take, wondering why they had even bothered to treat him.

The night was the longest that he had ever endured. On the next bed, Ormond sweated and tossed and turned just as hard, but she slept through until dawn; that was when Job, staring out of the window at snow that seemed determined to fall forever, finally lapsed into exhausted sleep.

When he awoke a gray-garbed figure stood at his bedside. Job was cringing away from it, ready to fight off more giant syringes, when he realized that the man cramped into the suit a couple of sizes too small for him was Skip Tolson.

Skip frowned down at him. "Thought you were never going to wake up."

"Am I dying, Skip?" Job automatically glanced across

to the other bed, and found it empty. Ormond's disappearance filled him with alarm.

"Dying? Course you're not dying. You only got one-seventy, you'll just feel rotten for a while. Ormond's not dying, either." Tolson had seen Job's look. "She got twice what you did, but she'll recover."

"Where is she?"

"In a private room. She an' Mannie Segal are like that" — he held up two fingers, close together — "an' Mannie's got Headquarters clout."

"She would have died, Skip, if she'd been left much longer. She would have suffocated before the radiation got her."

"Hey, you don't have to sell me nothing. And Mannie's already sold. The others on your work team told him what happened. They were madder than hell when you left 'em out in the snow an' they had to walk a mile to the other truck. Mannie got 'em even madder. He said you an' Ormond was worth the whole lot of 'em put together. That make you feel better?"

"I feel lousy. But thanks for coming to see me, Skip."

"Hey, this ain't no *social* visit." Tolson was scowling, dark brows a thick line across his forehead. "I come to make a *deal*."

"I have nothing to trade. Even if I had, I don't need a deal. I'm getting treatment as good as they're giving Ormond."

"Huh? What's that gotta do with anything? Joby, I guess you don't know *nothing* about this place. Everybody in Xanadu know you saved Ormond, and Mannie Segal's ready to kiss your ass. So, you're a big hero. So, in a few weeks you start to feel better. What you think happens next?"

"I've no idea."

"I tell you. You get sent back — to finish the training course. An' in your condition, that kills you. Tough? It's the Xanadu rule: nobody, I mean *nobody*, gets out of training early 'cept by dying. I did mine, Gormish did hers, you do yours. You got a fair dose of radiation, okay. You were lucky and you're gettin' treatment. Still okay. But last thing you want now is *another* fifty rads on top of what you just got."

Job lay back on the bed and closed his eyes. He had lived with hard rules all his life. The unbending code of the Tandy came as no surprise. But he knew one thing for sure: no one who had just received a dose of a hundred and seventy rads could survive the rigors of the training program, even in the mildest weather of spring. Already he could feel the radiation sucking at his bone marrow, ulcerating his mouth, wasting his limbs. The Decon Center program should help, but he would feel sick and physically weak for months. Another forty or fifty rads, or work outside in the freezing winter weather: either would be enough to finish him. Take them together, and he would not last a week.

"Don't you go noddin' off on me again." Tolson shook Job's shoulder. "You listening?"

"Not any more, Skip." Job opened his eyes. "I don't need to. You just told me I'm dead."

"Bullshit! I told you I come with a *deal*." Tolson sat on the edge of the bed, crouched down, and glared into Job's eyes. "You listen, and listen good. You get treatment here, an' in three, four weeks — five weeks, maybe, if Mannie an' Ormond swing you a bit more time — the people in Decon say, okay, we done all we can, take him away. An' you go back to training."

"And die."

"Yeah. And die. But you know radiation. You get it all at once, zap, you die. But you get it spread out, you can take it. So. After you leave here, you get better slow. You get hair an' strength back slow. Six months from now, when the weather is good, you begin to feel pretty good. You go finish training then, get thirty, forty more rads, so what? You eat 'em up, no trouble."

"But if everybody has to finish training —"

"They do. No exceptions. But they don't have to finish *right off*. Suppose some urgent job come up, somewhere in the Tandy, an' a new recruit's the only person can do it? Well, training stops, just 'til that other job finish."

Job's weakened condition was slowing his brain, but finally he was following Tolson. "You mean you can find work for me, something that will keep me out of training for a while, let me get better, then go back and finish?"

"You hear me. Tell you how it works." Tolson went to the window and stared out at the drifted snow, came back to close the door of the room, then sat down next to Job. He leaned close and spoke in a whisper. "Don't you talk about this, see, but the Big Three been havin' an argument. They got their followers scattered all over the Tandy, little groups of 'em. Bonvissuto says his people tell him Gormish been favorin' anyone who came into Xanadu with her. Pyle says his supporters complain, gettin' worst locations, worst jobs, worst equipment. Gormish says *her* followers claim they get slowest maintenance, lousiest service work. It's not that big a deal, nothin' to go to war over, but the Big Three sit down together an' they say, okay, let's get facts. We set up a mixed team, it goes out and surveys Xanadu, comes back and reports. An' then we sort things out between us.

"Now, one problem with that. People in the Tandy come from all over, and they mostly settle with their own sort. Don't talk to each other too good."

"Different languages?"

"You got it. Survey team gonna have a hell of a time. But suppose I pass word up the line. I say, hey, we got a new recruit here, talks every lingo you can think of. He should be on the survey team, pull it all together. Mannie an' Ormond put in the good word, too. You work the survey — no radiation — an' when it's finished, you go back an' finish training."

It almost made sense. But there was one problem. "Skip, you said you came to make a *deal*. What you said would be good for me, but I don't hear any deal. What's in it for you?"

"I'm doing you a favor." Tolson was looking away, out of the window. "You can just owe me."

"Try another one." Job felt he was becoming as cynical as Skip. "That bird won't fly."

"Hey, Joby, don't you know a good thing when you hear one?" But Tolson was grinning at Job in an embarrassed way. "All right, smart ass. Here's the rest. You're in Headquarters now, but you don't know nothin' about this place. I do. If you have to live in Xanadu, there's only one place to be: right here. Water's cleanest, dose rate way down, never an accident from a bad air drop. An' here's where all the power is. So you scheme an' struggle and fight to get in, an' you're makin' it on the inside, an' you sure as hell don't want to leave, even for only a few weeks. You lose an edge, that's all it takes."

"So that's it! *You* got picked to be part of that survey team, and you don't want to go. Come on, Skip, admit it."

"Yeah. Well, yeah, that's the way it's been shapin' up. Gormish picked me, an' acted like she was doin' me a *favor*. But I told her, she needs a real good language man, an' that sure ain't me. I got one language in my head, an' all the rest are animal noises. Pyle's bunch sound to me like dogs barkin' when they get together, Bonvissuto's lot might as well be gargling, an' there's a dozen other sets that's worse."

"So you're not doing *me* a favor — I'm doing you one."

"Don't you believe it." The certainty returned to Tolson's face. "You be savin' me a job I don't want. But I'm savin' your *life*. The survey will be all talk work, indoor work, easy on you. By the time you finish you know more about different bits of the Tandy than near anyone, an' Pyle an' Gormish an' Bonvissuto know you, know what you can do. After you done the rest of your training, that pays off. You make it here to Head-quarters in a year or less, record time — took me four, and that was *fast*." He stood up. "So. What you say? We got a deal?"

"Skip, you got me on ice. I have no choice."

"Yeah." Tolson was grinning again. "That's how I figured. So I go an' start the wheels rollin'. You oughta' have four easy weeks, maybe five, before they kick your ass out of here an' into the survey team. You better be ready." He walked to the door, opened it, and turned back to Job. "Hey, one other thing, Joby. Don't let 'em bring you no mirror. Your face looks like a plucked chicken's ass when you got no hair."

Job lay back on the bed as the door closed. *Four easy weeks*. Like hell. He had seen prisoners who had eaten a hundred and fifty rads and tried to keep going in the training program. None had made it. The treatment he was receiving would help a lot, but the next month was going to be murder. He ran his tongue over the inside of his mouth. Already the tender tissues of his cheek and tongue felt rough and fissured. In another day they would be a mass of ulcers. Swallowing would be agony, speech next to impossible. And *then* it would really start to become unpleasant.

Job tried to visualize his own hairless head as it would surely be in a week or two: swollen, ulcerated, purulent, covered with weeping radiation sores. Instead his mind fed him the bald, grinning gnome face of Wilfred Dell. Only then did Job realize that during the past couple of weeks the agenda set by Dell in the Mall Compound had disappeared from his thoughts. Dell himself was a mirage, a wraith, no more than the distant memory of a former life. *This* was the world that mattered, the solid reality of the Nebraska Tandy.

Dell vanished. Balanced on the edge of sleep, Job saw in his mind the face of Hanna Kronberg. He realized the other implications of a survey of Xanadu installations: If the team traveled *everywhere* in the Tandy, as Tolson had suggested, then Wilfred Dell's secret agenda might not be so impossible after all.

● Chapter Seventeen

In a moment shall they die, and the people
shall be troubled at midnight, and pass away:
and the mighty shall be taken.

— *The Book of Job, Chapter 34, Verse 20*

Four weeks were nowhere near enough. By the end
of that time the intravenous feeds had been removed
and Job was able to force down liquid nourishment,
but he was so weak that half a dozen steps left him dizzy
and panting. He was totally hairless, his face and chest
carried the red stigmata of radiation burns, and the
flesh had melted from his bones; his arms and legs
were stick-thin, their muscles no more than strings and
puny knobs of flesh. He could stand and walk, but a
breath of wind would push him over. As part of a survey team he was a dead loss; that would be obvious to
anyone.

Human inefficiency and the bitter Nebraska winter
saved him. When he was discharged from Decon Center and shipped to the main Headquarters complex,
two of the survey team's seven members had not yet
arrived. They were finishing an assignment for Bonvissuto. Five more days, the others were told. But five
days grew to two weeks, and it was not until the morning of the seventeenth day that word came from the
missing two. Their job was done at last. They promised
to be on their way that night from the far west of
Xanadu.

Before they could leave, the weather played its part.

A February ice storm raged in from the northeast and set its lock on the Tandy, dropping three feet of dry snow, halting all business, stopping all outside movement. The temperature dropped fifty degrees in eight hours. It was five more days before roads became passable and the missing two could be delivered to Headquarters.

Job had hidden away in the little underground room assigned to him, eating and drinking as much as he could stand, nursing his sores, keeping a low profile. By the time that the last two team members arrived he could walk up a flight of stairs — just. A meeting had been scheduled for the same afternoon. With the help of crutches Job struggled to the second floor, leaned panting against the wall outside the meeting room, and felt the tendons of his legs quivering like bowstrings.

As he had planned, he was the first person to arrive. When his heart had settled in his chest he hid his crutches behind the door, sat at the end of the long table, and adjusted his head dressing. Nothing could make him appear well, but if he appeared too sick they would not let him be part of the survey. The other team members appeared one by one and gave him a nod and a casual glance. If they thought he looked strange, they said nothing. Job made his own inspections and was not impressed. The two men and four women were healthy enough, but there was a dullness and a placidity to their eyes. The position of survey team member was not a coveted one. Maybe any smart Headquarters staff member would do what Skip had done, and find a substitute.

As soon as the team members were in position, three blue-clad men entered and went to chairs placed by the window. They were an odd trio, one Nordic, one darkly Latin, and one Oriental. They did not look at the survey team, and they did not speak. They sat, scribe recorders and notebooks on their laps, until Gormish,

Pyle, and Bonvissuto bustled into the room, talking to each other in the odd version of *chachara-calle* that was unique to the Nebraska Tandy. Job had seen the Big Three at mealtimes from his corner in the Headquarters food center, but it had been a distant and a hurried look from behind the partitions — he wanted to draw no attention to himself. The new closeup view was not reassuring. Gormish was a short, gray-haired woman with a heavy build and a thin-lipped, determined mouth. She gave Job no more than a passing glance, but he was sure that she had read his physical condition exactly. Pyle was snake-thin and sinewy, with a lantern jaw, hooked nose, and deep-set unreadable eyes. His black hair was thinning in front, but at the back it was grown long and tied into a short pony tail. He constantly fiddled with his hands, cracking the knuckles, picking at the nails, chewing the loose skin at their edges, but his eyes were everywhere.

At first sight, Bonvissuto was much the most congenial of the three. He was chubby and full-faced, with laughter lines at his mouth and around his brown eyes. He reminded Job of Colonel della Porta. His voice was just as cheerful, bubbling over with energy and good humor as he came into the room and greeted the seated team members. It was hard to dislike him, but Job had heard the rumors around the training center: behind that bonhomie was a deadly efficiency and coldness; to reach his position as one of the three rulers of Xanadu, Bonvissuto had set a Tandyman onto his own brother and dropped him alive into the Tandy's main acid dump.

The seats for the Big Three were on the window side of the long table, in front of their scribes. There was silence as they took their places. All three glanced briefly at each team member, then turned to gaze steadily — at Job. He tried not to panic. It was natural that they should look at him, they knew every other member of

the team from previous contacts. Yet his heart began to
pound in his chest, harder than when he arrived at the
top of the stairs.

"Job Salk, is it not?" Pyle, seated in the middle, spoke
first and in fluent German. "Your record when you
came here showed a gift for languages, and we heard
the same thing from a friend of yours. I hope for your
sake that it is not exaggerated."

Job's chances to speak German had been limited to
conversations with a couple of street *basura*, almost four
years ago, and their accent differed slightly from Pyle's.
He wondered at the man's birthplace and heritage —
Pyle was certainly not a German name — as he replied,
"I don't think that it is exaggerated, but in this language I am certainly a bit rusty. And my mouth is sore
from the radiation, so it is not easy to enunciate well.
Give me two or three days with others who speak German, though, and I will sound a good deal better than
this."

It was clear to Job that no one but Pyle and his scribe
had any idea what he was saying. Gormish and Bonvissuto were staring questioningly at the saturnine man
between them. He shrugged, frowned, and finally
nodded to Gormish. "Good enough. Your turn."

She turned to Job. "You have been in Xanadu for
almost four months. Tell me what you have done since
you came here, and what you expect to do during this
survey."

She spoke in Russian, fluently enough, but Job knew
that it was not her native language. It had been
learned, probably when she was in her early teens, and
although she spoke it well there were still small errors
in grammar and pronunciation. He made sure that his
reply was delivered a little slower than his usual
speech, and he avoided long words and difficult con-
structions.

By the time that he had finished and Gormish was

nodding her satisfaction to the other two, Job was more relaxed and almost enjoying himself. Bonvissuto's switch to rapid and graceful Italian came as no surprise. Job replied with the same speed and elegance, made a joke at the end of his explanation of how he had come to be hurt, and was rewarded with Bonvissuto's broad grin.

"According to my staff he has equal command of all the major languages favored in Xanadu," said Gormish. "Well? More questions, or are we ready to proceed?"

The conversation turned to the survey. Job sank back in his chair and drew a long, painful breath. The test was over; he had passed it. Unless he were called on to speak again he would keep quiet, and concentrate on listening to the others.

An hour of haggling, questioning, and harsh comment confirmed what Job already suspected: the other members of the survey team were nothing but dullards, given the job because they were trusted by Gormish, Pyle, and Bonvissuto. Or rather — Job could see how the lines were drawn — two were trusted by Gormish, two were Pyle's people, and the other two belonged to Bonvissuto. Job was the odd man out, the person who had no allegiance but happened to be needed. One scribe also belonged to each of the Big Three, and they fulfilled roles as more than simple recorders; occasionally one would lean forward and whisper into the ear of his boss. From the few words that Job could catch he knew that Gormish's assistant was speaking in Mandarin Chinese; Gormish herself, from the look of it, was no mean linguist.

By the end of the second hour of the meeting Job was coming to another conclusion. The Big Three of Xanadu certainly had their differences. They argued and grumbled about many things; but in one area they were totally in agreement. Whenever the outside world was mentioned, whether it was the air drops, or the influx of new prisoners, or even something as uncontrollable and impersonal as the ice storm that had recently swept in from the north, the bitterness and hatred in each voice could not be missed. Even Bonvissuto's joviality took on a chill edge when he spoke of "Outside," the world beyond the Tandies.

It was not surprising — Job could see the scars of old radiation ulcers on each face at the table, and his own weeping sores were too commonplace to remark. What *was* surprising was the sense of approaching revenge, of a long-awaited reprisal soon to be delivered. But little was said explicitly.

"The survey *is* expensive of personnel resources." That was Gormish, talking to Pyle. "But we will have an exact measure of our strength, and that measure is necessary. We are talking of the management of a very large area, though admittedly a sparsely populated one."

She could not be referring to the Tandy; the Big Three already governed that, and it was not large or sparsely peopled. Job found his thoughts straying to Wilfred Dell. That sinister cherub could be called many bad names, but he could never be called a fool. He had been convinced that something was going on within the Nebraska Tandy; something that might also affect life in the Mall Compound, otherwise he would have had no interest in the matter. For the first time, Job found himself agreeing with Dell. But what *was* going on? He could no more put his finger on it, here at the center of things, than Dell had been able to do with his space-based observations from three hundred miles up. Some central piece of information was missing.

At the end of the meeting that piece was still absent. The team was dismissed and told to prepare themselves for their next-morning departure. There was no proviso of "weather permitting." Gormish and Pyle blamed Bonvissuto for the delay so far, and they were not willing to see it continued.

Job intended his main preparation to be sleep, as much as he could manage. He waited until the others had left, then went to stare out of the southern window. Across the frozen wastes of the Tandy, less than a mile away, he could see the outer fence of Xanadu and the beginning of the outside world. But that world could not be reached, by people or machines. The guarding lasers made it as inaccessible as the surface of the Moon.

We are talking of managing a very large area. . . . That sounded as though it referred to the country beyond Xanadu. But what could Gormish and her colleagues have in mind that might conquer or even threaten a world that they could not reach? . . . *though admittedly a sparsely populated one.* With its four hundred million people, the country beyond Xanadu was far from sparsely populated.

It was all mystery. Job retrieved his crutches and made his way slowly back downstairs. He had not eaten since breakfast, but he was exhausted and had no appetite. On the way he stopped at the dining area and forced himself to spoon down a bowl of thick corn soup. It made him even more weary. He descended to the basement level and his own little room, lay on the bed, and waited for sleep.

When at last it came it was shallow and unsatisfying, full of disturbing dreams. Wilfred Dell was sitting next to Job. It was night, and they were squeezed together inside the driver compartment of a Tandyman, riding through towering mountains of glowing trash. "Do you want to see the world population double — again?" Dell was saying. "That's what it might do, if we could eat cellulose. It's nice to have plenty of young and poor, to look after the needs of the old and wealthy, but the biggest threat to all of us is *change*."

"*Change.*" Job awoke on the final word. There was

someone in his room, leaning over him and examining the ID badge on his chest. The man's touch was light but he had accidentally brushed against Job's arm, where the weeping sores were still exquisitely tender.

It was the blue-clad Oriental, the scribe and aide to Gormish. Job began to sit up, but already the man was hurrying away, out of the room.

Job felt for his chest. The plastic badge was still there, apparently untouched. When he went across to the light and examined the ID it appeared exactly as it had always been.

He lay back on his bed. Why should anyone come in and look at his ID? If they thought there was something wrong with it, why not check it openly, in the meeting or after it?

As Job fell asleep again he decided that today he had learned one thing of paramount importance: there were levels within levels at Xanadu, subtleties and interplays and cross-tensions of which Skip Tolson, and perhaps most others at Headquarters, understood nothing.

The location of the Nebraska Tandy had been chosen thirty years earlier, when disposal of toxic materials became a major public concern.

The site selection had been made with care. An ideal dumping ground for toxic and nuclear waste would be totally isolated. That was impossible, but at least the flow of water, on the surface and below, should be *into* a Tandy and not away from it. That meant a self-contained catchment basin, admitting runoff from outside but never discharging to it.

Those same facts now decided the Xanadu population pattern. A settlement close to the outer boundary enjoyed lower toxin and radioactivity levels, as far as possible from the lethal central dumps. Water supplies, draining in from outside, were most pure at the outer perimeter. Thus the towns and villages of Xanadu were set within an annulus, no more than a couple of miles from the circular outer boundary.

The survey team would proceed clockwise from Headquarters, visiting one or two settlements each day. According to the catalog of facilities provided to Job, that should bring them to the fenced installation that interested Wilfred Dell late on the third afternoon.

They started out an hour after dawn, in cold so intense that the truck's engine had to be kept ticking over even when they were not moving. Freezing air gnawed at Job's weak lungs and provided exquisite pain to any inch of his exposed and ulcerated skin. He wore multiple layers of clothing, a face mask that left only small eye-holes, and triple pairs of gloves and socks. As he waddled through the snow to the waiting truck he stared straight up into the cloudless blue sky. According to Wilfred Dell there was daily monitoring of Xanadu by the orbital imaging systems; if Job were outside for an hour, he would be spotted.

Maybe. Job was skeptical. He might be *seen*, but the chance that he would be *recognized* in his mask and present swaddling garb was negligible.

The more he thought of his escape mode from Xanadu, the more terrifying it became. When he decided to leave he was supposed to lie down outside, flat on the ground with arms and legs splayed, for at least an hour. He would be seen by the orbiting observation posts, identification would be made, and orders passed to the Tandy perimeter defense. That same night, between eight P.M. and two A.M., the defensive lasers would be turned off on the road at the eastern boundary of Xanadu. In that six-hour period Job must pass through the outer fence.

But suppose that the observation system was out of action for a while — it had happened before — and he was not seen? Or suppose that he was seen, but in his hairless and wasted condition he was not *recognized* by the imaging systems interpreters? Or what if the information were not passed on to the perimeter defense system? Or Job arrived early or late at the fence, when the lasers were in operation?

It could even be that Dell had already solved his problem in some other way, and no longer needed Job at all. (Job had no illusions about smiling Wilfred's magnanimity.)

He forced himself to stop. He could imagine a dozen other snags; if he allowed himself to accept any one of them he would never dare to leave Xanadu. He climbed into the waiting truck and settled himself delicately on the hard seat.

The first stop proved to Job that Skip Tolson had made a wise decision. Work assignments in the Tandy were on the basis of experience and competence, but the residents chose to live as ethnic groups. This community was ninety-nine percent Filipino. While the questions of the survey team were asked and grudgingly answered in the Tandy's own version of *chachara-calle*, the comments and conversation all around them went on in rapid *Tagalog*. Job, listening but rarely speaking, found out ten times as much about the community's real feelings as the rest of the survey team combined. People here were concerned that they did not receive their fair share of the new materials sorted out from the air drops. They did not like the foods grown in their area of the Tandy, and they would like permission to make changes. They thought that the quality of road repair was poorest in their region. Most of all, they worried because the community population was growing while resources were not; worried, not for themselves but for their children.

Job wondered if they understood the idea of a survey. He switched to *Tagalog* and began to explain, but he was soon interrupted.

"We know," said a man with two infants in his lap. He

was totally bald from radiation. "We were told, and we approve. The survey is needed for preparation. This place is enough for us, but these" — he smiled down at the children — "they cannot live here forever. We need freedom for *them*."

Job felt excitement in the air at those words, a sense of expectancy. He knew that this community was loyal to Bonvissuto, and it must be his promises, vague but glorious, that Job was hearing now. But he could not understand Bonvissuto's motive. The jovial fat man was presenting himself to his followers as a Moses, ready to lead them to the promised land — yet that land was unattainable, guarded by a wall of fire.

But it was not just Bonvissuto. The next day the team came to a community of a thousand people, all of Chinese origin. Their main allegiance was to Gormish, not Bonvissuto, their practical worries were different from the previous day, and yet their expectations were the same. The routine of the survey plodded on, statistics and census data and complaints, but all around it, invisible to anyone who did not speak their language, the people revealed their dreams. "It is all right for *us*" — the speaker's gesture was inclusive, sweeping Job into her circle of seated Chinese — "we can live in the Tandy as we live now, and then die. But what of the children? The little ones must not suffer shortened lives. They must have freedom."

Freedom. That word again.

They spoke readily to Job when they realized that he was fluent in their tongue. His weeping radiation sores were an added credential. He was one of *them*, tested and tried by the gods of Xanadu. One woman brought him her newborn, so that he could touch its head for good luck. He reached out with one tentative finger, while the rest of the survey team looked on in amazement. He was amazed himself. How long since he had touched a baby, or held an infant? Years and years. He put his forefinger to the tiny, scowling forehead, and was rewarded with a shriek of rage. Everyone in the group burst out laughing.

Job stared around him. He was astonished by the number of infants. They were everywhere. Xanadu was supposed to be a deathtrap, a grave for people without hope. But there was more hope here than he had seen back in the city. And the Mall Compound, he now realized, had no children at all.

As the people in the circle spoke, Job learned that *all* they had was hope. They knew no facts. They had no idea of anything that might achieve the longed-for release from the Nebraska Tandy.

But surely the Big Three had at least an *idea* of a mechanism. They could not hold out the promise of a bright future for very long, without something to support that optimism. And yet the mechanism remained as obscure to Job as it had ever been.

At dinner that night, the woman whose baby he had touched introduced him to her sister, Jia. She stood there shyly, a slim girl about the same age as Job. She was placed next to him during the meal. He felt ashamed when she tried to serve him with the best tidbits, and he had to explain that his throat and stomach could tolerate only the soft-boiled rice, and poorly at that; after the first mouthful he felt nauseated. She smiled understandingly, brought him a drink that was soothing and lukewarm instead of the spicy herbal infusion that the rest were drinking, and found for him a sweet, chilled mush to substitute for the chewy dessert. Job's mouth was sore, and he encouraged her to talk more than listen. But she hung on his every word, and took his hand in hers when she left.

Before he eased himself into bed that night, Job did what Skip Tolson had warned him not to do: he found a mirror, and stared into it. The bald, raddled nightmare that peered back at him made him feel

sicker than the boiled rice. A few wisps of thin dark hair
were appearing on his scalp, worse in Job's opinion
than total baldness. His eyes were like black holes in the
furnace-slag of his cratered face, and his receding chin
was a minefield of open sores. How had Jia even been
able to *look* at him, still less to talk to him without disgust, smile at him, and touch his hand? But she had
done all that, and invited him to visit the village again
when the survey was finished.

He climbed into bed. There was one possible
explanation: in the topsy-turvy-Tandy world, radiation
sores did not send a woman screaming away. They
were Job's saber scars, his mark of manhood, the scalps
at his belt, his red badge of courage showing that he
had been through stern testing and survived.

So far. But the real test lay ahead. Tomorrow the
schedule would take them to the mysterious fenced
facility.

Job should have been worried. Instead he drowsed
off oddly content, and slept easy for the first time in two
months.

• Chapter Eighteen

For now I shall sleep in the dust;
and thou shalt seek me in the morning,
but I shall not be.

— *The Book of Job, Chapter 7, Verse 21*

Morning brought a great change. While Job slept, high winds carried away the deadly cold of late February and left in its place a false spring that mimicked full summer. By eight o'clock snow was turning to gurgling rivulets, warm fogs rose to blanket the gentle slopes of the Nebraska Tandy, and birds were appearing from nowhere to peck at newly exposed earth.

As great a change had been taking place inside Job's own body. He overslept, to awake with an unfamiliar sensation. It was *hunger*. His mouth was sore and his skin itched, but for the first time in months he was eager to eat breakfast.

Everyone on the survey team was already in the dining area when he arrived. They too were responding to the outside changes with more animation than Job had ever seen before. Give us three or four days like this, they were saying, we'll be ahead of schedule, we can be back at Headquarters within two weeks....

Which was where all of them longed to be. They hated the survey — stupid questions, uninteresting people, jabbering away in unintelligible languages. Job was hurried through his meal and into the truck. By nine o'clock they were in the far west of the Tandy, passing through the boundary fence of the biggest town Job had seen so far.

He stared about him with quivering intensity. Here, at last, was Techville, the preferred home of scientists exiled to the Nebraska Tandy, the town where according to Wilfred Dell as many as three thousand of them lived. Job saw nothing unusual within the surrounding fence. The buildings were standard Xanadu construction, set in regular rings around a central cleared square from which the streets ran off like spokes of a wheel. Job stared along one of those streets as they arrived at the center. Follow it for three or four hundred yards, and you would reach another facility, this with its own boundary fence. Would the survey team be allowed to follow that road, later in the day?

If Job found the town interesting, his curiosity did not seem to be returned. In the other communities people had crowded around the truck. Here, the arrival of the survey team was noted with no more than mild interest. It was as though they had been expecting visitors, and knew just why the team was in Techville.

The group waiting in the central clearing confirmed that view, together with another impression gained by Job during the drive into town. This was not the ethnically uniform community that the survey had encountered in previous stops. Job saw many different racial types and heard a polyglot mixture of languages. The people who met the truck were just as diverse: an Oriental woman, a hulking red-haired male with a broken nose, and two dark-skinned men who looked like brothers.

The red-haired bruiser was the spokesman. "We know what you want," he said, after the briefest of introductions. "We have already prepared the census data, and listed the areas where we could most use help. That's written out in the packet here. So if we could just confirm your IDs . . . and of course, if you would like us to go over our answers with you, we'll be happy to do it." His manner suggested that it would be a waste of time.

The ID badges were collected from each team member and examined by the Oriental woman as census packets were opened and examined. Was Job's badge receiving an unusually intensive scrutiny? He thought so, but he told himself that must be his imagination. As the badges were handed back he became alarmed for a different reason. His companions were eager to press on to the next stop. The residents of Techville had prepared everything in advance. The survey team would have no reason to stay, and then —

" — and then you can take advantage of the good weather and be on your way," the red-haired spokesman was saying. "Leave now, and you'll be in Clydestown before noon."

Leave now, and make no visit to the interior fenced area. Leave now, and find no answers to Wilfred Dell's questions. Leave now, and maybe never have a chance to come back. The gates of Xanadu would remain closed forever.

His companions were putting away their packets after scarcely a glance at the contents. They were ready to go. How could he delay them?

By persuasion? Ridiculous. Even if he had a logical argument no one would listen.

The truck? He could disable it, given time and privacy . . .

Forget that. He had neither.

There was only one way to prevent his departure — a dangerous and irrevocable act, but Job was moving before he had thought through its consequences.

He put his hand to his head and staggered forward to collide with one of the dark-skinned men. Eyes closed, he stood clutching at the man's chest.

"Here. What's he *doing*?" That was the Oriental woman.

"He's radiation sick. He should never have been in our team." That was a woman from Job's own party.

He was surprised at the vindictiveness and satisfaction in her voice. Yet he could have predicted it — and not just from her. The other members knew each other's loyalties, and therefore how to behave, but Job was an unknown quantity, and therefore dangerous. "He can't go on with us," she continued happily. "He'll interfere with our work. You'll have to make arrangements to ship him to Headquarters. . . ."

Where he will be sent back to the training program, and die. Job could finish her thoughts. *If Gormish and Pyle and Bonvissuto and I went through training, he has to go through training, too. And if it kills him, that's his problem.*

The rules were implacable. But how many deaths in Xanadu over the years were due to the inflexibility of those idiot rules? In another month Job would be able to finish the training course and survive. Start tomorrow and it would kill him.

Job opened his eyes. Everyone was staring at him, but on no face could he see a trace of sympathy.

"Take him to the hospital," said the red-haired man. He turned to the rest of the survey team. "You can go anytime you want to. Don't worry about him. We'll arrange his return to Headquarters."

Fifteen minutes later Job was stretched out on the bed in an otherwise empty room. He lay back and closed his eyes.

I've managed to work my way right into the lion's den. Well, clever me. But what now? I feel a bit of energy for the first time in months, but I'm forced to lie here and do nothing . . . unless I can find a way to put my head in the lion's mouth, and get over to the fenced buildings.

A more sensible man would hurry back to the square and try to rejoin the survey team, hoping that they had not yet left, telling them that he felt fine, that it had been just a minute or two of dizziness. A more inventive man would send a signal aloft to the watching satellites, find a way to reach the Tandy eastern exit at the right time, and then make up some story to satisfy Wilfred Dell.

Job stood up and went across to the window. It was closed — and barred. The hospital bordered the central clearing, and he could see that the truck had already departed. Apparently he was neither sensible nor inventive enough.

And now the sky was clouding over. Dell had made it plain that Job could lie outside all day, but if the sky were overcast he would not be seen. There could be no escape from Xanadu tonight. As though to reinforce that conclusion a Tandyman came rolling across the middle of the square. Everyone hurried clear of it, and watched intently until it was far away in the distance.

Job was still standing at the window when the Oriental woman returned.

"Well," she said. "Not dead yet, eh?" Her cool manner had gone, and she sounded pleased with herself.

"I don't feel too bad. In fact, I'm getting hungry."

"Good sign. We can take care of that easily enough." She smiled. "I'm Frances Chang. You know, you didn't have to go through that little act outside. We already planned that you would not be leaving with the others."

For the past few weeks the sores on Job's face had encouraged him to show as little expression as possible. That helped now. He walked forward and sat down on the bed. "I don't understand."

"Of course you don't. That's why I'm here." She held out her hand. "Give me your badge for a moment."

He handed it to Frances Chang and watched in silence as she turned it over to show the back. "See that?" There was a little green line along the bottom. Job could not remember if it had been there when the badge was issued. "That says you're a candidate to work in Techville. We like to keep to ourselves here, as much as we're allowed to, but we have friends at Headquarters. When someone arrives in Xanadu who might be useful, we like to know about it. Normally nothing happens 'til the training program is finished, so your badge doesn't get marked 'til then. Your case was unusual. You popped up here ahead of schedule."

"Candidate for *what*?" Job opted for the least revealing thought in his mind.

"I told you, to come and work here." She did not seem surprised by the question. "I know you've had no scientific training, and you've been in trouble — we have your full record, we've had it since the day you arrived at Xanadu. But you have excellent aptitude. We try to pick up anyone with potential. You will have to go back to Headquarters and finish the training program, but before you leave we want you to have a feel for us, and what we do." She handed him his badge. "Come on, since you say you're hungry."

Warning lights were flashing inside Job's head as he followed Chang from the room. While he had been scheming to find a way here, someone had been waiting for him — more than waiting, *steering* him in this direction. People didn't do favors for nothing, outside Xanadu or inside it. Frances Chang could paint her innocent picture of Techville scientists, impressed by Job's aptitude and wanting to recruit him. But Job could see a far more probable scenario. These people had friends in Headquarters, just as Chang suggested, and one of those friends, the Oriental aide to Gormish, had tagged Job's badge. But the green line didn't say, "Promising recruit, treat him well, sign him up." Far more likely it said, "I don't know what this one is, but he's a late addition to the survey. Keep him around until you find out why he was sent to Techville."

One thing that Frances Chang had said to Job possessed a ring of truth: "You didn't have to go through that little act outside. We already planned that you would not be leaving with the others."

Job might be treated as a "guest"; but "prisoner" was a better description of his status. He would leave when, and if, his hosts decided that he should. And if they decided that he was too dangerous to release? Well, that was no problem. He had been left behind in Techville because of radiation sickness. What was more natural than his death here?

The next few hours confirmed his suspicion. Food was served in a different building, and although Frances Chang left him while he ate, three or four other residents always managed to be at his table throughout the meal.

They chatted freely among themselves, but to Job's surprise they did not ask him the obvious questions: why was he here, how long had be been in Xanadu, what was it like outside, did the *Quiebra Grande* still devastate the rest of the world? They must know he was a stranger, to Techville and to Xanadu. Their lack of curiosity was inconsistent with his earlier idea, that they would probe to find out why he had been sent with the survey. He ate in puzzled silence.

The answer when it came to him was not reassuring. It took the form of another question. Why go through the farce of polite queries when you had the truth drug? One dose of that, and Job would tell *everything*. And once they knew that he had been sent to Xanadu by the outside government . . .

Job had learned from the conversation around him that the hatred for the government of the Mall Compound was as strong here as anywhere in the Tandy, maybe stronger. The only "crime" committed by Techville residents was the pursuit of science; but the witch-hunts had grabbed them, declared them guilty, and sent them to Xanadu without even the pretense of a fair hearing.

Let the punishment fit the crime. Science was officially to blame for the country's worst problems, pollution and toxins; therefore by government policy, captured scientists should be sent to the country's worst Tandy.

It would be pointless for Job to explain to the people around him that he too was a victim, sent here against his will. They would learn that he had entered the Tandy as a spy for Wilfred Dell and that would be enough.

At the end of the meal Frances Chang appeared from nowhere and conducted Job quietly out of the dining area. They had reached the door of the building when a vanload of new diners came hurrying in. Job, one step in front of Chang, found himself suddenly face to face with a woman.

It was Hanna Kronberg.

She looked older and more worried than her pictures. The genial expression had vanished from her eyes, her gray hair was thinning, and she wore rimless glasses, but Job would have known her after far greater changes. He stopped dead, unable to resist staring at her point-blank. Fortunately she gave him only a casual glance, then looked right past his face and stepped around him to talk to Frances Chang.

Job went outside and stood waiting. His pulse was racing, his heart pounding up in his throat. After months of planning and anticipation, the first meeting had been an anticlimax. He had said nothing to Hanna Kronberg. What could he say — "Ah, Dr. Kronberg, just the person I was looking for. Tell me about the experiments that you are doing inside that fenced-off area"?

The air was warm, and the heaps of dirty snow were melting into the ground. The pulse in Job's throat slowed and became like a ticking clock. It was the clock of his own time, rapidly running down. The weather felt like early summer, but it was not yet even spring. In another day or two winter would return to set its grip on Xanadu, roads would again be difficult, escape impossible, and long before that, the truth drugs would have squeezed him dry.

Job did not speak to Frances Chang as she led him back to the hospital, except to say as they entered his room: "I'm sorry, but I'm exhausted. May I just rest here until morning?"

"You'll miss dinner if you do. The only place to eat is in the dining room, and it will be the last meal of the day."

"I don't feel up to eating again."

She nodded. "I understand. We'll talk in the morning." Even if *talk* meant *cross-examine*, she sounded sympathetic.

But sympathy had its limits. As she left the room the door closed firmly and Job heard the key turn in the lock. After a few minutes he went across to examine it. The door was solid. Even if the lock were of a simple type, Job had no idea how to pick it.

In any case, escape into the corridor was no solution. To get out of the building he would have to pass three or four rooms, each one occupied.

That left only the window. He went across to examine it. The room was on the second floor, and beyond the thick and yellowed glass of the casement were the vertical bars of iron. Job studied them. They were solidly planted in the window frame, each one a quarter of an inch thick. Skip Tolson might bend them; Job was far too feeble. But the bars had been spaced to prevent the escape of a normal adult, not one sickly thin and naturally hollow-chested. Job opened the casement as wide as it would go and pushed his head tentatively into the widest space between the bars. It might go through — just. And then by turning his body sideways, he might be able to slide his shoulders and hips through. At that point he would be hanging head-first above the ground, dangling over a twelve-foot drop onto wet black earth.

Job closed the window and went back to sit on the bed. Suppose that he worked his way through the bars and did not kill himself in the fall. What then? It would not be dark for another two hours, but the sky was completely cloud-covered and he could not signal the watching satellites. And if, miraculously, the sky were suddenly to clear and he could send his message, he must still travel to the eastern edge of the Tandy. It was at least fifteen miles, more if he avoided the deadly dumps at the center of Xanadu. He might not make it to the exit road before the two A.M. deadline.

Suppose, instead, that he stayed here until morning? Then he would surely be questioned, and the drug would make sure he told the full truth.

Problems.

Job climbed into bed and pulled the sheets over him. He needed sleep, but his mind remained furiously active. As the room darkened around him, he little by little decided what he had to do. He waited, eyes closed. At dusk, a stranger unlocked the door and looked in. When he saw that Job was lying quietly in bed he retreated without speaking. The key turned again in the lock.

Still Job waited. The roads and many buildings of Techville were not lit at night. By six-thirty the area below Job's window was completely dark. At last he moved his bed across, stood on it, and eased himself feet-first into the widest space between the window bars. The rough-edged metal scraped agonizingly on the sores of his hips and chest, but he kept inching forward. Within a minute he was holding a bar in each hand and turning so that his feet dangled down against the outside wall. His head was all that remained inside, but it stuck at the ears and temples and would not budge. His feet scraped for a hold on the wall of the building, and found nothing. The bars gripped him on each side of his hairless skull, tearing the skin from his ears. He wriggled and shivered and gave a last despairing push.

And then he was through. He lost his grip on the bars and dropped with a rush of air to sprawl full-length on soft, gluey earth.

As soon as he could breathe he rolled and scrambled away around the side of the building. Surely someone must have heard his feet, scrabbling away on the outer wall . . . But he saw and heard nothing. He waited thirty seconds, then crept away, around the building and towards the dining hall.

The street in front was disturbingly well lit. He hadn't noticed those lamps when he had been there in daylight. But lit or not, it was to the front of the dining hall that he had to go.

He watched while three small trucks drove up to the door, dropped off passengers, and left. At last the little van that he had seen earlier in the day came rolling up to the entrance. Hanna Kronberg and half a dozen others climbed out and went inside.

Job hurried forward. He had no time to worry about being seen. The engine was still running, and it was odds-on that the driver would be out again almost at once. At the side of the van Job hesitated. If just the driver reappeared, it made sense for Job to climb inside and hide at the back. But suppose that the driver was on his way to collect another group of diners? Then they would enter the van, and be sure to find Job.

He went around the truck and climbed onto the open iron frame at the rear. It was a primitive and home-made luggage rack, built of welded lengths of reinforcing bar. Even with the van stationary it was uncomfortable. Job crouched stiffly on hands and knees on the bare metal, and wished himself invisible. Despite the shadow of the van's body he felt conspicuous, but he dared not move.

The driver appeared at last. By the time the van was moving down the road Job's hands and knees were aching so badly that he wanted to scream.

The journey was mercifully short. When the van came to the fenced area and was waved on through the gate, Job was not sure whether he should be pleased or terrified. Certainly this place, inside yet another fence, should be the last location that anyone would search for him once they found that he was missing; they would first assume that he was making a run for Tandy Headquarters to report to his bosses. But if this seemed safe for the moment, instead of two barriers between him and Outside there were now three: one around this enclosed area, one around Techville, and the final and most lethal one around Xanadu itself.

He did not wait for the van to stop. While it was still cruising slowly between buildings he waited for an unlit patch and rolled off the luggage rack. The road was made of concrete. It knocked the breath out of him and delivered punishing blows to his left shoulder and hip. It was another minute or two before he recovered enough to crawl off into the darkness. He was scarcely to the side of the road before the van came roaring back with another load of passengers.

Months ago, Job's inspection of space photographs had shown him three buildings inside the fence. The middle one was three times the size of the others, but it seemed to be devoted to dormitories and recreation. The building next to it, farther to the east, had the most work activity — and it was where Hanna Kronberg had been spotted. Job headed that way, walked up to the building door as though he belonged there, and strode inside. If the staff went to dinner in shifts, rather than all at the same time . . . well, then he would be caught at once and not much worse off.

He found himself in a long, bare corridor with offices set off on each side. Most of the doors were closed, but as he walked he heard the sound of voices from behind one of them. Apparently at least a few of the staff were skipping dinner. At any moment one of them might have a reason to come out into the corridor.

He had to find a hiding place, but having come this far he wanted more than that. He stared at the closed doors as he passed. Each one had pinned to it a card bearing a person's name. He walked the length of the corridor to the narrow metal staircase at the end, but saw no card saying "Hanna Kronberg." He went up, treading as lightly as possible on the creaking bare metal, and found himself on a second floor that was all one big room. It was a laboratory of some kind, with computer consoles, electron capture detectors, chromatographs, and NMR equipment along one wall, racks of bottles and jars along another, and a dozen cages at the far end. Each cage was empty. Three of them were big enough to hold a large animal — or a human being.

In the corner nearest to Job stood another staircase. It led up to the third and highest floor of the building. Job hurried to it, ascended, and found himself in another corridor with a staircase at the far end leading to the roof. Three doors were along the right-hand side. Two bore unfamiliar names — but the middle one carried the painted number 36 and below it, "Hanna Kronberg."

Job pushed the door open and went in.

The room was empty. It was a plain twelve-by-sixteen oblong, with no pictures or decorations except a clock on one wall and a man's photograph in a frame over the desk. There were signs of recent occupancy. One of the three file cabinets had a drawer open. The computer in the corner was still switched on, displaying a complicated graphic of a biological organism. Jackets had been thrown carelessly on two of the chairs, and a pipe sat next to a pile of papers on the little metal table in the center of the room. It looked as though a meeting in progress had been interrupted for — or was continuing over — dinner.

There was one other exit to the room, a connecting door over by the file cabinets to Job's left. He went through it, and found himself in a file storage area filled with racks of cabinets and a dozen free-standing bookcases. He walked along the bookshelves, reading the titles. Predictably, they meant little to him. They were on molecular biology, physiology, genetics, organic chemistry . . . all subjects about which Job knew nothing. He went back to Hanna Kronberg's office and spent the next half hour examining the open file cabinets and the computer. It was the same story, the same words with a few new ones: hybridomas, recombinant DNA, mapping and splicing, commensalism, artificial symbiotes.

Job realized that real security in this facility was guaranteed not by protective fences and walls, as Wilfred Dell or the Big Three might think, but by the nature of the subject matter. Job could be left in this room all night, undisturbed, and at the end of it he would have only a vague idea what was going on. He had no trouble *reading* the papers in the files, but to him they were just strings of meaningless words. If he were to *understand* Hanna Kronberg's work, he would have to be told about it.

He went back into the storage room and examined it with a new eye. What he needed was a comfortable hideaway, one that would keep him from discovery while allowing him to overhear conversations in the next office.

Unfortunately, there was no such place. If he remained close enough to the door to hear speech, he would be seen by anyone who came in. Unless — Job looked up — unless he dropped any idea of comfort. The two bookcases next to the door were each six feet tall, three feet wide, and a foot deep. They were wood-framed, substantial and solid. If he climbed onto their shadowed top he could stretch out on them, uncomfortable but invisible unless anyone thought to look directly up to the bookcase tops.

He cracked open the door to the other room and looked around for something to stand on. There was nothing. Finally he took hold of the sides of one bookcase and gingerly began to ascend using the shelves themselves as steps. They creaked and bent, but held his weight. He dragged himself over the top and stretched out along the hard wood on his stomach, shoulder square against the wall. When he pushed his head forward it was no more than a foot from the top of the door to Hanna Kronberg's office. He could even slither forward, lean far down, and see the desktop and table at the other side of the room. In that extended position he was so uncomfortable that he could hold it for only a few seconds at a time. Job eased his way back.

In five minutes the hard wood was compressing the sores on his chest and legs. He shifted and squirmed, but found no relief. Before he climbed up he had worried that he might fall asleep and roll off. Now his concerns were quite different: could he endure this, until the return of Hanna Kronberg and her colleagues?

That return felt as though it was taking forever. Job, craning now and again to peer at the clock in the other room, knew that it was only half an hour until footsteps and voices sounded in the corridor outside. He pulled back close to the wall and lay perfectly still.

There was a scraping of chairs and a man's hoarse cough. And then another voice, a woman's. It was speaking, loudly and clearly.

And Job could not understand one word.

He lay frozen on the top of the bookcases. Of all the obstacles that he might have predicted in exploring the

mysteries of Techville, this was the least probable. And
yet it was one that Job should have been prepared for.
Here, as elsewhere in Xanadu, people stuck with their
ethnic groups. Hanna Kronberg and her colleagues
were no exception. They were talking freely to each
other — in their native language that Job had never
heard before.

He forgot his discomfort and *listened*, harder than he
had ever listened to anything. After a few minutes he
began to pick up words, cognates drawn from various
other languages. There was a hint now of Italian, then
a phrase like Turkish and another that sounded like
oddly pronounced Hungarian. The structure was
familiar, yet at the same time alien. Within a few
minutes Job's ear began to make the adjustment, and
his brain reached for a conclusion. What he was hearing was *Rumanian*, a language that he had encountered
only in written form, in one dusty book acquired and
pondered during his long years as a street *basura* and
vendor.

As the three people in the other room — Job could
identify two men's voices and one woman's — continued their discussions, other facts became clear.
Although they spoke Rumanian, most technical terms
were not translated to that language. They were
dropped in as English words. Job could hear the same
biological vocabulary that he had read in the papers:
hybridomas and recombinant DNA techniques and
symbiosis. Added to them were new mystery words: *airborne vectors*, *contagion and immunity*, and *antigerial effects*.

And one other fact became clear from the tones of
voice, independent of any language. These three
people had not returned for a late-night technical
meeting. They had come to continue an argument,
and it was a fierce one.

The voices grew louder. Job began to grasp tanta-
lizing scraps of meaning. *You are a slave of Gormish*. That

was Hanna Kronberg, addressing the gruffer of her companions, who coughed continuously whenever he was not arguing. *I know what she wants, and what Pyle and Bonvissuto want, too. But we have a* — Hanna Kronberg used a phrase that Job did not recognize. The book that he had studied so long ago had been written for children, with a child's limited vocabulary.

The argument grew more intense. Job risked craning forward enough to steal a glance into the next room. The three had their backs to him, crowded around the computer console. Hanna Kronberg was waving her hand at the screen. "*I can do it — I have proved . . . but it works only by . . .*" Directed something, that was the words she used. From the context and her gesture, it had something to do with *touching*. But touching what, and for what reason?

Job wallowed in words, clutching for the life raft of familiar phrases. "*. . . proof downstairs, as certain as I breathe*" . . . "*five years work, no doubt at all . . .*" "*Stupid, they have no idea what they ask us to do . . .*"

On and on it went, for another three hours. There was no agreement. The hoarse man was losing his voice. He began to bang his fist on the table to emphasize his points, and after a final outburst he swept out of the room. Hanna Kronberg and the other man followed, still arguing. The door slammed.

Job lay flat on top of the bookcase. He felt weak and dizzy. He had spent four hours in a concentration so intense that the world around him now seemed vague and distant. The only reality was the turbulent sea of words on which he had been so long adrift. He wanted to relax, but he was too uncomfortable. He flexed taut shoulders and began to ease his way down to the floor. There had been a sound of finality in the way that the door had been banged shut, but even if he were wrong about that he could not stay hidden forever. He went through into Hanna Kronberg's office and looked at

the papers strewn on the table, and at the display on
the computer screen. She had been pulling materials
from file cabinets to support the points she was
making, and had not bothered to put any of them back.
The same was true of her computer files. Data cubes
sat by the console, and one was still in the machine.

Job looked at the clock. Almost eleven; less than
seven hours to daylight and his first chance to send a
signal aloft to the orbiting monitors. He sat down at the
table. Finally he had an idea what the Big Three of the
Tandy were planning, and the role that Hanna Kronberg was supposed to play. But ideas were not enough;
he needed *proof*, enough to convince Wilfred Dell and
the Royal Hundred.

For the next five hours he studied the papers on the
table and called files onto the computer screen. Finally
his brain would absorb no more information. He
walked downstairs to the laboratory and went to a line
of glass-fronted cabinets. They were locked, but they
had not been built for strength. He forced two of them
open with a metal ruler and stood for a long time staring at their contents.

The two cabinets each held a dozen transparent vials
with color-coded stoppers. Within those tiny bottles,
unless Job had totally misunderstood the argument
among Hanna Kronberg and her colleagues, sat the key
to Techville and the reason for the fences around it. The
invisible microorganisms floating in their cloudy yellow
fluid were human designed — Kronberg's saver-of-
worlds, but also the Big Three's destroyer-of-worlds.

Job cautiously removed one plastic vial from each
cabinet, checking that the stoppers were tightly sealed.
The bottles went into his trouser pockets, then he continued to the first floor. He did not attempt to hide what
he had done. By morning his presence here would
have been noted in other ways.

He went out into the chilly predawn darkness and

walked quietly back to the fence. There was a guard on
duty at the gate, but he sat inside a heated kiosk, tilted
far back on his chair with a cap shielding his forehead
and eyes.

Job lay down in the soft mud at the side of the road
and slithered through the nine-inch gap at the bottom
of the gate. When he stood up he was shivering and
close to exhaustion, but he could not stop now. He
walked to the center of the town and into the dining
hall. It was deserted, and the lights within had been
turned down to a glimmer. Half a dozen leftover bread
rolls and a tray of leathery pieces of cold cooked meat
sat on one of the serving counters. He wrapped bread
and meat in a table cloth, tied the ends tight around his
waist, and went back outside.

He was afraid that the second fence, eight feet high
and running all the way around Techville, might be a
tougher proposition. At first sight, it was. The main gate
was closed and locked, with two guards standing by it.
But when Job, keeping to the darkest shadows, walked
along the line of the fence, he came to a place where the
recent thaw had turned the ground to a swamp. The line
of the eight-foot barrier was drooping outward. Job
splashed through six inches of icy water and put his
weight onto the place where the fence leaned farthest. It
tilted a few more inches, enough for him to scramble
partway up the steep side, hang on as it sagged farther,
and finally claw his way to the top and drop over into the
water and gluey black mud at the other side. He pulled
his feet free of sucking ooze and splashed onto drier land.
It took a second or two to get his bearings. There were no
stars or moon, but he knew that he had walked
counterclockwise around the Xanadu fence, and that the
entry gate was on the south side. If he kept going, he
would be heading in roughly the right direction. When
the sun rose he would learn where true east lay and
could set his course for the exit from Xanadu.

But that was still far off, in distance and in time. For the moment there were more urgent priorities. Exhausted, dizzy, and feverish, he walked away from the fence.

He had to force himself to do it. His legs did not want to obey his mind. He began to count steps, as he had done so long ago on the return from the incinerator and city dump. *One, two, three.* A dozen lifetimes ago, he had walked and walked and walked like this. *Nine, ten, eleven.* Forever. He had walked forever then. But now — *eighteen, nineteen, twenty* — now he did not have forever.

He cupped his hands over his aching eyes. The clock was running. Fast. He must be out of sight of Techville before daylight, and dawn was less than an hour away.

• Chapter Nineteen

*My bone cleaveth to my skin and to my flesh,
and I am escaped with the skin of my teeth.*

— *The Book of Job, Chapter 19, Verse 20*

Job walked to daybreak, and through it.

After the first half-hour his legs took on a momentum of their own, swinging his body forward across the dark, damp earth. If it had been hard to start walking, now it was much harder to stop. The need to keep moving, to travel, to press on towards the eastern edge of the Tandy . . . the urge was almost irresistible; only as the sun rose higher could Job force himself to halt.

The inducement was the shrunken remains of a snowdrift, piled against the north side of a dense evergreen shrub and protected from sunlight. Job knelt, took a handful of packed gray snow, and sucked it avidly. He held another handful against his forehead. No doubt about it, his fever was worse.

He stared east and made the calculation over and over. Less than a mile away the ridged trash mounds of Tandy Center rose above gentler hill slopes. He must circle that lethal central area and head east for another ten miles before he came to the fence around Xanadu. The total distance to be traveled was, say, fifteen miles. It would be dark again by six. The defensive laser ring would be turned off from eight P.M. to two A.M. Assuming that he started out promptly at sunset, he would have eight hours before the barrier closed for the last time and his chance to leave Xanadu vanished forever. Fifteen miles in eight hours; less than two miles an hour. It sounded trivial — if his legs could carry him so far.

And if the barrier around Xanadu could be opened.

Job sighed and lay full length on the ground, face up. He peered into the sky, into as deep a blue as he had ever seen. Somewhere in that void, hundreds of miles above him, unsleeping surveillance satellites stared back at Earth. Onboard sensors, if Wilfred Dell were to be believed, were even now scanning the Nebraska Tandy with their sensitive optics and cunning shape-detection algorithms, searching for the starfish form of a supine man against black earth.

Were they there? Would they see him?

Job forced himself to lie in the same place for two hours. The temperature gradually rose and the sun climbed higher, until even the gentle rays of early spring were enough to sting his ulcerated face. At last he crawled to the shelter of the scrubby evergreens and lay down by them. With the day to go before he could safely move on, what he needed more than anything was rest. But he was too feverish to sleep.

He began to munch on hard bread and tough meat, chewing with raw, lacerated gums and swallowing with a throat on fire with fever. The early lessons of Cloak House allowed him to endure the pain: *Eat when you can, not when you feel like it.*

He swallowed every scrap that he had brought with him, washed it down with mouthfuls of melted snow, and stared about in search of a safer hiding place.

There was nothing. The Tandy was too flat and open. Its valleys were broad and shallow, not enough to conceal a human, even one lying at full-length. The evergreen bushes might seem like the best hiding-place — but that meant they were the first place that any searcher would look.

Job rose to his hands and knees. A couple of

hundred yards to the southeast the spiky grass vegetation gave way to taller sedges and rushes. It suggested swampy ground. He crawled that way. As he came to the reedy area his hands sank deeper into cool, soft mud. He kept moving until he was at the center of a little depression. His hands were in above the wrist, and his knees and lower legs were covered, but the reeds and sedges were still not enough to conceal him. He had to burrow deeper. He lay flat on his back and wriggled, feeling his body sink slowly in the ooze until all but his head was covered. He reached out to each side, picked up handfuls of wet black mud, and daubed his burning face with them. Now he had become a man of earth, invisible from more than a few paces. He placed the mud-soaked cloth that had held his food over his fevered forehead, closed his eyes, and relaxed.

The cool embrace was exactly what he needed. As the day grew hot and the sun rose past its zenith, Job could feel the fever draining out of him, leached away by wet black earth. The soil above him dried and crumbled in the heat, while he drowsed and drifted and dreamed. He did not remember falling asleep, but when he opened his eyes the sun was suddenly a ball of orange fire, low on the horizon — and he was feeling human again.

He sat up. Time to be moving. And as he had that thought and stared around him, he learned that he was no longer alone. On the western horizon a long line of tiny figures had appeared. They were on the brow of a gentle hill, far off but steadily approaching. The line curved around him to both north and south.

He was hunted. And hunted in the most logical and inescapable way. Once Pyle, Gormish, and Bonvissuto had learned that Job had taken the vials from Hanna Kronberg's lab, they must have realized that their whole plan was in danger. Since they commanded the use of all the manpower in Xanadu, it would be easy to raise an army of ten thousand or more, send them to the outer border of the Tandy, and instruct everyone in the circle to walk inward. Only a hundred feet from each other at the outer perimeter of Xanadu, they would come closer and closer together as they approached the center. Nothing could escape them — not even a solitary man, lying flat and covered in mud.

Job could lie still, and wait for night. But only a fool would believe that they lacked flashlights and infrared detectors.

The behavior of the far-off line of men and women confirmed his assessment. They were in no hurry. They were convinced that they would find him, no matter where he hid.

And they were right. Job could not stay where he was. As the light faded he began to move in the only available direction — towards Tandy Center. He crouched low to the ground, seeking shelter from every meager bush or hummock.

He should have waited just a bit longer. As he was passing over the top of a little rise he heard a cry from behind him. Confirming calls rang out along the line.

Job stood up straight and began to run, taking the risk of being picked off by some sharpshooter. The main line was to his west. It was useless to run north or south — the cordon would surely continue there to form a full circle. All that he could do was run east, on into the central dump of Xanadu. Soon it would be totally dark, and already the tops of the trash mountains were beginning to merge into the sky. No sane person would pursue him into the deadly wilderness of the dumps. He could hide all night in Tandy Center.

His lungs began to burn in his chest, and he paused for breath. He could hide tonight, but to what purpose? Unless he had a way to escape in the morning it was pointless. In daylight, searchers wearing protective suits would have no trouble finding him in the dump, no matter where he hid.

He could not fault that logic, but his legs ignored his brain. He began to run again. Soon he was in a broad corridor that wound into the central drop-off zone. Chaotic mounds of unprocessed junk rose high on every side, providing an illusion of security from pursuers. They would not be reckless enough to follow into unknown dangers. But Job's own knowledge of Tandy Center had also been gained in daylight, and it was useless at night. He slowed his pace, staring in the sun's last gleam at twisted skeletons of metal, jumbled piles of contaminated aluminum sheeting, and seas of carboys and boxes and sharp-edged crates. He could see those clearly enough — what he could not see were the hidden dangers, the radioactivity and the toxins that permeated the debris.

At last the twilight faded to total darkness. Job squatted on the ground. Although he could sense the tangled wreckage on each side, he could no longer see it. Walking here at night was an invitation to disaster. He would have to wait until the tricky light of pre-dawn, then try to slip through the cordon.

It was the half-hearted decision of a man who already knows that he has lost. And as he made that decision, a booming roar sounded out across Tandy Center.

JOB SALK.

As he jerked to his feet he recognized the grotesquely amplified voice. It was Gormish.

JOB SALK. I KNOW THAT YOU ARE HIDING IN THE DUMP, AND WE BOTH KNOW THAT YOU CANNOT ESCAPE. YOU HAVE SHOWN GREAT INITIATIVE TO COME SO FAR. SURRENDER NOW, AND YOU WILL NOT BE HARMED. MEN WITH COURAGE AND SKILL ARE HARD TO FIND. COME OUT, AND I GUARANTEE THAT YOU WILL HAVE A POSITION AT HEADQUARTERS. YOU HAVE MY WORD ON IT.

Job sank back to the ground. Shades of Wilfred Dell and his promises. He and Gormish looked nothing like each other, but they were brothers under the skin.

COME OUT NOW, JOB SALK. THIS IS YOUR LAST WARNING. COME OUT, OR WE WILL COME AND GET YOU.

Those were the words that finally forced Job to action. He might die here in Tandy Center, but he would die according to his own plan, not Gormish's. For half an hour more he rested, then rose and began to pace cautiously forward. If his signal had been received by Dell the eastern barrier of Xanadu would open in one more hour. The middle of the dump could not be far away. Even though it was a forlorn hope, he had to reach that middle and continue across Tandy Center, to confirm that its eastern edge was blocked by the same line of pursuers.

He stepped on a piece of hard board that cracked under his weight with a sound like a pistol shot. Appalled at the noise, he stood motionless; and then he saw, like a glimmer of false dawn, a faint light shining through an iron lattice in one of the mounds.

Surely they had not pursued him here to join him in suicide. He stepped closer for a better view. As he did so there was a clash of gears and the growl of moving treads. Through the open metal grid Job saw a familiar towering shape.

Tandyman!

His legs wobbled under him and he sank to the floor.

The Tandyman's pincered arms telescoped out, as though the machine was stretching and flexing its muscles, then retracted to the sides. Twin searchlights in the cylindrical head swiveled and moved to narrow beam. Then Job could see that it was not heading towards him. It had turned, to run down a corridor parallel to the one in which he was standing.

He started in the opposite direction. Before he

could take more than two steps another rumble of treads came from his other side. He saw more lights, and heard more engines. All the Tandymen parked in Tandy Center were coming alive, one by one. Searchlights glared out, and behind them red crystal eyes glittered in the reflected beams.

They were after *him*.

He could see lights at each end of the corridor. Job was trapped. Desperately he scrambled up the steep side of the nearest ridge, ignoring cuts from sharp metal edges and the danger that the whole face would slide down to bury him.

At the summit he paused. He could see lights in all directions as a dozen Tandymen were activated and responded to their remote controllers.

One of them stood below the mound right in front of Job, no more than twenty yards away. He was about to run along the top of the ridge when he saw that the Tandyman was not moving. It had not yet been activated.

Job plunged down the side of the mound and straight to the Tandyman's back. He pulled open the spring-loaded door and squeezed through to the interior. It was utterly dark, but as he dropped into the seat the remote control console blinked to life. Job used its light to slam the lever into position for manual override, one second before the remote operator achieved full control.

The front and rear viewing screens turned on automatically. He took one quick look at the scene provided by the cameras. Four Tandymen were converging on his position. Without waiting to find out if they had seen him, Job sent his Tandyman straight up the side of the nearest mountain of trash.

The tracked wheels spun and raced. Six articulated legs thrust and jerked and scrabbled for purchase. Then they were at the top and over, descending the other side in a cascade of falling junk.

Job turned on the headlights, revved up to maximum speed, and roared away along a dark canyon through the debris.

He could see half a dozen pursuing Tandymen in his rear viewer, but they were a long way back. The remotely controlled units lacked the fine coordination of his manually operated Tandyman, and they could not take his desperate route over the top of the trash mountain. But their sensors were as good as his. They could certainly follow his lights and his sound. There would be scores of them after him, and they had all the time in the world.

Job had only one advantage: they could have no idea of his particular destination.

But where *was* that destination? The turns and twists within the drop-off zone had left him with no sense of direction. As his Tandyman roared along another corridor and into the open land beyond Tandy Center, he tried to find his bearings.

Before he had time to scan the land and sky ahead he had reached the line of men and woman guarding Tandy Center. They had been settling down for the night, but as the Tandyman roared towards them they scattered. Job heard the rattle of bullets on the metal around him, then he was plunging through the line. Two men and a woman did not move quickly enough. The rushing Tandyman hit them, and the vehicle lurched as it ground their bodies beneath its metal treads.

Job shuddered and drove on. He was desperately seeking a reference point. There was no moon. The Tandyman's range of upward vision was enough to allow him to see the stars, but he did not know how to use them to determine direction.

Soon it should be eight o'clock. The eastern road out of Xanadu would open, and Job did not know how to get there.

The rear viewer showed the searchlights of half a dozen Tandymen, following his path. They were far behind. He fixed a straight course away from the central dump and bent over the control panel. There was no compass — none had ever been considered necessary — but surely *something* in the controls would serve to tell him direction.

He examined every instrument. There was nothing. But the tiny ruby light showing the Tandyman to be under manual control gave him a last-hope idea. He stopped, turned off the engine, and shifted the lever to remove the robot from manual override. The remote control console began to blink; in the same moment Job was pushing open the door and scrambling outside.

He moved a few steps away from the Tandyman and looked up. The directional antenna on the metal body was moving, homing on the transmitted radio signal. It made a quarter-turn, then steadied around a fixed direction. While it was still locking in, Job was back at the door in the rear of the Tandyman and climbing inside.

The pursuing Tandymen were only a couple of hundred yards away when he took over manual control again, started the engine, and roared off.

The Tandyman were remotely controlled from Headquarters, in the far south of Xanadu. The antenna locking on the signal from that direction told Job that he had been heading the wrong way, towards the southwest of Tandy Center. He began to angle south, then gradually east, shifting his bearing little by little so that he did not run too close to the Tandymen who chased him.

He was at maximum throttle, but he could not increase his lead. The vehicles behind him had fanned out into an arc, always a couple of hundred yards away. They were being systematic in their pursuit. If he made a sudden turn towards any of them, the whole group would not hesitate to ram him. Tandymen were valuable, but tonight any of them was expendable.

Far to the north Job could see the lights of the cordon around Tandy Center. They provided him with a useful reference point as he spiraled steadily around to a northeast heading. He was following a long, curved path that would bring him tangent to the eastern road by which he had first entered Xanadu.

When he felt heavy vibration as the metal treads left the soft earth of Xanadu for the concrete surface of the road, he had a new worry. Was he too *early*? It seemed like hours since he had climbed into the Tandyman, but that was subjective time. Tandymen could run at more than thirty miles an hour, and he had been pushing along at maximum speed. It could be little more than half an hour since he left Tandy Center.

It was too late to change his mind. The fence was less than half a mile away, rushing closer. He was up to it in seconds.

If the ring of guarding lasers had not been turned off...

Job gritted his teeth and wondered if he would have time to realize that he was being vaporized before he died. Then he was through, with the fence behind him.

He was outside Xanadu.

Before he could take pleasure in that thought, he saw that his pursuers were still coming after him. They were at the fence — passing through it —

The night turned blue. Laser beams sprang out across the dark land. Where the Tandymen had been, fountains of sparks and blossoming fireballs illuminated the boundary fence. Watching in his rear viewer, Job saw fragments blown high into the air, to be hit again and again until they were reduced to a fine rain of exploded plastic and liquid metal.

He drove on. In ten minutes all evidence of the Nebraska Tandy was out of sight behind him. Job turned off the engine and leaned back in his seat. He felt in his pocket, took out the two vials, and sat staring at them in the control board light.

In Tandy Center he had been forced to action. But that action had still followed Wilfred Dell's agenda: enter Xanadu, learn what Hanna Kronberg was doing, and escape with proof of it. Job had done just that, and he had with him exactly what Dell needed to persuade others.

And now?

It seemed to Job that every action in his whole life had been forced on him by others. It was fear, death, and Colonel della Porta that first made him quit Cloak House. The drug delivery that led to his capture in the Mall Compound had been pushed on him by Miss Magnolia. Starvation had forced him to leave Cloak House for a second time; after his second capture, Wilfred Dell had made him go to Xanadu. Gormish's words had roused him to escape from Tandy Center. He had *always* been no better than a human Tandyman, driven along by remote control.

It was time to change. For the first — and only — time in his life he was going to make a decision of his own.

He picked up one of the vials. And then he hesitated. Maybe he was about to make a too-hasty action. But wasn't that always true? Was there ever enough time in life to evaluate any major decision completely?

He thought of Father Bonifant's words, from so long ago. *Remember, an easy question can have an easy answer. But a hard question must have a hard answer. And for the hardest questions of all, there may be no answer — except faith.*

Job removed the stopper from the vial. He had faith. He was doing the right thing. He poured the contents into the hollow of his hand and rubbed it onto his face and neck and the skin of his forearm.

The yellow liquid penetrated his open sores with agonizing speed. He was still gasping and writhing when a supersonic helicopter screamed out of the eastern night sky and feathered down to land beside the silent Tandyman.

● Chapter Twenty

So Job died, being old and full of days.

— The Book of Job, Chapter 42, Verse 17

The journey to Xanadu had been seven days of misery. The return to the Mall Compound took less than two hours.

During the trip Wilfred Dell made an inflight call to Job and asked three questions.

"Did you find out what's going on with Hanna Kronberg?"

"Yes." Job had seen Dell's puzzled look when communication was first established. The bald, mud-caked and suppurating object that Job had become bore little resemblance to the young man whom Dell had sent to the Nebraska Tandy.

"Is what you found out important?"

"Very." If Dell did not comment on his appearance, neither would Job.

"Did you bring proof — I mean *proof*, not hearsay and impressions — of what you found?"

"I brought proof."

"Good. I'm busy now. I'll set up a meeting for when you get here."

Dell was gone. Job lay back on the makeshift bed in the rear of the helicopter. He could feel the changes taking place inside him. They were bad, and about to get worse; he must endure them for at least a few hours more.

The helicopter pilot ignored the airport across the

river and flew directly to the Mall Compound. It was still one hour short of midnight when Job found himself again in the glass-sided elevator, ascending the tall, square-sided tower that dominated the Compound. Dell's office when he entered had changed a little. The top of the wooden desk had been cleared, and different oil paintings hung on the walls.

But there had been no visible change to Wilfred Dell. The cherub's face above the massive dwarf's body still carried its half-smile as he greeted Job.

"Welcome back. I thought your return deserved something of a formal reception." He spread his short arms wide to take in the three other people in the room. "The Honorable Reginald Brook. Senator Graydon Walsh, Senator Horatio Waldo Nelson. This young man — a little the worse for wear — is Job Napoleon Salk. He is here to present the report of his trip to the Nebraska Tandy."

The nods to Job were barely visible, but there was curiosity in their eyes. What could this ragged, battered wreck have to offer, of possible interest to *us*? It was clear to Job that Dell was playing for effect, stroking the egos of the other three by pointing out that they were to hear the report as soon as anyone.

"You mean he went right, er, *inside* the Tandy?" said Senator Walsh. He and Reginald Brook were Job's mental image of a powerful political person: tall, lean, aristocratic, and languid. But their eyes lacked Dell's luminous intelligence.

"Right inside, and back out again." Wilfred Dell was beaming. "But only just. Five minutes earlier, and the perimeter defense would have annihilated him. Did you know you were so early, Job?"

"No. I thought I was almost too *late*. Everything a few seconds behind me was wiped out."

"Naturally. At my direction." Dell glanced smugly at the others. "I decided that we were only interested in the *first* vehicle to emerge. The rest could be destroyed; it was not my intent to encourage a mass exodus." He turned again to Job. "The hour is late, and the senators and I have another engagement tonight. Keep it short. Details can wait until morning."

"I'll be brief. But I have to give you a little background." Job sat down uninvited. Flakes of dried mud fell off him onto the chair and into the thick pile of the pink carpet. "I don't know what was originally intended when the Tandies were used to exile criminals and undesirables, but I can tell you what the effect has been. There have always been people in the world who hated government, or were cruel, or were indifferent to the needs of others. Those people used to be mixed in with everyone else. But with the Tandy exile program, the hatred and cruelty and indifference have been *concentrated*, distilled out and sent to a few isolated sites. And now all that hatred is directed *outward*, to the world beyond the Tandies."

"Get on with it," said Dell impatiently. "We know all that, and it's not important." Already Senator Nelson was fidgeting in his seat.

Job took a deep breath. He had rehearsed this mentally for two hours, but he could not say it all in thirty seconds. "It's important now, Mr. Dell. Your intuition was quite correct. The Nebraska Tandy *is* dangerous — to everyone. Its leaders are full of hate. They have been working on a project designed to kill every person in the country, perhaps in the world. Only Tandy residents will be spared."

He had certainly regained their attention.

"Xanadu is different from most Tandies," Job went on. "It not only serves as a concentration camp for ordinary criminals, it is also the main exile point for *scientists*. So far as they can, most of those exiled still pursue their scientific work. There is particular capability in biological research, and some outstanding minds have been sent to Xanadu. A few years ago, the Big Three who control the Tandy decided to take advantage of those talents. They demanded a synthetic plague, one with a hundred percent kill rate, which only those with prior immunization — people inside the Tandy — would survive. I don't know what pressures the leaders of Xanadu applied to the scientists, to make them do what they were told, but it worked. The researchers did almost exactly what was asked of them. They took natural microorganisms and modified them using recombinant DNA techniques; they gave the leaders their artificial plague."

Job reached into his pocket and pulled out a sealed vial with an orange stopper. It was full of cloudy yellow liquid. "Here it is. The killing contagion. It's a lethal variant of an old, extinct disease called smallpox. The only other place in the world where it exists is in the Techville labs of the Nebraska Tandy."

Reginald Brook was backing up in his chair. He turned to Wilfred Dell. "You mean you let him bring that in here when we're — "

Only Dell seemed unmoved. The trace of a smile was still on his face. "I'm sure that bottle is tightly sealed," he said quietly. "I told him that we needed *proof*, and that's just what he brought us. Job, you said that the scientists did *almost* what was asked of them. What did they miss?"

Job had forgotten the precision and subtlety of Wilfred Dell's mind. The other three might regard Dell as no more than their hireling, but he could think rings around them.

"The plague lacked one property," Job replied. "They are still working on it. As you know, no one leaves the Nebraska Tandy. The perimeter defense system makes sure of that. But at the moment the plague is contagious only by *direct contact*, person to person. Outside the human body, the microorganism survives for just a few seconds. To do what the Xanadu leaders want, the plague needs to provide *airborne* contagion. The microorganism must be able to survive outside the body for days, not seconds. Then the Nebraska Tandy can infect the whole world simply by releasing a spray into the air high above Xanadu, and letting the winds blow it at random. There are enough people in the world to guarantee the spread after that. Second and third stage infection would be guaranteed. The residents of Xanadu would know that they had succeeded when there were no more airdrops and the perimeter defense stopped working. Then they would emerge from the Tandy — and claim the world."

Job stood up, went across to Wilfred Dell's desk, and placed the vial gently on top of it. "I am sure that you will want others to study this in a controlled environment. As you can see, I have been careful not to break the seal."

When he returned to his seat he saw that hatred had replaced fear on the faces of Reginald Brook and the two senators.

"You were quite right, Dell," said Brook. "Damn them. We'll provide you with authorization. Make sure the Techville facility is flattened. The whole Tandy, if you want to."

"I don't think that will be necessary." Wilfred Dell's smile held genuine pleasure. "The razing of Techville — together with Xanadu Headquarters — should be adequate."

Job realized that this task, at least, was to Dell's taste. What old score was he paying off, to someone who had escaped him by exile to Xanadu Headquarters?

Job thought of Hanna Kronberg and the rest of the scientists. Would they have time to escape? If they were wise they would have abandoned Techville already, the moment they learned that Job had taken the vials and managed to leave the Tandy. But scientists were *learned*, not necessarily *wise*. Job had learned the difference long ago from Alan Singh. Some of them, obsessed with their work, would surely stay in Techville until it was too late.

Headquarters was on the target list, too, but Job was less worried about Skip Tolson. With Skip's nose for trouble he was probably hidden away already in some new bolt-hole, far from danger.

Wilfred Dell had stood up and was moving across to the desk. He picked up the vial and peered into it. "A good piece of work, Job. I'll send this out for full analysis tonight, and we can continue tomorrow morning. But now I must fulfil other commitments."

"There's more to tell. Don't you want to hear how I rode a Tandyman to get out of Xanadu?"

"I do. But that can wait." There was a glint of lust in the gnome's eyes. "The senators and I have an appointment with some friends of yours. Should I offer your regards to Miss Magnolia, over at Bracewell Mansion?"

Job stood up, too, and walked towards Wilfred Dell. "I don't think she'll even remember me. If she does she probably thinks I'm dead. A few hours ago, I thought I was, too." He reached out, took Dell's hand, and shook it. "I just want to say, it's good to be here. I don't know if you are surprised that I made it back, but I am."

Dell had looked startled when Job shook his hand. He nodded. "I am surprised. And impressed. I admit it. As I told you before you left, good men are all too scarce. I'll arrange for you to receive the best medical treatment that we can give. You need rest now — a bath might be a good idea, too. In the morning we will talk about your future."

Dell ushered the other three men out, leaving Job standing alone. He went back to the chair, sat down, and covered his face with his hands. He had held up this long, but it had taken all his strength.

One more step, he told himself. One more step; and then I can rest forever.

* * *

Job had learned on his first encounter with Wilfred Dell that the man needed little sleep. Bracewell Mansion must have occupied much of the night, but it was no surprise to Job to find himself summoned to Dell's office at eight in the morning.

Job had already been up for three hours. He had gone to bed at once, still unbathed, but by four o'clock the nausea that had started at midnight was much worse. Long before dawn he went to the medical room in the lower basement of the building to demand sedatives and pain killers. They were provided without objection, but the doctor who spoke with Job gave him a brief examination and shook his head.

"There's nothing much we can do for you here. Are you seeing specialists?"

"Later."

"Do it soon. This is going to knock you flat." The doctor could hardly find a vein for the needle, in Job's ulcerous and wasted arm.

Job winced as the injection went in. "How long is the pain killer good for?"

"Five or six hours."

"Fine. That should be ample."

"That's not the point! You ought to be in bed."

"I'm on my way." But Job went upstairs to the twenty-four-hour cafeteria, where he ordered a pint of milk and four raw eggs. The pain killers were beginning to work. They allowed him to force eggs and milk down his blistering throat. The sedatives overrode his nausea, enough to permit him to keep what he had swallowed.

Back in his room he soaked for two hours in a luke-warm bath, and worried.

He had no doubts that it had been right to give Wilfred Dell the vial, and explain its contents. In their anger, Gormish, Pyle, and Bonvissuto were willing to destroy everyone in the world, guilty and innocent alike. They were implacable. When people spoke of the Nebraska Tandy and quoted a life expectancy for new arrivals of a year and half, they had no idea that the Big Three were *causing* most of the deaths. With a more humane policy toward the treatment and training of new prisoners, the average life in the Tandy could be drastically increased — perhaps to the point where it was as long as life outside. But Gormish and her colleagues were fanatics. If they would not try to save people who had been condemned to the Tandy with them, how much less would they care about everyone else?

Job had been given the chance to stop them. He had taken it. There was no doubt in his mind about that decision.

But what about the *other* vial, and his own action?

That was Father Bonifant's hardest question, one that Job could not answer; but he knew the reply that Reginald Brook would give, and he could not accept it.

He at last forced himself to leave the tub. The warm water had soothed and relaxed him, but overall he felt worse. Dressing, even in the softest and loosest clothes, was an exquisite agony. When he was clothed he went to sit by the window and stared at the city, spread below him in the morning sunlight. Already a thick haze hung over it. From this distance it was less pleasant a prospect than the clean plain of the Nebraska Tandy.

When the call came from Dell, Job was ready. He placed the empty second vial in his pocket and walked gingerly across to the other side of the building. He knocked and went into the luxuriously appointed office.

This morning the only man with Wilfred Dell was Reginald Brook.

"The senators are still a little under the weather." It was apparent from Dell's manner that he was not. "We'll begin without them. Let me start by saying that a first examination confirms what you said. The bottle contained a genetically modified form of the *variola* virus — the smallpox virus, to us simple folk. It will take a while longer to confirm the potency of that new virus, but there's no reason to doubt what you said. So much for Dr. Hanna Kronberg, and her 'great love' of humanity."

Job shook his head, and felt new pain in his neck and chest. "She didn't develop that virus. The work was done before she arrived in Xanadu, by other scientists. Hanna Kronberg was actually *opposed* to plague virus development — believe it or not, she really does love people. I was there when she had a big argument with the others in the lab. She wanted to *hinder* development of an airborne contagious form. What she wanted them to work on, without telling the Big Three, was something quite different — another tailor-made microorganism."

Dell snorted. "Still chasing her old idea, making us so we can all chew wood like a bunch of beavers?"

Job saw Reginald Brook's pop-eyed look. It must be his first exposure to Hanna Kronberg's pet project.

"Not that. For three years she has been after something new. Her latest organism is designed as a symbiote to the human body, to live inside people and help repair damaged structures. It grew out of her earlier work on cellulose digestion. She had started to wonder, what was the point of more babies if all they had to look forward to was disease and early old age? She managed to produce a symbiote that strengthened the immune system and inhibited the aging process, but there were problems. Simulations, confirmed by lab tests on human subjects, showed that the symbiote would produce side effects: diminished sex drive and reduced fertility. And there were other difficulties, ones that she was never able to solve."

"Well, they're all history. She'll do no more experiments." Wilfred Dell glanced at his gold wristwatch. "Her efforts will end in three and three-quarter hours, precisely at noon today — when Techville and Xanadu Headquarters are blown off the map. She'll never make her symbiote."

"She already made it." Job reached into his pocket with shaking hands and carefully took out the vial with the yellow stopper. The pain killers were still working, but Job's condition was deteriorating. He could feel new ulcers and blisters erupting on his tongue and inside his mouth. In another hour speech would be impossible. He held the vial out towards the two men.

"I stole this, too, from the lab. Hanna Kronberg's latest genetically tailored microorganism."

Reginald Brook was beginning to repeat his action of last night and flinch away in his chair, but after a moment he frowned and leaned forward. "Wait a minute. That bottle is empty!"

"Quite right. It is empty — now." Job could hear his voice slurring the words. "It wasn't, though, when I took it."

"What did you do with it?" That was Dell, the urgency in his voice showing that he was jumping ahead of Job's explanation.

"When I was still in the Tandyman, I poured it over my hands and rubbed it on my face. It's inside me now. You see, Hanna Kronberg never found a way to make an air-carried version of this, either. It can only spread from person to person by actual body contact."

"God*damn*." Dell was glaring at Job. "You may have killed us all. *Body contact.* Last night, when we were leaving, you shook my — "

"That's right. Inside me, and now inside you." Job giggled like a drunkard. "Sorry about your sex drive, Mr. Dell. You'll miss it more than most. I hope you avoided body contact last night at Bracewell Mansion."

Dell gasped. "You *fucker*! You're dogmeat, Job Salk.

I'll see to it *personally* that you're dead before I eat dinner." Every veneer of sophistication had gone from his voice. His speech was pure *chachara-calle*.

"Sure. You think you can make me in worse shape than I am?" Job sighed. "Don't threaten a drowning man with water torture, Mr. Dell. Can't you see I'm dying? That I'm dead *already*? I wanted to explain last night, but you were so eager to go over to Bracewell Mansion, you didn't want to listen. I blundered around the central Xanadu dump, the hottest part. *I rode a Tandyman to leave Xanadu!* You hear me? If you want to live, you don't go near a Tandyman without a protective suit. I knew that. I didn't want to die. But I didn't have a suit, and I was carrying something so important that I *had* to get away. Last night I ate thousands of rads. Thousands and thousands."

"Fuck you and your thousand rads! It's a pity you didn't fry on the spot." Wilfred Dell was shaking all over. With rage or fear, Job could not tell.

"But if you shook Dell's hand . . ." Something was finally getting through to Reginald Brook. He was holding his hand in front of his face and staring at it in a puzzled way. "And he shook hands with *me* when I left last night, and then *I* shook hands with Walsh and Nelson . . ."

"Welcome to the club." Job laughed again, a dry rattle that tortured his throat. "How many of us are there this morning, Mr. Brook? How many will there be by tonight? Don't you *want* a symbiote to stop you aging and make you live to a healthy old age? Most people would love it. I thought for an hour or two that it might even help me. But it can't work miracles."

"An antidote! Something to reverse the action. There has to be one." Dell snatched the bottle from Job's hand and dashed out of the room.

"Don't bet on it," Job croaked after him. "Hanna Kronberg doesn't think it can be removed from the human system. And she's an awfully smart woman."

He stood up and walked slowly across to Reginald Brook. Frozen in his chair, the other man raised his hands in front of his face. "Get away from me!"

"I just wanted to take a good look at one of the *real* owners of the world." Job stared at Brook for a few seconds, then walked back to slump in his own seat. He was feeling dizzy, and the light in the room had become a patchwork of light and dark spots.

"You never visited the Nebraska Tandy, Mr. Brook." Job closed his tired eyes. "You never will. But I did. And you know something? Life goes on there. You take the worst poisons and the worst radioactives and the worst pollutants in the whole country, and you pour them all into one little area, twenty miles across. And you know what happens? The earth fights back. Life fights back. *People* fight back. They have children, and they worry about their future. They seem as happy there as they do here.

"I sat in the Tandyman last night, after I escaped from Xanadu, and I thought about you and the Royal Hundred. I knew that if I gave that vial to Wilfred Dell, he would take it, and study it. But what would you do next? I knew the answer. You'd *restrict its use*. You and a few friends would get the benefits, along with the Royal Hundreds, whoever they are, of other countries. *You'd* like the fit life and the healthy old age — but you wouldn't want it for everyone, because the big side effect is *reduced fertility*. Hanna Kronberg talks about a future world population that will stabilize at one and a half billion, instead of increasing past twelve. That's good for most people. They'll be better off, because they won't *need* a whole bunch of kids to look after them in their old age — they'll able to manage for themselves. And Earth will be better off, too. It needs a breathing space. It fights back, better than we deserve, but it can use a rest from too many people."

Job opened his eyes. Reginald Brook was staring at

him open-mouthed, with the terrified and hopeless expression of a rabbit facing a snake. Job rested his aching head on the soft seat back.

"Did I say *everyone* will be better off? I don't mean quite everyone, do I?" His voice was an unintelligible mumble. "I mean, everyone but you, and a handful of others like you. What *you* fear, you see, more than anything, is *change*. But when the world population shrinks, change is one thing that's absolutely guaranteed. 'It's nice to have plenty of young and poor,' Wilfred Dell told me, 'to look after the old and wealthy.' He meant *you* — the Royal Hundred. You need the status quo. But what will your kind do when the supply of young and poor dries up? Will you cook your own meals, and clean your own house, and mend your own clothes?"

There was silence. Job opened his eyes. Reginald Brook had left. Job was alone.

"It's the hardest problem of all, isn't it?" Job went on muttering, his head lolling forward onto his chest. "*Who should run the world*? There's no easy answer, no magic solution. There never is, to a really hard question. Who should run the world? Hanna Kronberg and her friends would *like* to run it, and they can make gadgets that help; but they don't understand *people*, so they don't know how the gears work in the real world. Wilfred Dell is different. He knows *how* it operates — the trouble is, he wants to operate it *himself*. And that's enough to rule him out."

Job sat up and stared around. It was clear daylight, but the room seemed to be filling with a pink fog, blurring the outlines of everything. When he tried to speak, his throat produced no sound.

So who will run the world? The question rolled on, inside his head. *There's only one answer. No one knows if there's a 'right' way for the world to work, so* **no one** *can be allowed to run the whole thing. But* **everyone** *plays a part.*

Hanna Kronberg does her bit, trying to make things change for what she thinks is better. Maybe she's right. Reginald Brook and Wilfred Dell fight every change, doing their best to keep things just the way they are, and maybe they are not always wrong. Even Skip Tolson has a purpose, hanging on when there's no hope and no reason, surviving when he ought to die, clinging to life, never giving up. He does his bit.

And I did mine.

It was the answer that faith provided, and it was the right answer. Job was sure of it. Because although Reginald Brook had left the room, Father Bonifant had taken his place in the chair opposite. And Mister Bones was smiling.

Wilfred Dell returned in fifteen minutes, gray-faced and furious. He had three armed guards with him. But he was too late. Job had already slipped away.

ROGER ZELAZNY
DREAM WEAVER

"Zelazny, telling of gods and wizards, uses magical words as if he were himself a wizard. He reaches into the subconscious and invokes archetypes to make the hair rise on the back of your neck. Yet these archetypes are transmuted into a science fiction world that is as believable—and as awe-inspiring—as the world you now live in." —**Philip José Farmer**

Wizard World
Infant exile, wizard's son, Pol Detson spent his formative years in total ignorance of his heritage, trapped in the most mundane of environments: Earth. But now has come the day when his banishers must beg him to return as their savior, lest their magic kingdom become no better than Earth itself. Previously published in parts as *Changeling* and *Madwand*.
69842-7 * $3.95　　　　　　　　　———

The Black Throne with Fred Saberhagen
One of the most remarkable exercises in the art and craft of fantasy fiction in the last decade. . . . As children they met and built sand castles on a beach out of space and time: Edgar Perry, little Annie, and Edgar Allan Poe. . . . Fifteen years later Edgar Perry has grown to manhood—and as the result of a trip through a maelstrom, he's leading a life of romantic adventure. But his alter ego, Edgar Allan, is stranded in a strange and unfriendly world where he can only write about the wonderful and mysterious reality he has lost forever. . . .
72013-9 * $4.95　　　　　　　　　———

The Mask of Loki with Thomas T. Thomas
It started in the 12th century when their avatars first joined in battle. On that occasion the sorcerous Hasan al Sabah, the first Assassin, won handily against Thomas Amnet, Knight Templar. There have been many duels since then, and in each the undying Arab has ended the life of Loki's avatar. The wizard thinks he's in control. The gods think that's funny. . . . A new novel of demigods who walk the Earth, in the tradition of *Lord of Light*.
72021-X * $4.95　　　　　　　　　———

This Immortal
After the Three Days of War, and decades of Vegan occupation, Earth isn't doing too well. But Conrad Nimikos, if he could stop jet-setting for a minute, might just be Earth's redemption. . . . This, Zelazny's first novel, tied with *Dune* for the Hugo Award.
69848-6 * $3.95 _____

The Dream Master
When Charles Render, engineer-physician, agrees to help a blind woman learn to "see"—at least in her dreams—he is drawn into a web of powerful primal imagery. And once Render becomes one with the Dreamer, he must enter irrevocably the realm of nightmare. . . .
69874-5 * $3.50 _____

Isle of the Dead
Francis Sandow was the only non-Pei'an to complete the religious rites that allowed him to become a World-builder—and to assume the Name and Aspect of one of the Pei'an gods. And now he's one of the richest men in the galaxy. A man like that makes a lot of enemies. . . .
72011-2 * $3.50 _____

Four for Tomorrow
Featuring the Hugo winner "A Rose for Ecclesiastes" and the Nebula winner "The Doors of His Face, the Lamps of His Mouth."
72051-1 * $3.95 _____

Available at your local bookstore. Or you can order any or all of these books with this order form. Just mark your choices above and send a check or money order for the combined cover price(s) to: Baen Books, Dept. BA, P.O. Box 1403, Riverdale, NY 10471.

Name: _____

Address: _____

_____

I have enclosed a check or money order in the amount of $_____.

MICHAEL FLYNN

**What if it were all a plot?
What if there really *were* a secret conspiracy
running things behind the scenes ... and
they were incompetent?**

It is a little-known fact that over a hundred years ago
an English scientist-mathematician named Charles
Babbage invented a mechanical computer that was
nearly as powerful as the "electronic brains" of the
1950s. The history books would have it that it was
unworkable, an interesting dead-end.

The history books lie. In reality, the Babbage Machine
was a success whose existence was hidden from view
by a society dedicated to the development of a "secret
science" that could guide the human race away from
war and toward a better destiny.

But as the decades passed their goals were perverted—
and now they apply their knowledge to install themselves
as the secret rulers of the world. Can they do it? Even
though their methods are imperfect, unless they are
stopped their success is assured. *In the Country of
the Blind*, the one-eyed man is King. . . .

PRAISE FOR
IN THE COUNTRY OF THE BLIND

"A marvelously intelligent scientific thriller. . . . This is a book to read, and read again."   —Faren Miller, *Locus*

"A tremendous amount of historical research went into this book as well as a large amount of thought into the implications of a secret society that was able to predict the future through mathematical models. . . . The result is an engrossing mystery that always has the ring of authenticity. . . . In all, this is a highly recommended book. Four stars."
—Danny Low, *Other Realms*

"Flynn's first novel is a white-knuckle roller-coaster ride of a conspiracy thriller, chock-full of alternate history, mathematical prediction and philosophical speculation. . . . An impressive debut, both as SF and as thriller."   —Scott Winnett, *Locus*

"The [Babbage] Society, and the idea of a scientifically guiding history, are the best parts of the book for me. There is an incredibly involved espionage plot, which becomes funny as the original Society keeps finding more and more similar societies trying to do the same thing, not always for the same reasons . . . Recommended . . ."
—Robert Coulson, *Comics Buyers Guide*

"This is the Faustian heart of modern SF."
—Russell Letson, *Locus*

HOW TO IMPROVE SCIENCE FICTION

Want to improve SF? Want to make sure you always have a good selection of SF to choose from? Then do the thing that has made SF great from the very beginning—talk about SF. Communicate with those who make it happen. Tell your bookstore when you like a book. If you can't find something you want, let the manager know. But money speaks louder than mere words—so *order* the book from the bookstore, special. Tell your friends about good books. Encourage *them* to special order the good ones. A special order is worth a thousand words. If you can prove to your bookstore that there's a market for what you like, they'll probably start to cater to it. And that means better SF in your neighborhood.

Tell 'Em What You Want

We, the publishers, want to know what you want more of—and if you can't get it. But the people who order the books—they need to know first. So, before you buy a book directly from the publisher, talk to your bookstore; don't be shy. It doesn't matter if it's a chain bookstore or a specialty shop, or something in between—all businesses need to know what their customers like. Tell them: and the state of SF in your community is sure to improve.

And Get a Free Poster!

To encourage your feedback: A free poster to the first 100 readers who send us a list of their 5 best SF reads in the last year, and their 5 worst.

Write to: Baen Books, Dept. FP, P.O. Box 1403, Riverdale, NY 10471. And thanks!

Name:_____

Address:_____

_____

Best Reads	Worst Reads
1)	1)
2)	2)
3)	3)
4)	4)
5)	5)